COURT
OF
ICE
AND
ASH

By: LJ Andrews

Cover Design by: Bianca Bordianu at Moonpress.co

Editing by: Jennifer Murgia

Formatting by Clara Stone at Authortree.co

For rights and inquiries contact Katie Shea Boutillier at Donald Maass Agency: ksboutillier@maassagency

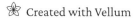 Created with Vellum

To those who love a little romance with their magic.

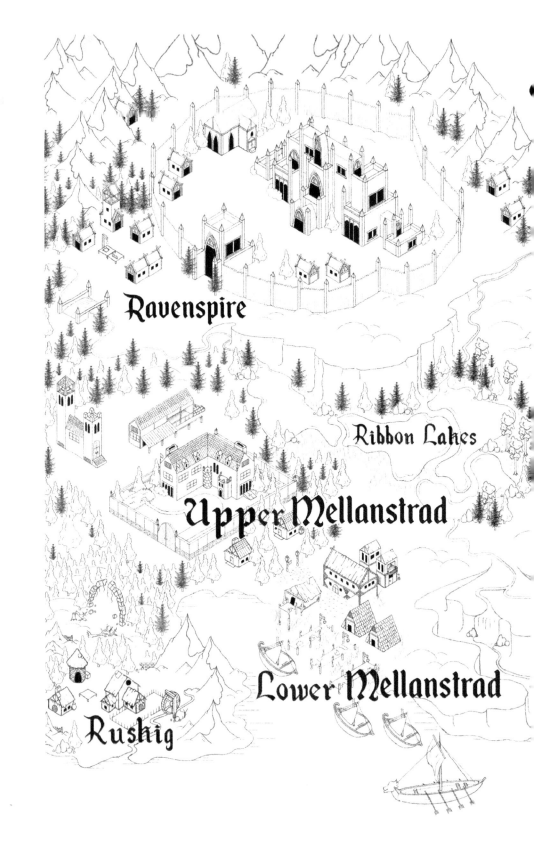

Ravenspire

Ribbon Lakes

Upper Mellanstrad

Lower Mellanstrad

Rushig

AUTHOR NOTE

Hello wicked darlings, for audiobook listeners who also read along, take note there have been slight changes to some passages since the recording. It in no way changes the meaning, but it might not align perfectly with the audiobook. Should be a wild ride either way.

CHAPTER 1
NIGHT PRINCE

L ust for blood was still there. Heavy and palpable each time I rested a hand on the black iron axes tethered to my belt. A mute creature still lived, wanting blood, desiring the pain of it. As if the curse went on too long and now a bit of me would always be deadened to the warped beast I'd embraced time and again.

I had grand plans to keep the truth of it to myself.

Seated on a boulder in the trees, I breathed in the tang of copper mingled in the damp. Blood was there in the last remnants of the storm. I inhaled it all, soothing the tug in my chest, desperate for more.

"What is the point of this?"

I glanced over my shoulder at Tor. He scraped a whetstone over his dagger, glaring at me. Like he used to when I was nothing more than a tagalong boy to him and my older brother, Sol.

Back when life made sense.

"I liked you better when you bowed to me." I turned away and rested a hand on one axe.

"Yes, a fleeting moment, a bit of gladness to have a curse lifted and memories restored." Tor stopped sharpening his blade and came to my side. "Tell me something, My Prince, what will this accomplish?"

My thumb stroked the now useless black seer stone around my neck. I had no answer, and in truth, I hated admitting I didn't have a sure plan. Somehow, I managed to school my voice into one of confidence. "Losing another caravan will be a dent in the false king's coffers. It will build agitation and mistrust."

Tor rolled his eyes and I nearly laughed.

Memories speckled my brain in a clear image of Tor arguing with Sol and rolling his eyes much the same. Moments kept forming as time went by. Sometimes one of us would pause, rub our forehead, then describe the new memory.

We'd either laugh or use it to fuel our lust for vengeance.

"I think this brings us too close," Tor said, voice low. "You said you wanted to leave her in peace, yet we keep returning to those closest to her."

One fist clenched at my side as things that drew out a strange fear in my chest took hold. Things I couldn't risk, and certainly couldn't want.

She could have nothing to do with me, the Guild of Shade, or this endless battle to avenge the blood of my family. It wouldn't be fair. At least that is how I justified the idea in my head. Closer to the truth was Elise Lysander would take away the last of my bloodlust and I wasn't ready to bid it farewell.

So, I'd go on as if I were utterly indifferent.

I glared at Tor, glad to see him lower his gaze beneath my scrutiny for once. "This has nothing to do with the Timoran."

"The Timoran? I'm glad to hear you talk like that because she is Timoran. No matter what *Kvinna* Elise did to break the curse, she is the blood of King Eli. His damn namesake. If you want to move forward, then we do it alone. Yes?"

My eyes dropped to the red cloth in my hands.

"Unless you'd rather admit to a change of mind, perhaps a change of heart." Halvar materialized from behind a tree, licking grease from his fingers and tossing aside the slimy bone of a waterfowl. "In which case, I vow to the skies, I will not say I told you so. Even if I have told you so many a time."

"Elise has no place here," I said more to convince myself than them.

"I agree," Tor said. "She played her role, and now will be better off away from us."

"I do enjoy listening to the both of you say thoughts out loud. Almost as if you're convincing the fates that brought her to us, as if they care what you think. Elise is his *hjärta,* the song of our prince."

"Really? When did you turn so soft, my friend?" Tor said, snorting a laugh.

"Ah, I've always been the best lover of us all. There is nothing soft about me. And deny it all you wish, Torsten. You are the one among us who has had your own *hjärta* and should recognize it better than me. But I think you, too, have tried to close off that blackened little heart of yours."

Halvar grinned with a touch of wickedness when Tor tried to strike his arm. After moving a safe distance, Halvar looked to me. "I stand by what I said, and I shall enjoy watching you fight against the draw you have for *Kvinna* Elise, Prince Valen. Truth told, I plan to say I told you so at least a hundred times once you—"

"I wish the curse had muted him," Tor interrupted.

I tightened my jaw to keep from grinning. I missed this. Knowing one another as we once did. I didn't even mind that I'd been the younger nuisance and these two had played horrid tricks on me. I only wished Herja and Sol were still here. My sister would be my defender, and Sol would know what to do better than me. He'd know how to make New Timoran pay for our people's blood and suffering.

"Let's move." I paused and narrowed my gaze on Halvar. "And Elise is not my *hjärta*."

He grinned, like I was a ridiculous child once again. "As you say, My Prince."

It was a romantic notion. A favorite among Night Folk so long ago. Legends spoke of old fury that would connect two lovers in such a way their souls seemed to bond like a song's harmony. Unbreakable.

It was ridiculous.

It ached.

My father always called my mother his heart's song. She'd been Timoran. Perhaps . . .

No. I had no business connecting myself to Elise Lysander. I used her with intention to break the curse. We'd succeeded. It was done.

I lowered to a crouch, narrowed my eyes, focused on the rough trade road that wound beneath the rocky ledge. A discreet road, tucked between black oaks and willows and evergreens. The tops of trees cut through a gathering fog like fingers tangled in the hair of a lover. Hazy as it was, I still tracked the black coaches well enough. My eyes had grown keener at night since the curse released my fury and memories, but it was what I'd been known for in a life long gone.

The Night Prince, sovereign born under a crescent moon, prince of the shadows, keeper of earth fury. I'd always favored dusk over dawn and still did.

Three coaches bounced and rocked over the raised roots and brambles of the path. Each followed by a line of weary travelers on foot.

The blood is there. Dozens of Ettans dressed in Ravenspire blue carried ribbons and satins; some carried heavy canvas sacks on their shoulders. Others carted bags of endless fabric, feathers, pins, and needles for tailors and seamstresses. Few of the serfs had shoes. Most were bent over, fumbling across the bits of sharp rock and dust on the road. Even the smallest among them.

My lip curled into a sneer.

A girl, made of nothing but skin and bones, carried a grain sack as big as her. All the while, the Ravens sat on their plump asses, guarding the caravan without noting the suffering people at their feet. My people.

I could not be their prince. At least not the prince they wanted. But I could be the villain on their behalf. A rogue who brought Castle Ravenspire to its knees.

Then, I'd be free of this godsforsaken place.

This was not the Etta of my childhood. This was a land I didn't recognize, and I felt little love for it. Its people, I held a degree of loyalty to, but I could not—more, I would not—rule them.

By the time I took my vengeance, I'd be as unfit as the false king who sat on the throne.

"Why the hells are we going for textiles? Where are the treasury carts?" Halvar muttered.

He hopped from an upper ledge and came to stand beside me. Dressed like a Shade, his mouth and nose were covered in black, so he faded into the night.

"It's all part of the game, you bleeding idiot." Tor slid down the side of the ledge and crouched in the darkness ten paces from us. His fingertips sparked with pale blue flames, then dissolved when he clenched his fists. Pyre fury was one of the more difficult veins of power to control. In a way, after his memories were recalled, Tor had to relearn how to balance his magic.

Halvar sniffed. "I'd rather hit the false king where it hurts most—right in the coffers."

"In due time, Halvar," I said dryly. "Due time."

From the moment the curse lifted, we'd taken to driving a thorn into the side of King Calder—a fool and boy who'd murdered his own father for the throne.

First with the guards he'd sent to the Black Tomb once the curse had lifted. I knocked away the tightness of remorse thinking of the moment. They'd been sent to discover what had happened, and they'd discovered the ends of their lives instead. All but one. We'd let him live to stagger back to the castle with tales of the Blood Wraith and the Guild of Shade.

I'd wallow in the title Blood Wraith; it was a means to the end. I couldn't be Valen Ferus, couldn't shoulder that weight when all I needed to do was avenge the deaths of my family.

Their blood soaked into the soil of Old Etta, and I could not sleep over their cries.

I wanted Timoran to crumble.

"What is the best way to bring about the downfall of a kingdom, Halvar?" I asked in a low voice.

He folded his arms over his chest, studying the caravan. "Light it on fire, rob it blind, cut off the head of the king? I do love your riddles, My Prince, but do tell me. I can wait no longer."

I grinned. Gods, he hadn't changed. Curse or no curse, Halvar talked too much, loved too thoroughly, and was loyal to the end. "You drive a wedge between its people and its king, my friend. Unmask his incompetence. While they suffer, he grows rich."

"You want us to bring suffering to Ettans?"

"Timorans," I said. "Our people already suffer. But Timorans, the common people, they already see their supplies depleting while their king and their nobles bask in wealth."

I faced the trade road again, grinning. By the time we finished, Timorans wouldn't have faith in their king. They'd see him for the sniveling snake he was. They'd oust him, and leave way for fury, for the blood of Etta to come forward again.

We just needed to find a Night Folk willing to take the crown of such a battered kingdom. I'd rescind my claim. The land would choose another by my word.

Fury chose the royals of Etta. A gods' given gift, and it was only natural it should be the deciding factor in the sovereign of the land.

Halvar squatted beside me. "She's going to know it's you."

Words like a dagger to the chest, so swift and harsh it was

impossible not to react. Like I buried the call to blood, I could bury this too.

But such a longing for a such a woman proved a fiercer beast to tame.

"It doesn't matter." Ah, but it mattered a great deal, and I hated it. "Let her despise me. Then she will be free of me."

Halvar closed his lips—for once—and simply shook his head.

I turned away from him, studying the red mask in my hands. She hated this, even vowed to give me a different color. Back when we dreamed of being free of this land together. I closed my eyes, buried the disquiet until my heart burned and rage took over the soft memory of her lips, of her skin on mine.

I covered my chin, mouth, and nose with the red cloth. The threads were heady in smoke and sweat and blood.

I breathed deeply.

I tugged the black hood over my head. An ache grew, one that yearned for my heart to bid farewell to Elise; the same as it always did before I attacked. True, she'd know I was the one causing pain amongst her people. It was for her benefit. I was not the man for her. I *wanted* to wallow in blood.

Forgive me, the unbidden thought came as I spun an axe in hand.

Tor opened his palm so a cool flame coated his skin. Halvar spun the storm clouds above us with air fury.

I gripped my axes. If I revealed I could bend and break the earth, I'd be known. But no matter. I didn't need to fight with fury and took more pride in attacking bone and flesh.

A wicked kind of grin curled my lip beneath my mask. The

caravan passed directly below us. They'd never reach Castle Ravenspire.

"For Etta," I said, voice dark and low.

"For Etta," my friends repeated.

I took the first step down the ledge.

Blood was calling.

CHAPTER 2
ROGUE PRINCESS

Cursed hells! Again?

I gritted my teeth and tugged on my own leg, knee-deep in sticky, potent mud. A loud suction broke the silence of the night. All gods, it smelled. My nose wrinkled at the harsh reek of refuse and rot. Each shift of my step released a plume of stink into the air until my stomach turned and I strongly considered vomiting, so it might help the smell.

Murky bubbles of sludge popped and gurgled as the swamp slowly released my foot. But I'd pulled hard enough, when the boot slurped free, I fell backward and now my hands, head, and backside were coated.

A snicker from the reeds deepened the frown on my face.

"I don't want to hear it, Siverie," I snapped. A shiver ran the length of my spine and pin pricks of cold coated my thighs where my wet, muddy hose clung to my skin.

Siv emerged from the tall grass, grin wide and white. She'd hidden her pine needle colored hair beneath a black brimmed hat and had lifted the sharp collar of her woolen coat, so it hid the sides of her face.

I'd thought to be clever and lithe by wearing sturdy leather boots, a black tunic and cowl to hide my icy hair. Now I wished I'd have listened to Siv's warning of the cold and wetness on the prison trails. I shivered in the sludge, soaked to my bones.

At least my skin was masked now. Nothing worse than having a Timoran complexion that practically reflected moonlight like a lantern when stealth was key to everything. I held tightly to Siv's shoulder, stepped where she stepped, until we were back on the spongy bank.

"You have terrible night eyes," Siv whispered. "That is the fifth time you've stumbled into the water. At this rate we may as well wait until dawn and bring back his ashes from the pyre."

I frowned even if she couldn't see it in the dark. "Everything is the same shade—night. I can hardly make out the path, unlike you who's memorized it."

"When your people are constantly arrested, the road to the prison becomes second nature."

She'd said it lightly, but it wasn't a jest. Siv was an Agitator. Folk who hated the current king and his predecessors. Folk who believed the fae prince of old was the true heir and would restore this land into what it once had been as the Kingdom of Etta. A time before raids and Timoran rule.

Agitators despised royal Timorans, and being a lesser princess, I'd been horrified to discover Siv, my friend and former maid, was an Agitator sent to slit my throat. But Siv had proven her friendship. Because of it, we were both outsiders to her clan. Now, we were being proved. And I wouldn't fail. Not because I wanted the Agitator clan to let us live, but because others were depending on our success tonight.

I wouldn't be the one to let them down.

But in truth, life would be wholly more convenient if we could tell the Agitators the truth: the fae prince they worshipped was alive.

Valen Ferus. The Night Prince.

A man who'd desired me. Made me desire him.

A man who'd trusted me and taught me to trust.

A man who'd chosen revenge when I'd chosen him.

I shook my head to chase away thoughts of Valen. Thoughts of the Night Prince usually ended in tears or a rush of anger, fierce enough to make me throw knives.

Neither would be helpful.

I ducked behind a fallen log when we made it to the base of a stone wall surrounding the prison. Made of wood and wattle, with rotted beams and iron bars on each window. Prisoners would endure the elements, frost, and heat, without proper protection. Most would die.

Torches lit the courtyard, and in the center a wooden dais was raised, along with a device to splay the arms of victims. Rusted blades were laid out on a bloody, stained table.

Bile burned the back of my throat. Already the wood was stained in blood. A wagon below the dais held three bodies set for the prison pyres. On the opposite side of the dais a line of broken people awaiting their fate snaked around the damp yard.

Siv held up a finger, then gestured over the shadowed knoll. I bit the inside of my cheek, forcing myself to remain silent once I found him.

A little thinner. A ratty beard on his chin. Rags for clothes.

"Mattis." My chest cinched for my friend, the carpenter, and roared in a new hatred for my own sister.

Two weeks ago, Siv and I had slipped back into Mellanstrad seeking to bring Mattis to the Agitator clan, only to learn he'd been claimed as an enemy of the king.

Runa. My sister had helped her betrothed, Calder, murder the king and steal the throne. Once I was not found amongst their cowardly supporters, Runa had Mattis arrested, no doubt with torture. But even more, she and Calder burned the Lysander manor to the ground, uncaring whether any serfs or maids or cooks were inside.

Runa might be worse than Calder, the false king. False because Valen should hold the crown.

In my heart I knew he'd unite this broken kingdom. I could not believe otherwise.

"You've got that look again," Siv whispered as she readied an arrow in her bow. "We focus on Mattis and the elder and getting out of here alive tonight, then we can worry about Prince Valen."

"I wasn't thinking of the Blood Wraith."

She rolled her eyes. "You shouldn't call him that. He'll take the throne eventually. It's in his blood."

"Tell that to Ari."

Weeks ago, we'd been cornered by the head of the Agitator clans. Ari, a powerful fae illusionist, had claimed the throne, claimed he'd returned life to the land. The people accepted him as the new king. They believed the Ferus bloodline was truly dead.

"Ari will concede," Siv said after a pause. "Deep down he wants what is best for Etta."

I wasn't so sure. Ari seemed to enjoy his new title. Made clear by sending us into this bleeding, damp forest without argument.

"Why not let the Night Prince have a bit of revenge along the way?" Siv asked.

I replied with a long sigh. Valen wanted to destroy the throne of Timoran in the name of his parents, brother, and sister. He wanted retribution and revenge. He wanted more blood. I understood. In truth, I wanted Runa and Calder to pay for the lives they'd taken, but at what cost?

When he'd sated the call for blood, what sort of man would be left? The strong, kind, and gentle man I'd known—or a new version of Calder, except Valen had fury.

I have not forgotten for whom my heart beats. He'd said the words moments before he'd shoved me away. Still, he remained. The fury in his blood, the very smell of his skin, was like a shadow I could not touch.

My heart, my temper, could not take much more.

Siv tossed a satchel at me. "Let's go."

Together, we positioned ourselves at the top of the knoll. From the satchel, I removed a small crossbow, and locked in a bolt. I wasn't skilled enough to use other bows and arrows like Siv, but I'd been practicing. Since Valen made the decision to leave us, I made the decision to fight my way back to him.

On the dais, a holy man from the royal shrine of the gods read sagas of the great hall that awaited in the Otherworld as Mattis was brought toward the bloody center. I took a bit of pride. My friend didn't flinch. He strode to his fate with the bravery of warriors.

Siv murmured a prayer under her breath. One folk said to protect those they cared for. She'd never admit it, but I had my own suspicions the carpenter had burrowed into her guarded heart.

"We move swiftly," Siv said.

I nodded my agreement and lifted my bow. The executioner shredded Mattis's tattered shirt from his back. Through my teeth, I blew out a breath, and let my bolt fly.

Right after, Siv freed her first arrow.

Shouts rang in the prison yard like growing flames. The executioner rushed for one of the blades on his table.

Bleeding hells! He was going to kill Mattis where he stood.

Or so he thought. Mattis was no small man. His work with heavy beams and iron tools had given him enough stamina— even weakened as he was—to reel back and strike the executioner in the nose.

Guards rushed the dais. Siv fired an arrow, ripping out the throat of one raven. I released a bolt and it hit a shoulder.

Half the patrols rushed to secure the prisoners trying to escape their ropes. The rest aimed their attention at the knoll. Siv took a few steps back, firing arrows. I retreated, my stomach in hard knots. We were not meant to be alone.

Where were the others?

Like a fist to my stomach, I realized we'd been left to fend off the ravens on our own.

This was a suicide task.

Ari had given us a directive. Our task was to interrupt the

execution of an Agitator elder. We negotiated, of course, to free Mattis. *Damn, stand-in king.*

I'd misjudged the playful, cunning fae. If I had to guess, death was exactly what Ari hoped for us. They never planned to accept us, and now Mattis would die too.

"Siv!" I screamed when a patrolman reached the top of the knoll. His face was painted blue and black. Head shaved with intricate runes tattooed on the sides extending from his temples. With a sneer, he removed a slender sword from his belt.

I fumbled with my bolts. Siv dropped her bow when the guard swatted it away. My fingers trembled. With two missing fingertips, I'd learned how to adjust my grip on things, but in the moment my palm was slick with sweat.

All at once the gates of the prison yard clanged open. The guard hovering over Siv pointed his attention as a swell of Agitators rushing the yard.

About bleeding time, Ari!

Siv's fist curled around my wrist. "Elise! Hurry! Mattis and the elders are still caught in there."

Agitators fought against the miserly guards at the prison gates. Some of the prisoners had taken hold of knives, rods, and branches. Some stood still, possibly too stunned to fight. Others fled. But those, like Mattis, fought the guards with terrible rage. The weeks, months, turns, of suffering at their hands burst out in jabs, and strikes, and cutting blows.

Siv sprinted to Mattis. I turned to the man with a silver beard and a gray birthmark below his eyes.

"Elder Klok!" I screamed. "This way."

The man wasn't terribly old. A few leathery wrinkles

battered his skin, but his body seemed strong enough, his eyes clear. The man took me in for a few breaths, took note of my bow and bolts, then followed my gaze to the open gate where the Agitators broke through.

"You are with the clan?"

"In a sense."

The elder grinned, revealing one broken tooth at the front. "Good enough for me."

He dropped the wooden rod in his hand and rushed for the gate. A few Agitators shouted his name in a strangled kind of glee.

I didn't wait for him to be free before I ran back to Siv and Mattis. She reached the carpenter as he swung a wooden board at a guard's head. Siv shoved his shoulders when shouting his name wasn't enough.

Mattis fumbled to the side. His eyes were wild when he glanced back. A few breaths passed before he beamed beneath the scruff of his beard.

"Siverie." His voice was hoarse and dry. "You've come for my jokes."

"You stupid fool!" she shouted at him, a touch of desperation in her voice. "Get out of here! Hurry!"

Mattis chuckled and accepted her hand. His eyes caught mine and his smile changed into something softer. "*Kvinna*."

"There are no *Kvinnas* here tonight, my friend," I said as I picked up my pace and ran toward the gates.

I didn't look back. Didn't want to watch the slaughter of the prison guards. Doubtless some prisoners deserved to be locked away and we'd freed them.

"You . . . came for me," Mattis said, gasping over his knees. "I always knew . . . you cared Siverie."

"Shut up," she said, voice trembling. "Or I will gladly return you."

Mattis started to smile, but it faded as quickly. I followed his wide gaze to the edge of the trees. From the shadows a row of darkly dressed men materialized. At the front was a handsome man with wheat-golden hair to his shoulders. His tanned skin smooth and coated in dark stubble. The darkness in his eyes was unique and ringed with gold. When he grinned, the white of his teeth caught the moonlight, the same way the gold piercings did in his pointed ears.

"You lived," he said. His voice was like silk, cool and soft. But beneath it all was a jagged edge waiting to strike. "Consider me . . . impressed."

"Ari!" I narrowed my eyes and took a step closer. "You left us to be slaughtered!"

"I'm offended. Did I not warn you this would be a test of fate? Naturally I assumed you would know there would be danger involved."

I clenched my fists. "You wanted us to die."

He studied his painted black fingernails. "I was indifferent." Unbelievable. Ari grinned that smug grin he used to win over everyone in his clan. "Don't be sour, Elise Lysander. You survived and now you shall have a warm bed to rest your pretty, royal head." Ari flicked his eyes to Mattis. "This is your boon companion?"

I pinched my lips. I didn't trust them, not in the slightest, but Night Folk were notorious for being truthful, and clever, and wicked. He said we'd be welcome, but for how long? I didn't know. We would need to negotiate a better deal soon. "Mattis will come with us. He is welcome the same as we are, yes?"

"He is Ettan. Of course, he is welcome."

Mattis kept glancing at Ari, then Siv. Sometimes me.

"Night Folk? *Agitators*?" he said after a pause.

"We prefer to think of ourselves as revolutionaries," Ari said. "Castle Ravenspire and Timorans are the true agitators of the land."

Mattis ignored Ari and turned to Siv. "You're an Agitator?"

"Mattis—"

"You were an Agitator with the *Kvinna*. No doubt sent there for a reason."

"To kill her," Ari said dryly.

I shot him a glare. The stand-in king had no tact, and I was positive he did it on purpose when he winked at me.

"I tease a great deal," Mattis said through his teeth, "but I do not lie. It is a disgusting habit I have little patience for."

Mattis walked away from Siv and came to stand beside me. I touched his arm gently. "Mattis, she—"

"Don't," he said. "Not yet, Elise. Not yet."

He wanted to be angry. And who was I to say he couldn't be? For weeks he'd been a prisoner. Tortured. Now, a person he cared for was revealed as a liar.

I knew the feeling.

"Come," Ari said, grinning. "No doubt we have much to discuss. I have a feeling you might want to hear the most unusual news I've just been given."

"I doubt it."

"No?" Ari lifted his brows. "Even if it involves one of your former *interesting* connections?"

"What are you talking about?"

Ari squared against me. I caught my breath when he gripped my arm. He was stronger than he looked, but never lost his grin. He reminded me of Legion Grey at times. Even if Legion didn't know he was truly Valen Ferus, the Night Folk love of mischief had been rife in his mannerisms.

I swallowed the knot of nerves when Ari took a step closer. "You have unseemly friends, Elise, do you not?"

"I don't know what you're talking about."

"Were you not taken in by the Blood Wraith and his guild? Did you not form some wretched partnership with the man?"

My body stiffened. "I . . . how did—"

"I have my own disconcerting friends." Ari's grin widened. "Come. We need you to help us find him. I have a proposition for the Blood Wraith."

CHAPTER 3
NIGHT PRINCE

"Fate had different plans, little brother."

"No, Sol. No. Leave him, you bastards!" I shouted, struggling against my bound wrists. The raiders surrounded my brother.

Sol's blue eyes grew dark, like the black parts of the sea. "Fight Valen! You fight like you've never fought before! Fight like the gods! I'll save a space for you in the great hall!"

The door slammed between us. The pit where they'd kept my family, where they'd kept our knights and members of the gentry for months and months, settled in a dreary silence.

Those of us left alive stared, unblinking, at the door. Sol was meant to be the next king. The rightful, strong king.

But now . . .

My father had gone through that door. He'd returned bloodied and dead. They'd blocked my fury with spells and strange magic, but even still, the ground shook with my pain.

I was alone.

I was the last Ferus. No doubt, I wouldn't be breathing for much longer.

A pain in my middle woke me from the flash of a memory. I blinked my focus back to the caravan. To the fight right in front of me.

A bulky raven tried to kick at my ribs again. My axe cut through the guarders over his shoulder. He let out a shout of agony and scrambled back.

My chest tightened. The scrape of steel on steel danced down my spine. Smoke from pyre fury thickened in the air. Blood, the sweet tang, the desire to be closer to it, tugged at the beast inside.

The caravan had been ready for our attack.

False King Calder was using his few brains at long last. The moment we'd lunged off the ledge, weapons were raised, and the caravan circled around their supplies. The feeblest Ettans shrank to their knees, expecting to die. No doubt they still ran stunned when the Guild of Shade broke their tethers and attacked their captors instead.

Thoughts of my brother replayed in my head. I fumbled out of reach when another raven joined in against me.

Memories came at odd times, but remembering such a

horrid moment, now, with blades drawn, was wholly incon-
venient.

The guard swiped a short blade at my neck. I parried and
drove one axe between his lower ribs. The raven fell back, gasping, blood dripping between his fingers. A groan rumbled in my
throat. Desire to shred the flesh until more blood spilled was
there. Not as potent as the curse had been, but it was as if
memories of the creature I'd become still lived in my head, a
disease festering that could burst if I was not cautious.

My breaths came heavy behind the red mask, and my grip
tightened on the handles of my axes.

When the second guard met my eye, fear was there. Did he
need to die? I could practically hear my mother's voice begging
for peace, asking me to be the greater man. The way she'd tried
when the Timoran raiders invaded and destroyed our land. Her
pleas fell on deaf ears. They cared little that her skin had been
fair. Her hair like winter frost—like Elise's. They'd taken her;
they'd dragged her like a dog to the Timoran king.

She'd wanted mercy from both sides. From her people, and
her husband's.

The raiders, her own folk, didn't listen. Now her cries were
from the grave.

Did this Ravenspire guard deserve to die? Yes. He did.

Lithely, I dropped one axe against the soft nape of his neck.
He'd hardly budged, as if he knew I'd strike and there was little
he could do to stop it.

Fight, Valen. Fight like you've never fought before. Beneath my
mask, I sneered at the chaos we'd caused the royal caravan.
Perhaps we'd descended into nothing but thieves and killers,

but when Timorans suffered, when their loyalty for Calder faltered, then it would be Etta's time to rise again.

I would fight as Sol demanded of me. I would not stop until those who'd viciously robbed my people of their freedom lost everything.

Halvar laughed behind his black mask, his hood falling back as his air fury spread Tor's flames in hot waves around fleeing Timorans and Ravenspire guards. We'd trapped the caravan and could do as we pleased now.

Until new cries entered the fight.

From the distance, a few dark figures burst from the surrounding field. They appeared from the tall grass and rushed the lone textile cart that had found a way to break through the flames. Not ravens, they were . . . Agitators.

Cursed hells. My insides twisted. There was no time to deal with these fools now.

"Blood Wraith!" an Agitator cried. I could not make out his face, but the glee in his voice made it clear he thought us to be on the same side.

We weren't.

They were a nuisance. A deadly one, but a nuisance all the same. And they were tearing apart the cart. The driver was slaughtered before we could even stop them.

"Get back you bleeding fools!" Halvar shouted. It took a great deal to draw out his anger, but Halvar had little patience for Agitators.

An Agitator rushed toward me, breathless, unafraid of my black iron axes leveled at him. "We saw you attack, and we knew. We knew you served Etta! You serve the true king."

The true king?

"The main coach is there," said the Agitator. I tried to resist, tried, but my eyes followed his pointed finger. The coach was nothing but a supply wagon.

"Textiles," I grumbled.

"No. The false king has been transporting his nobility and supporters in inconspicuous caravans for weeks. But a new wave of raven patrols is coming, Blood Wraith. We do this now, or not at all."

My skin prickled at the notion we were somehow unified with these rogues, but I didn't correct him. Instead, I studied the unimpressive wagon. There was nothing to hint that a Timoran noble was inside. But if there were, well then, the night would get more interesting. I did not mind tearing down the Timoran noble lines vine by vine until they grew so weak and brittle, they would crumble beneath the feet of Ettans.

I whistled at Halvar and Tor, jerked my head at the covered coach, and stalked to the side. A quick swing of my axe broke the bolt on the door. Tor ripped it off the weak hinges. I planned to strike fast and mercilessly.

But small screams drew my attack to a halt.

Children?

A girl, no older than twelve, huddled at least five young ones behind her skinny body. She wore a fine woolen gown, hemmed in silver thread. A band of rowan berries crowned her pale hair. The children behind her wore shoes, stiff trousers, and sturdy woolen tunics. Their cheeks were plump and rosy, proof they did not miss meals.

I hadn't realized the Agitator had come to stand at my shoulder until he laughed viciously.

"Ah, the precious ones of the royal court." I turned my glare to the man. He lifted a brow and drew a knife. "Nobility, Wraith. Isn't that right, little witch?"

The Agitator reached for the oldest girl, taking her by the hair. The younger children screamed as he dragged her away. She winced but remained silent. Brave, for a Timoran. I closed my eyes for a heartbeat. Like Elise.

They were nobles. They'd grow to be vicious, no mistake.

Then again, Elise had not been vicious. She was a rarity, a ray of light in a sea of darkness. These littles, I had few doubts they'd be raised to be ruthless. But could I kill children?

King Eli had not hesitated.

Fight, Valen.

My pulse raced in my skull.

"We . . . have done nothing to you," said the girl, a tremble in her voice. She spoke Ettan roughly, but the Agitator understood enough. "We go to the court for schooling."

"Ah, you won't make it, love."

Fight, Valen.

This would be a fight like I had never experienced before. Slaughtering young ones, giving the Timorans a taste of what my folk endured.

I tightened my grip on my axe. The iron grew heavy. The blade head twitched at my side. I'd make it painless. Swift. I'd spare them from a coming war where they'd watch their families be tortured and killed in front of their eyes.

How many times had I wished to die as a young man after I'd been locked in the quarries?

Bloodlust called. It would keep the creature inside sated. The girl's eyes jumped to mine. Fear was there, but a strength, too.

Dammit!

In one smooth motion, I pressed the cutting edge of the axe against the Agitator's throat.

He turned a look of astonishment my way.

"We don't kill young ones," I said.

Halvar and Tor moved in, whether they agreed with me or not, they'd defend me.

"They are Timoran pups," the Agitator said. "They'd kill you without a second thought should the tables turn."

I was once these children, hiding from monsters in the dark. All gods, I hated them. I hated me for even considering cutting them down.

"Let them go." I pressed the axe blade to his throat until a drop of blood broke free.

The Agitator gawked at me, wholly surprised, but obeyed. His grip unraveled from the girl's hair.

She scrambled back toward the littlest children. "Go, out the back, hurry now."

The Agitator's face contorted into a grimace. He shook his head and ran off into the trees. Let him be angry.

Perhaps we were a little wicked, but there were lines in the sand, and I'd drawn them. Damage had been done; we'd destroyed much of King Calder's trade. Another cut at his weak empire. We didn't need to spill young blood to do our work.

"There! That one. There!"

The girl's shriek startled me. All gods! I cursed myself. The curse had made me complacent in my battle instincts. Enough I did not notice the flames dying, nor the new rush of approaching ravens.

The child I'd just saved pointed her slender finger at me. "He's the leader!"

A guard sliced my arm, splitting the guarder on my shoulder. Blood rushed and soaked my tunic. The sting ravished my skin. All those turns as the Blood Wraith who could not die, I'd hardly felt the burn of steel on flesh. Now, it seared like fire lined the edges.

The guard struck again. I stumbled, swung my axe defensively, and missed. Cursed hells, I'd lost the upper hand in a foolish moment of sentimentality.

I should've let the Agitator slit the girl's throat.

The guard reeled back again, but a gust of hot, fierce wind blasted his face with dirt and debris.

"Go!" Halvar shouted and shoved me back. He stood in my place, a growing circle of ravens at his sides.

The creature inside stirred as I scrambled to my feet. I planned to stand by Halvar, then rip everyone's flesh from their bones piece by piece.

"Air fae!"

Before I could take another breath, the ravens surrounded my friend and wrestled him to the ground. Halvar cried out. Something heavy burdened the air. A strange magic flickered in my own fury, creating a sensation like I would hit a wall should I try to bend the earth.

But Halvar didn't have time for me not to attack.

"Go!" I heard him shout in the crowd of ravens. "Bindings. Go."

Bindings. My throat grew dry. Horrid memories of fetters that wreaked havoc on fury, burned the flesh, and kept the strongest magic muted pummeled my brain.

In a panic, I lifted my hands. Halvar would not be bound again. Not when we'd only just escaped. I'd split the earth and swallow the ravens whole.

But arms wrapped around my waist and tossed me back.

"You bastard!" I shouted from the ground.

"Get up," Tor said in a harsh rasp. He nudged my shoulder. "Hurry. We must go."

"Have you lost your bleeding mind? We're not leaving Halvar!"

Tor dropped any titles between us. For a moment I was not his prince, he was not my subject. He gripped the back of my neck, forehead to mine, and hissed through his teeth. "You reveal yourself, then Halvar will be known. Right now, he is nothing but a rare Night Folk. The king will want to use him, and he'll live. If his connection to the Night Prince is made known, then he dies without question, and war, before we have any standing, begins. Go. We'll plan. We'll return for him, make no mistake."

Halvar was being dragged toward black prison coaches, unable to use his fury. More guards rushed back to Tor and me. My body trembled in hatred, and I cried my rage to the sky.

I turned toward the trees and ran.

Without Halvar.

Gods, I hated Castle Ravenspire. I hated the false king. I hated this land. *Every* Timoran would pay for this night. Young and old alike.

CHAPTER 4
ROGUE PRINCESS

"Allow me." Ari winked as he wiggled his fingers until his fury split a heavy briar shrub, revealing an unhindered path.

I glared at him. Impossible to say how old he might be. His face was young, his body strong and lean. Cleverness lived in the gold of his eyes, maybe a touch of mischief. I lifted my chin, refusing to be bothered the way those eyes laughed at me, and shoved through the split briars.

"What do you want with the Blood Wraith?" My insides had grown sharp and angry, like jagged glass since Ari mentioned the monstrous mask Valen Ferus wore.

"Patience," Ari said. "We shall talk soon. But I would ask you about the relationship you have with the bane of Timoran? Friendly? Lovers? Does he wish you dead? A great deal hinges on knowing how pleased the Blood Wraith will be to see you again."

My fingernails dug into the meat of my palms as I closed

my eyes, took a breath, then hurried ahead of Ari, hoping he would not catch a glimpse of my unease.

"I see," Ari went on. "So, I should not expect a warm welcome?"

"You should not expect anything," I said. "There is a reason we parted ways, and he is not a man who takes pleasure in being bothered."

"You ran, didn't you? Escaped him? Or perhaps the siege at Castle Ravenspire divided you and you cannot find each other."

"Any theory you conjure will be wrong."

"Then by all means, tell me. I do love a good story, Elise."

"No."

"No?"

"Yes, no."

"I could order you."

I snorted a laugh. "You could try."

If he could break the fury tying my tongue, I'd welcome it. But if I had to guess, the Night Prince had the stronger magic of the two.

Instead of anger, Ari's irritating grin widened. "You are difficult. It will be such a joy to crack you. Oh, don't mistake me, I don't mean violence. But I sense a great deal of resistance from you. I look forward to the day when you realize I am not the enemy here. If the rumors I have heard about you are true, if you help Ettans, then I daresay we're on the same side, *Kvinna* Elise."

True, a bit of desperation to find the Night Prince burrowed deep inside, but not this way. Not when the Agitators had no idea who they would face. For one thing, the Blood Wraith would not join any cause of theirs—not when I was here. For another, if Ari learned he was not the fae who'd returned life to the land, I worried a new battle of thrones might begin.

Still, I did desire to see Valen Ferus again.

I hated it.

Mattis hung back, surrounded by some of the prisoners who'd escaped and joined the Agitator clan. He'd said nothing and was clearly avoiding Siv. She walked a few paces behind me, eyes on the ground, a distraught shadow in her countenance. Perhaps we were better off before the Agitators intervened. Perhaps Siv, me, and Mattis ought to make our own way, away from the clan.

"Are you still angry, Elise?" Ari asked, interrupting my thoughts. He picked up his pace until he walked with me, shoulder to shoulder. "About our handling of the prison?"

"We went in good faith to that prison, and you left us to the hands of Ravenspire. Tell me something, *King* Ari, would you have allowed your elder to die if you did not reach us in time?"

"What do you think?"

"Trust me, you do not want to know what I think of you."

"You speak out of line, Timoran," said an Ettan man at my back. He couldn't be much older than me and bore a scar across his throat. As if someone tried to slit him open but didn't succeed.

Ari laughed and I hated the pleasantness of it. "Stand down, Frey. Elise Lysander is still in the habit of being the resounding voice. We shall forgive her a little longer."

My teeth clenched. Ari mocked my position in the Timoran royal courts often, but little did he know, I had no resounding voice there either.

Ari moved another bramble out of my path without fury. "We kept our bargain, Elise."

"You hid in the shadows waiting for us to die."

"Not true. Did I want to see how you fared against your own people? Yes. It was a strange kind of surprise to see you fight against the ravens for our elder."

"And Mattis. I was there for him."

"A half-Ettan," Ari said. "I'd heard rumors, you see, that one of the Timoran royals sympathized with the true people of this land. I had to see it for myself. You did not disappoint."

"Is this a game to you?"

"In a way, yes. We are all moving pieces in a game of power." Ari paused, his dark eyes smoldering in a new heat. "To answer your other question, yes. We would have saved Klok with or without you. And we would not have let you fall to the ravens. You're too interesting."

I bit back a curse over his tests and trials of fate. Risk his own life all he wants, but do not risk mine and those I care about.

Ari accused me of being arrogant, but he was more so.

And I didn't much care for the way he grinned at me, as if a witty remark were always on the tip of his tongue. It made him seem too much like the old Legion Grey. Like Halvar. Too approachable.

The ground sloped. Trees thickened and slowed our pace, forcing us to maneuver over fallen logs and narrower paths. A chill prickled the skin on my arms the deeper we went into the trees. Ari paused at a vine-wrapped structure. It reminded me of an old archway. Runes carved the rock, and the keystone at the curve of the arch had fallen away, leaving the bow incomplete.

"Wait here," Ari said, I assumed to me since he placed a hand on my shoulder as he walked by. His touch was warm, fury in his fingertips left me wanting to obey his every word.

My temper flashed, red and raw. Hells, I tired of Night Folk and their manipulation.

"I would've waited without being forced," I snapped.

"See, this is what I mean," Ari said. "We must get to know each other before I can trust you to follow such basic commands."

He placed his palm on the broken stone. In another breath, the runes glowed like molten gold. A rush of air whipped against my face. I closed my eyes, bracing against the wind. By the time I opened them again, Ari was ushering the others forward through the arch.

One side of his mouth curled into a playful sneer. "Welcome to Ruskig, Elise Lysander."

I tried to smother the thrill of stepping into an unknown. Ruskig was always spoken like it was some mythical plot of land in New Timoran. A place where Night Folk lived in peace, free from the sights of kings and queens. I had no reason not to believe it existed, but in truth, I'd started to think it was a place of fantasy.

To step inside was . . .

"You've managed to keep Ruskig concealed all this time," I said, dryly. "Impressive."

Ari chuckled again, his teeth bright against the darkness. "Strange how your near-compliment is so satisfying. Why would I want your approval I wonder?"

"Who can say? To me, it sounds like a personal problem, this need to be accepted." I didn't look at him as I hurried through the archway.

As much as I feigned indifference, I couldn't hold in the gasp once I was through the rune stones. All around silver moonvane burst in beautiful, reaching branches. Velvet petals glimmered like starlight. The world was different here. Trees were thicker, damp with bright, green moss on rich, black bark. The grass was coated in silvery dew drops. Blossoms of lavender, of blue rose, colored the darkness next to the moonvane.

The snap of branches. The whisper of grass bending underfoot. This place was alive. Magical.

"What do you think?" Ari whispered.

I didn't realize he'd come so close. Unable to resist, my fingertips ran across spongy moss on a nearby tree. "It's . . . so alive."

He beamed, satisfied. "It is. This is what fury can do for this land. What it will do once again. We plan to restore life the way the gods intended. Come, we have things to talk about."

"Wait," I said, glancing over my shoulder. "I should bring Mattis and—"

"Bring them," Ari said. "We have open courts here, as King Arvad once did."

I swallowed the scratch in my throat. This, *this* is what Valen could help restore if he would cease his vengeance. Tears stung my eyes as I wove back through the line of Agitators, looking for Siv and Mattis.

The Night Prince needed to take his place.

I needed him.

I pushed the thought away, hardening my heart. Sentiment would do little good now.

Mattis had faded from the crowd and studied a lush shrub of moonvane.

"Where is Mavie? Where is Legion Grey, Elise?" Mattis asked without turning around.

My chin trembled. "They . . . they're gone."

Mattis crossed his arms over his chest, body stiff, as if barring himself away from the truth. We stood in silence for at least ten heartbeats. I didn't want to explain anymore about Legion or Mavie. I let him think of them as gone together.

"I hope they found peace in the great hall," he whispered at long last.

I reached out and touched the back of his arm. "Are you all right?"

"No. All this time I trusted . . ." His eyes broke into me when he glanced over his shoulder. "How did you find out?"

"At the siege of Castle Ravenspire. Mattis, Siv could have killed me many times, but didn't. I know you're angry but speak with her. Let it go because we need each other. Ari wishes to speak with me, and I need those I trust with me."

Mattis furrowed his brow. "Why does he think you have connection to the Blood Wraith?"

I sighed. How would I explain anything? How could I? Mattis took Siv's betrayal so harshly. What would he do if he knew Legion Grey—whom Mattis had trusted too—was the Blood Wraith? "He . . . he took us to safety after the siege."

"You aren't serious?"

"I am. I suppose the Blood Wraith held more of a grudge

against Timoran folk like Calder, than second daughters of the second royal family."

Mattis dragged his fingers through his dirty hair, shaking his head. "Elise, what happened to you?"

"A great deal, I'm sure." Mattis and I turned together. Ari stood with his makeshift royal guard. Frey, and four more bulky Ettans held roughly shaped swords and glowered beneath mantles of wiry fur and animal skins on their heads.

"But would you mind chatting later?" Ari went on. "We really do have a schedule to keep if we're to move forward successfully."

Behind Ari was Siv, head still down. Matti's jaw flinched, but he folded his arms over his chest. "You helped get me out, so I'll listen to what you have to say. But to be clear, I am loyal to Elise."

Ari lifted a brow. "Even if we welcomed you into our home? Even as an Ettan?"

"Being Ettan, or Timoran, or Night Folk, does not make the person trustworthy. It is heart and actions. I am loyal to Elise. Perhaps, eventually, I will be to you as well."

At that, Ari grinned his slyness again. "I like you, Carpenter. How glad I am you were not spliced on the rack tonight. Follow me."

Ari led us to a longhouse surrounded by thick trees. The roof was made of mossy sod and moonvane branches. Inside an inglenook already had a fire burning against the chill in the air. Ari removed his weapon belt, letting it clatter atop a narrow table in the center of the house. The others stripped their furs. Frey poured ale from a wooden ewer and passed out horns as his king plopped into a wooden chair, lifted his boots onto the table, and crossed his ankles.

"Better," Ari said, accepting a horn of ale with a nod. He made a gesture to the remaining seats. "Sit. Please."

We took our places with a touch of caution. Siv sat on my left, Mattis on the right. Neither had spoken to the other and it raised the hair on my neck. I craved a touch of normalcy, and these two were the last of it. Divided, I didn't know how we would survive any of this.

"As promised, I have information on the Blood Wraith. At first, I would not think much of such reports, but after discovering he not only took you from Castle Ravenspire but attacked one of the false king's captains to save your neck, it made me wonder if the Blood Wraith has more purpose in his attacks than we thought."

"Your pardon?" Mattis said, eyes wide. "Elise, what happened?"

"Jarl," I whispered harshly. "Long story."

"I expect to hear it."

I waved him away as Ari went on. "First, I have a question, Elise. Is the Blood Wraith Night Folk?"

"Why would you think that?"

Ari's smile faded. "Weeks ago, some of our people were . . . infected by a strange blight. They went mad, almost as if they could not control themselves. They attacked Mellanstrad— they attacked your lands."

My mouth dropped. Memories of the crazed Agitators biting out the throat of one of my father's guards still haunted my dreams. I'd known something strange had taken those people. The blackness in their eyes, their mouths, their blood.

"I remember," I said softly.

"Yes." Ari cleared his throat. "We tried to heal them ourselves, but nothing helped. We tried to track them, to bring them back, but by the time we reached them it was too late."

"What does the Wraith have to do with it?" I bit the inside of my cheek. I told Halvar I saw the Blood Wraith that night, but he'd quickly dismissed the idea. Now, I was certain a cursed Valen had been there. Halvar likely returned to our lands to protect me against his own prince.

"It's curious," Ari said. "But there were some who saw the Wraith. They saw him use fury. A powerful fury that stopped the madness. Of course, it likely killed our people, too, but what sort of life would they have had in such a state?"

Was it possible? Even being in his cursed delirious blood-lust, was it possible that Valen had reached into his fury without knowing, and stopped the attack? The Agitators had all fallen at once that night.

"So, is he fae?" Ari asked again.

"I-I-I'm not positive." Fury kept me from giving his true name, but not that he had magic. Still, for some reason, I kept quiet. About it all, the curse, his ploy to take me. I didn't know if I protected Ari and his people, or Valen. "What you should know is he is deadly, strong, and hates Ravenspire."

"Then we have a great deal in common," Ari said blithely. "We wish him to join us, Elise. No doubt you've heard of the Guild of Shade attacks around the kingdom as of late. I know what he's doing—he's attacking supplies. He's starving Timorans, breaking their trust in their new king. He's perfect."

"He won't join you," I hurried to say, grateful for the nod Siv offered in support. "He prefers to be alone."

"I'm sure," Ari said. "But he's suddenly desperate, and I think he might be willing to negotiate."

"Desperate? I don't understand."

"Don't take my word, take it from our witness." Ari lifted a hand to the back of the house to a man in a flowing hood. "This is Ulf, one of my scouts. He'll tell you."

I hadn't noticed Ulf before now. He removed his hood from his square head and stalked to the edge of the table.

"I was there," he said, his voice husky and rough. "Tracked the Guild of Shade to a textile caravan that was a cover for transporting the little bastards of the Timoran gentry. Thought the Wraith was there to take them, but he was surprised. He bleeding hesitated to kill the young ones and it got one of his Shade taken by Castle Ravenspire. The other Shade had to practically drag him away. Never seen a man so filled with rage as I did when the ravens trapped his guild rat. It's a dangerous kind of desperate. The kind where a man is at the edge and he's about to jump off."

My breath caught in my throat. I whipped my eyes to Siv. She'd gone pale, her bottom lip between her teeth. Who'd been taken? Halvar? Tor? What would happen if Calder realized they were not typical Night Folk, but they were centuries old members of the Ferus court?

Worse, I believed Ulf. The Night Prince had lost everything but his two friends. To lose one of them to Ravenspire would unhinge him, no mistake.

Valen, where are you?

"So, you see, Elise," Ari said. "We know where they take captured Night Folk. We meet the Wraith as he goes for his Shade, we help him, and he joins us."

I shook my head. "I don't think it will be so simple."

Ari grinned, savagely. "I can be convincing."

Fear prickled up my arms. How far would Ari go to convince Valen to join him—hells, what would happen when he discovered the Night Prince was alive and destroying Timoran slowly?

There was no talking them out of it, I could see that. They wanted my input on the Wraith, not my permission. Doubtless the Agitators were going to use me to get the Blood Wraith. To bring Valen out into the light.

Our time apart was at an end.

CHAPTER 5
ROGUE PRINCESS

H alvar was being held at the fury quarries.

At least the latest report from Ari's scouts was an air fae had been taken there. It answered the question on which of the Shade had been taken.

Ari grew more pleased at the notion of having rare fury in Ruskig. I grew more irritated. The strength or talent of Halvar's fury didn't matter—he did.

And we were running out of time.

The journey was over a day's ride on horseback, and nearly three on foot. There was no telling what would become of the playful Shade in that time.

I didn't wish either Tor or Halvar to be taken, but Tor had such a disposition, I was certain he'd slaughter anyone who touched him. Halvar would try to befriend them.

A grimace tightened my face. He'd survive. He'd be fine. What had Valen told me? Halvar was the son of the first knight. He was bred to fight, even if he did so with a grin.

I couldn't believe otherwise.

Strange how important not only Valen had become, but the Guild of Shade too.

Tor and Halvar had been cursed as much as Valen. Their part was, perhaps, more gut-wrenching. Being forced to slice and brutalize their brother to satisfy the need for blood was a cruel kind of torture all its own.

I secured a knife into the weapon belt Frey had given me. Anger burned, slow and deep, thinking of Halvar being harmed at the hands of Castle Ravenspire again.

They'd pay.

If they didn't know who Valen was yet, they never would. Not from Halvar, at least. He'd never give up his prince. But his silence would prolong his suffering, and meant we needed to move. Reservations on seeing Valen again, in being there when he denied Ari, when he denied me once again, needed to be pushed aside for the sake of Halvar.

I dipped my hands into a clay basin. The cool morning had chilled the water enough it cut with cold. I splashed my face, stirring my senses awake. My fingers twisted my damp hair into a tight braid.

Ari had offered a small hut near his longhouse. The walls were made of tree limbs woven into mats, then packed in damp moss, sod, and mud. As if it could not help but spread, some of the walls were dotted in small blooms of moonvane. I grinned and stroked one of the silky, silver petals, then tugged on boots, a size too big.

In the corner, a small stove had been shaped out of river stone, and a tricky fae came in the night before and warmed the stones until the hut heated pleasantly. Not a pyre fae like Tor, but it was fascinating to watch fury brighten the stones into glowing embers all the same.

I had a bed and mattress padded with furs and dried grass. A few clay pots, and a kettle for dandelion tea.

I'd been given my own place amongst the Night Folk, and I still could hardly believe it.

Siv pulled back the bearskin over the doorway. "Elise, we're ready to leave."

"Coming."

Siv reached for a bowl made of bone. In it, Frey had mixed beeswax with charcoal into a sticky kohl. She took the frayed end of a stick and dipped it into the bowl. "May I?"

Tension squeezed in my chest, but more from excitement than worry. The charcoal paint was used for warriors. How long had I yearned to find a place in this land? Among the nobility of my family and bloodlines, I had no standing. No voice. Here, though, I could embrace the ever-present urge to be true to the boil of my blood; the call to fight for this land that was not truly mine.

Siv brushed the frayed end of the twig over my forehead, down the bridge of my nose. My chin. When she finished, I painted her face. Long strokes over her bronze skin. Protection. Strength. Jagged lines for a bit of malice.

Perhaps we weren't going to war. Then again, perhaps we were.

Outside of Ruskig there was no telling what awaited us.

"Finished," I whispered and returned the bowl to the small table. Only the haze of dawn lit the outside. No shadows of guards, no Ari. Still, I lowered my voice to a harsh whisper.

"What will happen when Ari discovers the Blood Wraith is no ordinary man?"

Siv's eye twitched. "I don't know. To me, it seems Prince Valen is not revealing his fury. We would have heard by now. Odds are no one will recognize him as anything but common Night Folk."

"Ari already suspects he is more than common because of the attack on my lands. Do you think he could've caused the darkness?"

"Sagas say Prince Valen is a Bender. Likely the first one in centuries. Whoever infected the clan, they do not have earth fury."

I took a bit of comfort in her response. Valen broke the earth, molded clay and bedrock to his bidding. He could not cause such a disease.

Outside, frost hung in the air. A dry wind prickled at my face, whipping pieces of loose hair against my skin. Horses were packed with quilts, furs, canteens, and ale horns. Mothers with their littles around their skirts bid farewell to fathers, uncles, and brothers.

Night Folk in Ruskig were not those with powerful fury. The raids had watered down magic, but a chill trickled down my spine at the sight of so many fae armed with axes, knives, and daggers. Most with runes and black lines painted across their faces, much like mine.

Even with little fury, they would be formidable now that they were rising at long last.

The same could be said for the Ettan folk. Women shaved half their heads. They braided the rest in tight, intricate rows. Their shoulders were bulky with pelts and woolen mantles.

Black surrounded men's eyes. Beards were beaded in bone and silver. Runes tattooed on shorn scalps.

Beaten by Timorans for too long, the Ettans and Night Folk were finding their place. They had always lived in peace together for lifetimes, one half with magic, the other without. Until Timorans stole the land from them all. Now, the folk of Old Etta were taking back their homeland.

I hated how the first thought I had at such a sight was how much I wished Valen could see it.

Across from me, Mattis helped secure a short blade to the body of a roan. He'd cut his hair, so only a ridge of chestnut curls was left in the center of his skull. The carpenter left the beard he'd grown in prison, shorter than other men, but he'd added a chain of bone beads in the center and blackened the lids of his eyes.

He greeted me with a grin, until he noticed Siv. The smile fell and he tugged a black hood over his face, turning away.

She let out a long sigh.

"Give him time," I said.

"He is living among Agitators, befriending them, yet he shuns me."

"I know." I paused, letting a sly twist play on my lips. "But in truth, I'm surprised it matters at all. I thought you didn't care for Mattis."

Her eyes flashed with a gleam of frustration. "I don't." Siv shouldered her pack again. "Don't mistake me. I think he's simply behaving like a child and that is aggravating."

I grinned as she stomped away.

"Elise." Ari stood beside a white horse. He'd braided the sides of his golden hair, drawn his eyes in kohl, and wore a thick cloak made of russet fox fur. "You shall ride with me. And might I say how vicious you look. Truly inspiring."

My face heated at the praise.

Truth be told, I could say the same. Ari's smooth skin was painted in blue and black lines, as if someone dragged their fingers from one temple to the opposite edge of his jaw. He was every bit a warrior as the rest of his clan, and too handsome for his inflated self-importance. No mistake, he would put up a wicked fight to get what he wanted. If only he knew what he wanted was the Night Prince.

I patted the withers of the horse, frowning. "I ride fine. I don't need a companion."

"Ah, but we don't have enough horses, and I'd hate to see those royal feet stumble across such uncharted roads."

"My royal feet are perfectly capable."

Ari grinned as he tossed the harness over the horse's head. "All the same, join me. We will make vastly swifter time, and as such it is not even worth arguing this point."

I lifted my chin, refusing to let on how grateful I was not to be walking. "Only because you fear I will successfully out-argue you."

He laughed, lacing his fingers beneath my heel to boost me onto the horse's back. "I have no doubt, then again I am told I have a convincing tongue myself."

I scooted back, giving Ari room to settle onto the horse. My pulse quickened when I curled my arms around his waist. He was warm. His skin breathed like the forest, clean with a bit of spice. The stand-in king was aggravating, but intriguing, too.

"Who tells you such a thing?" I asked. "You, to your own reflection?"

Ari glanced over his shoulder. "Frey tells me I ought to cut your tongue from your head, Elise Lysander."

Unbidden, my arms tightened around him, as if his body would shield me from his words.

Ari laughed and the shudder of it rumbled through my insides. "I told him I rather like your tongue, of course. It stays. But I will say I am gaining many holes in my fragile kingly confidence the more you speak."

A reluctant smile curled in the corner of my mouth. From a small house several men each carried a stack of wooden spheres. My eyes widened on second glance. "All gods, are those . . . shields?"

"Yes," Ari said.

With care the men handed out round, wooden shields marked in runes, with bronze or iron points in the center.

"Are we going to war?"

Ari chuckled. "Perhaps."

"I have not seen such a shield but for . . ."

"Portraits? History books? Yes. It is rather fortunate Night Folk have such incredible lifespans," Ari said, lightly. "We also seem to have a proclivity to collect."

"Are you telling me those are from the raids?"

"Why yes, I am."

My blood burned with a thrill, as if the warrior inside yearned for what was to come. A black shield with white runes was laced to the saddle pack of our horse. I touched the edges gingerly. A war. Was I joining an uprising against my blood?

I'd never truly given time for the thought to sink in before, but I was.

With a wink, Ari urged the horse through the veiled canopy

of moonvane and beyond the protected archway of Ruskig. The night was thick and cold. Trees there were thin, weak. After witnessing what fury could do for this land, the beautiful landscapes I'd enjoyed all my life were brittle and dull.

Empty.

I didn't realize how tightly I held onto Ari's waist until his hand covered mine. "I do love a woman's body pressed against my own, but perhaps we could loosen our grip slightly. Unless you are attempting to suffocate me, in which case I applaud you for such a devious attempt at assassination."

"All gods, are you ever serious?"

"I should hope not."

I adjusted and loosened my grip as asked, all the while despising how the stand-in king made me laugh.

As we rode into the night, I fought against thoughts of what we might face. The plan was to lure the Blood Wraith with the notion of rescuing Halvar. The tips of my fingers tingled with numbness.

No matter what happened, something told me very soon I would see Valen Ferus again.

CHAPTER 6
ROGUE PRINCESS

Valen and Sol are hiding something. The two princes are constantly sneaking into the forest. I have questioned Dagar, the first knight, many times since his eldest son, and young Torsten join them. And now, by the gods, they are taking Herja.

No one knows what mischief they are managing. No matter what threats Arvad and I spew at them, my three loyal children will say nothing to what they're up to. But there is a heaviness in Sol's eyes.

Perhaps it is the burden of taking the crown. His father often reminds him of his duty as future king. Necessary, but it could be too much. He has only reached sixteen and . . .

"What is that you're reading?"

My eyes snapped up from Lilianna's journal. Ari's shape blurred through my tears. This was the first entry

Halvar and Tor were mentioned. Strange to read about their past lives and know them now.

I didn't expect to miss them, yet I did.

"Three hells," Ari said, his eyes wide. "What has upset you so? I did not think anything could break you, *Kvinna* Elise."

Ari settled on the fallen log beside a shallow stream. We'd stopped to water the horses and to eat a meager meal of berries and dried herring. We were in Calder's territory now. The roads grew narrow, overgrown, and rocky enough I doubted any ravens would patrol.

I forced a tight grin at the king. "Nothing. It's nothing."

With care, Ari peeled the tattered journal from my fingers. I went to object, but he was already scanning some of the entries.

"Bleeding hells," he said under his breath. "Is this . . ."

I nodded when he went quiet, understanding his stun. "Queen Lilianna's."

His eyes were devoid of playfulness, he was purely astonished. "How did you come by this?"

"You have shields. I am of the royal line. My uncle had many artifacts," I lied.

"And this upsets you?" He stroked the spine reverently.

"Yes, but not for what you think." I smiled when he handed the journal back. "It's foolish."

"I don't believe in foolishness. Simply different thoughts. I vow upon my mother's grave I shall not mock you. Why does the former queen upset you?"

For a moment—I trusted Ari.

I licked my lip and clutched Lilianna's journal to my chest. "I've read countless times by now how Arvad and Lilianna once ruled. I was raised to think of them as vicious, cutthroat, and killers. But in truth, they were fair, they loved each other, they loved their children." I stared at the ground. "And my people destroyed them. I simply want this land to be what it once was."

Ari paused. For once without a thing to say. His voice was low and steady when he finally spoke. "You are a surprising Timoran, Elise Lysander. We, at last, agree on something. It is my oath, to all people, that this land will once more thrive as it did under the Ferus line."

"Yes, but what of the Timoran people?"

"There are more who think like you, I'm sure of it. Lilianna was Timoran." He tugged on one of his locks of golden hair. "I am Night Folk, but clearly my own bloodline is not fae alone. There will be war if I have anything to say about it, but I pray to the All Father of gods that we can heal the scars of this land. Together."

I opened my mouth to respond, but words turned to ash. Ari was fair, and a knot gathered in the back of my throat. If Valen would not take his place, then Ari might be the best chance we had. It was not a disturbing thought. Oddly reassuring, in fact.

He tapped my knee and stood. "Are you ready to continue? We wish to reach the inn before dawn."

I nodded and gathered the journal, shouldering my satchel, and followed Ari to the horses. Siv rode with Frey, Mattis with Ulf.

They had yet to speak, but I had to believe Mattis would defend her even angry as he was.

Once Ari settled in front of me again, he waved the clan

forward. Sharp aches burned and cramped in my bones from riding hard. I gritted my teeth and held onto his waist.

"Ari," I said after we took the lead. My voice slipped and stammered as the horse rocked over uneven ground. "How . . . how do we explain ourselves t-t-to an innkeeper."

I let out a choked squeal when the horse fumbled over a raised step in the path and squeezed Ari until he let out a grunt.

"Hells woman, did you not insist you were a skilled rider?"

"I am!" My crushing grip said differently, but I was inclined to argue. "Just not when the creature is attempting to scale a mountainside."

"Have more faith in Vit, Elise. He may be old, but he is strong." He chuckled, patted the horse's neck, as if we were not about to topple off the side. "And have more faith in me and my plans. Where we go, few questions are asked."

Soon enough the paths leveled, the forest thickened, and when the pale dawn crested the horizon, I understood.

Sven's alehouse came into view.

"You know this place?" I brushed a few wild locks of hair out of my eyes when Ari dismounted and tethered Vit to a post.

He grinned and held a hand for me. "I told you, Elise. I have unseemly connections, same as you."

"Is he . . ." I wrung my hands in front of my body, unable to finish. Was Valen inside? Would he be pleased to see me? Angry? I would hate to see the light and affection he once had in his eyes darken.

Ari rested his hand on the small of my back, nudging me forward. "I believe we are alone. For now." He lifted his brow, studying each twitch of my cheek. "Does he frighten you? You never did tell me if you ran *from* the Blood Wraith."

"Yet here we are whether I did or not," I said with a touch of bitterness.

"We must take risks."

I closed my eyes. Heat turned my insides upside down. "I did not run from him, Ari. At least not that time. But it does not mean the Blood Wraith will be pleased to see us."

He dipped his chin, a cautious grin on his face. "Understood. Still, I believe he is needed. Ravenspire fears him, and those are the people we need on our side."

To that, I had no answer. It was unnerving at times how much Ari played feckless to hide his logic and cleverness. Aligning with the adversaries of Calder's crown was the wisest choice, but only two of us knew the consequences of unmasking the Wraith.

Then again, this could be the nudge needed to push the Night Prince toward his fate.

Ari opened the door to the alehouse. I held my breath and followed.

Stale wine, ale, and unwashed skin hit my face. Beneath the stained floorboards was a constant damp in the air. A faint hint of coppery blood. My fists clenched and unclenched. Stains on the floor painted the boards in splatters of dark black from old blood. How much of the grime was left behind from endless nights of Valen's torture?

The curse demanded blood and the Guild of Shade took it under this very roof.

I swallowed bile, staring at the table where I'd faced Legion Grey for the first time as the Blood Wraith, where I'd demanded he return my missing fingertips.

A hot spark of pain bit at my heart as I touched the foggy

glass and stared outside where I'd lain next to Valen after his cursed night. Where he'd kissed me before we went to the Black Tomb.

Before everything changed.

"Well, look who came back."

My eyes flicked to the countertop. Sven sneered as he scrubbed a drinking horn.

"Sven." My voice cracked. I lifted my chin and stepped to the counter.

"I keep my mouth shut."

A furrow gathered between my brows. "Your pardon?"

The aleman winked and returned the horn to a dusty shelf. "I keep my mouth shut. I can sees you're about to tell me not to mention times we last saw each other, girl. I keep my mouth shut."

"Wholly unfair," Ari said. "Now you have admitted there are secrets between the two of you, and my curiosity is piqued to dangerous levels."

The aleman snickered and clasped Ari's forearm. "You pay me, and I'll keep your secrets too."

The stand-in king clicked his tongue. "I suppose that's fair. But I assure you, Elise, I will pester you ruthlessly."

I shook my head. "You're a child."

Ari grinned, as if pleased I'd insulted him. We waited for the others to saunter inside. Soon enough the room was packed with sweaty, travel worn bodies. Siv found me, offered a curt nod to Sven, but said nothing.

Mattis hesitated. His eyes went to us, then the clan. In the end, the carpenter came to stand at my other shoulder.

"Ulf said this is where the Blood Wraith frequents," he said, voice low. "You came here?"

"After the siege, yes. I didn't think he'd still return, though."

"You speak as if you know him well." Mattis scratched his chin. "What aren't you telling me? Why would the Blood Wraith not only save you, but take you here? Why keep you with him?"

"Mattis—"

"Sit," Ari interrupted. He grinned at the packed room. "The aleman will tell us what he knows."

Sven's leathery face wrinkled. Something close to a smile, I'd guess, but perhaps the turns of snarling kept him from showing a true grin. "You come here to stand against Ravenspire?"

"As I explained in my missive," Ari said.

"You came to . . . assist other patrons?"

Ari didn't falter. "As I explained in my missive."

Sven puckered his lips. "Then I'll tell you a bit. I don't give up secrets, but the ways I see it—this is life and death."

"Couldn't agree more," said Ari. "Where can we find the lost Shade? Or better yet, the Blood Wraith?"

"I don't knows where he's gone," Sven said. "The Wraith that is. But I knows where he's going. As I explained in *my* missive, your best chance at meeting is at the fury quarries. It's warded, though. Tricky magic lives there, keeps in all the Night Folk the king don't want to kill just yet. Knowing the Wraith as I do, he'll wait until dark."

"And you're sure he attacks tonight?"

Sven shrugged. "Best guess, yes. It's been nigh a week since his Shade was taken. Tonight is when they switch out the ravens. It's a weak point during guard changes. Seems the best night to act if you ask me."

Ari slumped in his chair. "Guesses. I don't like working on guesses."

"It's all you'll get," Sven said. "Not like me and the Wraith are thick as thieves. I give 'im a roof and cover, he gives me *shim*."

Sven turned away and began wiping the dingy countertop. Ari waited a moment, but when it was obvious the aleman was done speaking, he faced his clan. "The Wraith must know how to enter the prison. We find our own way in—best case—we reach the captured Shade first. Prove our intentions. Elise."

My mind had wandered, but Ari's voice drew me back to the moment. "Yes."

"What do you think? Do you agree with the aleman about the Wraith attacking tonight?"

I glanced around the room, shrinking under the scrutiny of so many. "I can't say. Truth told, I'm surprised he has not burned half the land of Timoran to the ground already."

"His Shade mean that much to him?"

"They are loyal only to one another," I said. Siv shook her head and glanced at the floorboards. I hated saying it, but it was true. Valen, Tor, and Halvar would fight for each other. I did not belong among them.

Ari's jaw tightened. He stood, leaning over the table. "We go tonight, then. If the aleman is right, then it will be the best opportunity to enter the prison. Take a few tolls to rest. We leave soon to face whatever fate the Norns have been spinning for us."

Fate. Such a fickle thing. The magic of the girl in the cage—

Calista. What had she called herself? A storyteller. A spinner of fate in her own way. Perhaps she was descended from the three Norns at the base of the great tree.

I thought of her often, wondering if she'd ever been freed from her prison. She'd fought for Valen, for me. But she told me fate had grand plans for Valen Ferus.

Tonight, I would either aid those plans, or alter his path entirely.

CHAPTER 7
NIGHT PRINCE

"This is beneath you."

I bit into my tongue to keep the laugh inside. "You mean, it is beneath you."

Tor narrowed his eyes, adjusted the sack of grain he carried, and scratched at the linen tunic covering the belt of knives on his waist. "My first order of royal business is outfitting serfs into something not spun in bleeding husks. All hells, how do they wear this?"

"I believe it is because they have no choice."

Tor let out an irritated sound, but clenched his jaw, going silent.

We hobbled with other pack serfs bound for deliveries to the fury quarries. After we discovered Halvar would be held there, we'd spent days and nights planning this moment. The trouble was not getting into the prison but getting out. Here, Castle Ravenspire kept the richest fury. Night Folk locked away to be of use to the false kings that took its throne. There was no telling if more pyre fae, air fae, or dark fae suffered in these walls.

My hold tightened around the musty sack of grain in my arms. How often were Night Folk tortured until they would use their magic for anyone simply to make the pain stop?

The Night Folk in here—I could not count on them being loyal against the ravens or the false king. If they were manipulated enough, then to them we might be the enemy.

Guards halted the caravan at a large wooden gate, checking the supplies.

Towers marked points along the top. Flames from torches cast raven guards in a harrowing light. Mentally, I checked their positions. Three towers. Four guards in each. Two on the outside of the gate, doubtless two more on the inside door.

More than ravens, there would be rune spells, and we'd need to be on our guard. Bindings lived here. I closed my eyes, wishing the memory of the burn had never returned.

I didn't know how many months the unbreakable fetters bound my wrists during the raids. Truth be told, I didn't want to remember each detail. Made of iron from this earth, but warped with some fury, some magic I didn't know. A wretched kind of spell powerful enough to block even earth fury as mine.

Those bindings added to our trouble getting out of the prison. Halvar would be bound, I was certain. We'd need to steal one of the keys used to remove the bindings.

A key, no mistake, the warden of this place would have in his keep.

Three men against the most heavily guarded, cruelest man

COURT OF ICE AND ASH

in this godsforsaken pit. The odds were not in our favor. But I never did care much for acting on the odds of fate. It had never been kind to me, so I would make my own.

"Bag." A guard prodded the grain sack in my arms.

I kept my head down, a knit cap pulled over the points of my ears, a dye in my eyes to brighten them. The guard whacked the grain with a wooden rod, chuckling when I grunted against the strike.

He pounded the end of the rod between my shoulder blades. "Keep moving, then."

My feet stumbled, but my mouth lifted in a sneer. Worthless bastards. Two paces behind me, Tor passed his own inspection and humbly sauntered like a downtrodden serf.

The prison gates were spiked on top. A few skulls jutted above the rest on pikes. Omens of raven feet, teeth, and bones, hung from leather. Beneath our feet mud caked the thin boots we'd stolen from a farmer's stable in the last township. A familiar reek of piss and mold hung in the air, no different than it was when I'd been trapped in these walls.

Anger tasted like acid on my tongue. I looked forward to the day this place burned to the ground.

Tor cleared his throat and gave a subtle nod. In the archway the serfs crowded one another, perhaps to stay warm, perhaps they feared being trapped here. No matter the reason, the swarm provided time for us to slip away through a covered bridge connecting the outer yard to the main prison.

Together, we kept our heads down, hurried our steps, and ducked behind stacked ale casks halfway down the bridge. Two torches provided little light, but fifty paces forward we'd find a small stove room where raven guards took respite. From there, corridors honeycombed to guard rooms and the warden's chamber.

We didn't need a map.

We had memories.

"How much time?" I hissed through my teeth.

Tor lifted his eyes to the velvet sky. "Moon's nearly at the high point, so within the hour."

I nodded, adjusting so I could crouch easier behind the casks and keep watch on a lancet window straight ahead.

"You trust this man to give the signal?" Tor asked.

"No. But he will."

"And if he doesn't."

"We follow through with the consequences. As promised." I'd follow through on any threat. This was the sort of thinking Elise told me she feared. She'd been right, of course. Now I had no doubt I'd sell my soul to avenge the wrongs of my people, to free Halvar.

She was better off away from all this.

Since parting, I'd heard word the second *Kvinna* lived on. Heard she'd found refuge in Ruskig. I'd also heard her future brother-in-law had taken her for a second wife. Another that her corpse decorated the gates of Ravenspire.

The latter was false—I'd made certain of it before I could ever give this night enough focus—so who was to say which rumors were true?

Tor smacked my chest. "We ought to dress."

I withdrew a knife from my boot, grinning. "If my mother were alive and she saw you hitting me all the time, you'd be buried alive, Torsten."

"Your mother loved me more than you, *My Prince*." Tor stabbed his grain bag at the seam and began splitting the threads. "Hells, you were always crying to the queen."

I thrust my knife into the grain sack, shredding the canvas until my boots were buried in oats. Inside the grain sack, my grip found the handles of the two axes, my cowl, two knives, and the red mask. "I regret nothing. I barely survived childhood because of you and my brother."

Tor smiled, but it was distant as he dug through the mess of oats and corn in his sack for his mask and hood. Silence thickened between us. This place had a chill in the air that I was certain only the two of us felt. As if ghosts from the past encircled our every move. Sol had belonged to Tor as much as me.

Emotion scratched up my throat. "Do you ever wish he were here instead of—"

"No," Tor interrupted. "I do not waste time with wishing." With that, Tor cupped the back of my head, eyes locked with mine. "I am nothing but cruel, broken pieces of what I was because Sol is gone. There is an eternal hole in my chest, but you are my brother, and not once have I wished anyone else stood at my side."

I cleared away the knot, patted his face, and gave him a curt nod.

Crouched behind the casks we stripped the serf clothing with care. Once or twice, we paused when a few ravens sauntered past, yawning and off their duty. I'd finished securing the battle axes to my belt by the time Tor struck my shoulder again.

"Look." He pointed at the window.

A new flame on a single candlestick glared through the glass. "That's the signal. Ready?"

"Days ago."

We kept low along the wall of the bridge. Once we reached the end, Tor pressed his back on one side of the door. I took hold of one axe.

This place was one of the hells.

I gritted my teeth and kicked the door hard enough the worn latch snapped.

The next steps blurred. Tor ducked into the room in front of me. His blade stabbed a half-dressed raven before the guard finished snapping his trousers. There were five guards in the room. All disoriented at the sudden attack. All in various states of dress and weapons.

Shouts rang in my ears. Fear. Surprise. A guard lunged at me. His blade met my axe. His unsteady stance became his undoing. I knocked his strike off course, then swung my axe against his neck.

Tor cursed when a guard gained a hit over his shoulder. I threw my axe and didn't wait for the blade to sink into the raven's spine before I had the second blade in hand. Wet, sticky blood coated my hands as the fourth raven fell.

The fifth guard had his back pressed in the corner. Shoulders heaved; his body trembled. Gods, he whimpered when I crossed the room to him. Bleeding fool.

I pressed the end of the axe against his throat, voice rough. "Where is it?"

The guard avoided my eyes, muttering prayers under his breath as he reached into the folds of his tunic. He pulled out a crumbled, folded piece of parchment. "I . . .I want to know she is un-unharmed."

I snatched the roll from his hand. "I keep my bargains. Your mistress is safe now, but I doubt you'll survive the night."

His eyes went wide in fear. "You promised! I give up the cell blocks and you don't harm me or Tira! Wraith, you—"

I chuckled darkly and leaned in. "She's safe. At your wife's home. It is not my problem your woman did not know you'd taken another. I've never been so frightened than when she discovered the truth. May the gods be with you when you wake."

With the butt of my axe, I struck his head. The guard crumbled at my feet.

Tor came to my side, holding a linen cloth to his wound. "How did Sven know this one would be the weak one?"

"His mistress is an acquaintance of Sven. A little digging and I knew he'd be the one. And I wasn't lying. His wife is terrifying. She'll bury him come dawn." I flicked my eyes to his arm. "Is it deep?"

"Nothing I won't survive."

We sprawled the parchment over the small table in the center of the room. A rough drawing of the different cell blocks was marked with the types of Night Folk locked inside. Air fae were kept below, near the water, and away from windows.

"This stairwell is our best chance," Tor said, pointing to the east side of the prison. "I remember always being brought to cells from the west. The ravens frequent the west side. These, I believe, are used for removal of the dead. See how it leads to the river? Traffic will be less."

"I agree." I folded the parchment again and retrieved my axe from the spine of the dead guard.

"Valen, what if fury won't work?" Tor asked.

"It must. We have no time to hunt the warden for his bleeding key."

"We must be prepared for the bindings."

Muscles in my jaw pulsed. Halvar would be bound, I was sure of it. Removing them would be a problem without a particular key. "Let's worry about getting him out first, then we'll worry about finding the runes to break his bindings."

"And if we don't, then the option is using dark, twisted spells from dark, twisted seers and sorcerers. Not Night Folk."

"Yes, and we might need to sink to the underbelly. Are we not desperate the same as the wretches?"

Tor pinched his mouth and stared at the doorway for a breath before facing me. "You are a *king* by birth and by right, so no. You are not the same. Do not risk dark tricks of magic. Me, nor Halvar want that."

"No," I said, gripping the collar of his shirt. "Sol was a king. I was born to kill for him. Now are we done? We have a man to save."

Tor let out a long breath. "Yes. We're done. For now."

"Then, hurry. When these guards do not report to their post an alarm will be set."

We made it inside, now we'd focus on getting Halvar before I worried too much on getting out. One step at a time.

We'd take the canals beneath the prison as our way out. It would be dangerous, but with enough iron bars, I believed I'd be able to bend us through most cages there. It was a decent plan. Made in haste, with few resources, but despite the risks it was the safest way out.

But as always, fate was fickle.

Roars of guards in the distance froze us at the door of the guard room. A horn echoed in the night. Another followed.

My brow furrowed. Tor ran to the window and peered out.

"Dammit," he cursed under his breath.

"What?"

Tor's eyes darkened when he looked at me. "Our plans will need to change. The prison is under attack."

CHAPTER 8
ROGUE PRINCESS

Ari stood at the head of a ramshackle table made from boards and stones. The clearing was damp, cold, and concealed the prison wall from view. The quarries were nothing more than a labor mine. Nothing of import was buried in this earth. Good stone for building, but no gold, no copper, no silver for shim.

I'd always wanted to know why the kings of Timoran bound Night Folk here. Did hard labor squelch their fury? Or were they tortured out of spite?

Since being in Ruskig, there were enough rumors I could guess kings experimented with fury in the quarries. Through torture and manipulation, they tried to take a gods-given gift for themselves.

Valen had been trapped here once. Younger then, but he'd watched his family be slaughtered. As a Bender, doubtless King Eli tried to take the Night Prince's fury.

I closed my eyes against the pain he must've suffered.

Sweat and death masked the blooming moonvane around us. It turned my stomach in sick knots.

I paced behind the wall of men huddled around the table, leaning forward as Ari spread out a weathered map of the fury quarries. Their bulky shoulders blocked most of my view, but I couldn't stop moving.

Did I trust the scouts on the ridge well enough to sound an alarm if anything unusual happened at the prison?

Yes. Mattis was one of them. Yes. I could trust them.

No matter how many times I repeated it, I couldn't stop pacing.

"Berger, tell them what you told me," Ari said.

A thick man with his beard split in two and tied with the teeth of a wild dog replaced Ari at the head. An Ettan, and a fearsome one at that. I knew little about him other than he was one of Ari's spies and had knowledge of the inner workings of the quarries.

Berger pointed to a spot on the map. "Three times a day this door is opened by the prison serfs and two guards. They keep it concealed by a wall and alcove to protect the natural spring. It is where they gather fresh water."

"How many serfs?" Ulf asked.

"No more than five. Unarmed. Usually women."

"That means nothing. Women can be fierce," Siv said, crossing her arms over her chest.

Berger hardly glanced at her. "The guards will be armed, but they are grunts. And I have doubts they look closely at the faces of the serfs. This, My King, this is where you send them inside."

Ari's eyes flicked up from the map to me. He curled his

fingers, calling me to his side. I didn't want to obey, for it made his head too large, but pacing was doing nothing but heating my blood.

"Elise, you will need to cross to this alcove," Ari said. "You're willing? Capable? Bored? Tell me your thoughts."

I followed his finger on the map. The door wasn't marked, nor was the spring. Simply a wall. If Berger was mistaken, we'd be out in the open with no way to get inside. Still, there weren't a lot of options when sneaking into a guarded quarry. "It is a good plan. A good way in."

"It is," Berger said. "Inconspicuous."

"How will you fare at the main gates?" I asked.

Ari grinned and slapped a hand against one of the round shields. "There is always a risk when one is used as the bait, but we will be fine, *Kvinna*."

"If you two do your part," Ulf said with a grunt. "You will be the ones to signal us away."

"How does it feel, Ulf?" Siv asked snidely. "Knowing your life is in the hands of a Timoran and—what was it you called me—a treacherous witch?"

Ulf narrowed his gaze. "My faith is not in you; it is in King Ari. This is his plan, and I will hold to that."

"Yes, I am rather impressed with it myself," Ari said. By now, I was keen enough to recognize he covered disquiet with humor and a witty tongue. His eyes had darkened and gave away his unease. "And even if none of my men feel the same, I hold enough faith in you, Elise and Siverie, for the lot of us."

"Unless we leave you to be captured. It is a good opportunity to be rid of you, after all." I said, grinning.

"Very true." Ari stepped closer and lowered his voice. "But I know you are concerned for the Shade who was taken. I don't understand it all, but I trust you will not jeopardize him. Besides, I have the key for the bindings he is surely wearing, so I urge you not to leave me to rot. I was not born to be in a prison cell. I'm too intriguing."

My smirk faded. Now was not the time to speak untruths. "You're right, I do care. About more than the Shade. I will not betray you."

"There, you see?" Ari faced his men. "Good enough for me." Ulf snorted his disapproval, but Frey winked at me as Ari reached for one of the shields. "Make ready, then. We have a gate to breach."

Siv and I covered in long cloaks and hoods, then waited while a unit of the clan gathered shields and made a box formation.

Ari barked commands to ease into a synchronized forward march. I crouched beside Siv and watched the Agitators lift the shields in a wall on the sides, the front, and overhead. It was an old strategy. One used by Timorans and Ettans alike. Walls of shields and bodies gave a charging unit the chance to advance with few casualties.

With Night Folk using fury to manipulate the senses of nearby guards, they might be unbreakable.

Ari wasn't the true king, but he was as wise and strategic as any noble I'd known.

The instant they broke the tree line a bellow of horns signaled the warning of the assault. Through limbs and brambles, Ravenspire guards sprinted at the top of the gates, archers tipped arrows over the ledge, and shouts broke the melancholy of the quarries.

"We need to hurry," Siv said.

Together, we darted through the tall, dry grass toward the gate. The slats weren't wide enough to slip through, but before we gathered in the forest some of the Agitators had split a post in two, so it could part and open enough for us to slip inside.

I ran one palm down the beams until a board slipped out of place, and my hand shot through the hole. "Siv, here."

I held up the board and Siv went in first. Two watch towers at our backs were empty. Ari's distraction had pulled the guards away as planned. With no eyes on us, we sprinted for the spring wall.

At the corner of the prison, shadows from torches gave away approaching ravens. My legs ached. The mud swallowed my boots.

Reach the wall.

We had no other choice. I pushed harder, faster, feet sliding on the refuse of the quarries. Shadows grew. Shouts rang in my ears. At the final step, I lunged behind the wall and hit hard enough the jolt shot down my spine.

I didn't breathe.

A unit of ravens appeared in the very spot we'd been with blades raised, racing for the front gates.

My knees wanted to give out, but I forced each step. The wall created a type of alleyway that sloped toward the trickle of water. I removed my dagger, held up a hand for Siv, and together we crept toward the sound.

Women in plain wool skirts kneeled at the edge of a clear

pool. They filled wooden buckets, one hummed a sad tune, and no one noticed our approach.

My breath locked in my chest, and as I released it, I hooked an arm around the neck of the nearest serf. Before she could make a sound, I clapped a hand over her mouth. The others let out shrieks until Siv pointed her bow at them, one by one.

"Do not speak a word," I hissed against the woman's ear. "Two of you must give us your skirts and pails, then run for the north gate. there is an opening. In the trees you shall find your folk, Ettans. Be free with us, or you may scream for your guards, and we will kill you."

The woman trembled beneath my grip.

"Anyone wish to scream?" Siv asked, low and dark, her arrow aimed at the four remaining serfs.

No one moved. They hardly breathed.

"I'll take my hand away," I told the woman in my grip. "But I leave the point of my blade in your back. Undress. Quickly."

Siv gathered another serf who was near her own height. The woman whimpered, but obeyed. We hurried to swap our robes with their skirts.

"You other three will lead us to your guards. Remain with us and you will be free this night as well."

One serf nodded with more conviction. A bit of light returned to her dark eyes as I turned to the two we'd traded with, and shoved them in the direction of the broken fence post. I gathered the abandoned pails the moment the iron door slammed against the stone wall.

"Get a move on it," said a tall, brutish sort of raven. He hocked a brown glob at one of the serf's feet, then gnawed on a frayed twig. A hunger in his gaze brought a bit of bile to my mouth.

Ulf guessed right. The guards never glanced at our faces; their lust was pointed elsewhere. Just as well, neither guard recognized two of their serfs hid rune paint underneath dirt smudges and ash.

Inside the quarry prison, the air was heavy with mold and rot. But the hum of fury shot a thrill in my heart. How many Night Folk were locked away in here? Releasing more would be a good strategy Ari ought to consider if he ever planned to take Castle Ravenspire.

"Go." A guard shoved me from behind. I stumbled up a set of stairs, spilling some of the water. He gripped my hair and wrenched my neck back. "Sloppy little whore. Now you've gone and made a mess."

The guard tightened his grip, forced me to my knees, and pressed my face a hairsbreadth away from the puddle.

"Lick it up."

"Knut," the second guard said. "There is no time. The gates."

Knut seemed to care little about the front gates. His fingers tangled deeper into my braid. My jaw tightened. My fingers walked down the length of my waist, reaching for the dagger sheathed to my leg.

The raven's hot breath touched my neck. "I said *lick* it up. Like a dog."

The tips of my fingers brushed against the pommel of the dagger, but all at once something heavy smashed against the side of the guard's head. He grunted and fell over.

Siv wound up her bucket again, aiming at the cursing

second guard. I ripped the dagger from its sheath. Heart racing, hand trembling, I thrust the point through the ribs of the raven.

He gasped, and swung at me, trying to grab my braid. Trying to grab anything.

I shuddered and tightened my grip on the dagger. Inept at killing, I froze, stunned in sick and disbelief. Like the last time I took a life.

Blood dripped onto my hand. When the guard fell, I fell with him.

He suffered. The wound killed him slowly. I could not take the sound of his rattling breath or his uttered prayers any longer. I clenched my eyes tightly and pressed the dagger in deeper until it all stopped.

"Elise." Siv scooped me under the arms and pulled me away.

My body shook. This was for Halvar. For the throne. If I could not keep my wits in a fight, then I had no business being here.

I dragged a few deep breaths through my nose, then found my step again. With the burn of bile in my throat, I pulled the dagger free and wiped the blood on my skirt. The other serfs hardly grimaced at the blood and surrounded the man Siv had pummeled with her bucket to pick his pockets of shim.

"The lower cells," Siv shouted, pressing her knife to the throat of one serf. "Where are they?"

The girl gulped and pointed down a narrow passageway. "There. At the bend there is a door, take it and the stairs will lead you down. But there is no way out down there."

"Yes," Siv said, withdrawing her blade. "We know. If you wish to be free, go out where we came and run to the trees."

The three women gave a single look at the unmoving guards and paused for a mere breath before they ran back to the spring door.

"Elise," Siv said as she rested a hand on my arm. "We press forward."

For Halvar. For the throne. For Valen.

I nodded. "Forward."

CHAPTER 9
ROGUE PRINCESS

E choes of the attack rang in the passageway. The door to the lower cells was ajar, as if guards ran up the stairs so swiftly, they forgot to lock it behind them. Damp moss soaked the steps and only a few torches lit the staircase. Shadows played games, dancing and jumping like Marish demons sent to haunt our dreams.

The stairs opened to the lower cell blocks. Each cell was made of wooden doors or iron bars. It was silent but for a steady drip of water in the darkness. Wet straw perfumed the air with mold and a thick cloud of unwashed skin. With open windows and cracks in the stone, the cells held little warmth, and each puff of breath clouded in front of my mouth.

Siv took the left, I took the right, peeking into doors and cages.

"Halvar!" I called out when we'd checked at least a dozen cells. Most were empty, two had corpses, the rest held Night Folk who wouldn't roll over to look at us. I dragged my fingers through my hair, panic rising in my chest. "Halvar, answer me!"

Nothing.

At least not right away.

"I am not surprised you ask," a raspy voice responded after a few heartbeats. "For whom would not enjoy the sound of my voice?"

I let out a wild laugh and darted to the cell tucked in the corner. He laid out on a wooden cot, one knee propped up, one hand behind his head.

A smile cut across my face, and I was taken aback how relieved I was to see Halvar Atra again.

He rolled his head to glance at the bars, the familiar cleverness in his eyes. But after a breath, the smile wiped off his lips, and he pounced from the cot. "Elise? All gods, am I seeing things?"

I chuckled and reached a hand through the bars. "You're not seeing things. We've come to get you."

"I don't . . . how are you here? How did you know I was taken? Wait, are you with him?"

"No," I said, defeated. "No, we heard of your capture another way. Hurry, now. We have one chance to get you free from this cell."

"Wait, Elise." Halvar curled his grip around the bars. For the first time I noticed how a few fingers were bent and bruised and on his wrists were silver bands. Runes were etched into the bands and his skin was red and irritated underneath.

"Halvar." I traced his bruised knuckles. "Have they hurt you?"

"Oh yes," he said lightly. "Expected in this pit, though."

I swallowed a swell of anger and pointed at the bands. "What are those?"

"Bindings. They make me terribly ordinary by blocking my magnificent fury. And they burn like the damn hells."

Those were the bindings Ari spoke of, the ones he insisted he had a key to remove.

"We'll get them off once you're out."

He shook his head. "I'll stay."

"What? No."

Halvar was pallid, his lips chapped. The glossy waves in his hair were matted and covered in a fine layer of dust, but his grin was sly as ever. With a heavy sigh, he flopped back onto the wooden cot. "I am flattered by the gesture, truly. Not surprised, of course. I knew you missed me most, but if you have come, no doubt my guild shall be arriving shortly. In fact, the way the guards ran from here, I would not be surprised if they are already here."

"You idiot," Siv snapped. "The guards left because of us! We have the clans outside causing a distraction, risking their bleeding lives to save you. Now get up and get out of here."

"The chaos is you?"

"Yes," I said with a sigh. "Siv, the powder."

Siv dug into her tunic and removed a pouch of tied pig skin. We had no key, but what Ruskig provided were hidden talents of skilled poisoners. It was rather frightening, in truth. Oda, an old man with a beard to his navel, had mixed the powder for us. Ari assured us it would be as effective as any key.

With a small spoon I scooped some of the red poison and sprinkled it onto the hinges on Halvar's cell.

"Careful," Siv said shrilly when I spit into the spoon. "Don't let any of the wet powder touch your skin."

I nodded and tipped the spoon onto the dry powder until it became a bloody paste.

Almost right away the powder hissed and snapped, and a bit of white smoke billowed up. Halvar took a step back. So did we. A stink of ore and ash covered the damp cells. It didn't take long before the hinges melted and the door on the cell slumped, maneuverable enough Halvar could slip out.

"Where did you learn a trick like that, *Kvinna*?" Halvar looked delighted.

"Ruskig has a lot of interesting folk. You must hurry."

He hesitated. "He will come for me, but if I'm not here, he will tear this place apart."

Siv groaned.

"Halvar, right now it is us who came for you," I said.

He closed his eyes, mouth tight. "He does not want—"

I wouldn't learn what the Night Prince didn't want. A clang of the door at the top of the staircase startled us into silence.

I withdrew my dagger. "Halvar, we're leaving."

"Right." He shook out his hands and climbed over the broken cell door. "Blade?"

Siv provided him with a narrow knife. He seemed ready to protest but spun it into his grip instead.

Cries of two others rattled in my head. I wished we had enough to free them all, but Oda told us the burn powder was tricky and expensive. We had one cell to use it on and no more.

At the stairs, Ravenspire patrols spilled into the cell block. Their dark leathers and guarders were damp with blood. They screamed at us to stop, then charged, ready to kill. My mind went blank. From fear or instinct, I couldn't say. I simply jabbed, cut, and parried. Siv handled a battle well, but Halvar was mesmerizing.

Not once did he stop grinning. Even with broken fingers, he danced around the guards. His blade tore out a throat, stuck in ribs, in the heart, the belly as if he did not even need to think. The last guard fumbled back after Halvar's knife sliced the side of his neck and the body smashed into me.

Halvar caught me by the arm and winked. "Tis so good to see you again, have I told you?"

"Yes," I said, glancing at the dead guards at our feet. "And I can see now why your people were the first knights."

Halvar chuckled but held a finger to his lips. "Naughty. Keep those secrets, dear Elise."

"I can't say anything detailed. I'm lip-locked by fury."

"Ah, still a sore subject for you, I see."

I rolled my eyes and ran after Halvar, grateful he was alive. Ragged, perhaps, but alive.

"Um, may I ask, my sneaky Agitator," Halvar began when Siv took the lead, "where exactly are we going to get out of the prison?"

"Up," was all she said.

We climbed the staircase back to the level with the spring door, then turned into another staircase. Up here, the shouting from the clans bellowed through every hall. Guards shouted commands; archers fired again. Outside, flames rose and the angry clash of steel on steel gave way that the shield walls had broken. The Agitators were fighting.

"Here," Siv shouted. She skidded in front of a window next to a torch on the outer wall. With the point of her elbow, she smashed through the glass and lifted the torch from the sconce, waving it back and forth.

"You're certain this is the one?"

"Yes," she said, breathless. "Five down from the center of the prison."

A horn blew in the distance, the signal for the clan to pull back. If they were still able to at this point remained to be seen.

Siv flicked her fingers. "Back up!"

From the trees, a bolt attached to thick rope whistled through the window and into the wet stone of the prison wall. Siv checked the tautness of the line, stepped onto the window's ledge, then unbuckled a boiled leather belt she'd fastened to her leg. "I'll go first."

Siv slung the belt over the rope, secured the buckle again, and slipped into the strap. She adjusted and secured it underneath her shoulders, then pounced off the windowsill into the night. Siv skidded down the line, legs tucked, and avoided the points of the gate by a few paces.

"Here." I turned to Halvar, gathered the serf skirts in my fists, and removed a similar belt from my leg. Once it was secured over the line, I gestured for him to come close. "Make sure it's under your arms."

"I am not leaving you here," Halvar said.

"I'm right behind you."

Reluctantly, Halvar stepped onto the ledge. I helped secure the loop over his head, careful of wounds sliced into his body I hadn't noticed before, and his injured fingers. He glanced back at me, doubtless ready to argue, but his eyes widened.

He shouted my name, then everything blurred.

A fist struck the back of my head. I fumbled as my eyes

darted between the raven who'd surprised me and Halvar who was trying to escape the makeshift harness and fight for me.

I bit the inside of my cheek and shoved him.

Halvar cursed as he was pulled out the window. He shouted my name again, but it faded with him.

Once he was on the ground, I slammed the edge of my dagger against the rope, cutting it before the guards used it to track where the clan hid.

A guard's thick arm curled around my waist. I screamed, kicked, bit. Anything to get free, but failed when his hand clapped over my mouth, and he dragged me away into the fury prison.

CHAPTER 10

NIGHT PRINCE

T he prison was a storm of screams, battle commands, and blood. The heat of it, the taste of it, stirred the call to the lust inside.

I rolled one of my axes in my grip. *Not now.*

More than ever, we needed to get to Halvar and disappear. Tor paused in a long passageway and glanced out the window once more.

"They're Ettans," he said.

"Ettans?" I followed him to the window, careful to remain out of sight. From where we stood the invaders were visible. They carried painted wooden shields and rammed the gate again and again. Not with a battering ram, with something else. The spark of fury was in the air. It didn't make sense. "Tor, Night Folk are with them."

"They're rising up?" He seemed as astonished as me. "Why after all this time?"

I shook my head. We had not done all we planned to weaken Ravenspire; not yet. But here was the outcome we'd wanted all along, and it was unraveling before our eyes. A pitiful army, no mistake. Small, but organized.

They must've been led by someone with skill and clear plans.

"We need not worry about them," I said. "We use this to get out with Halvar. Hurry."

In the lower cells the few air fae locked inside were banging on their bars and shouting curses at the gods. As if the chaos of the battle had stirred something awake in them.

"Halvar!" Tor shouted.

"Hells," a tall fae grumbled. "Him again. Give another a chance. He's gone."

I ignored him at first, until we arrived at a shattered cell in the corner. The hinges glowed like embers, and steam came from the iron. It was empty and Halvar was nowhere in the block.

Fury heated my blood. Had they discovered his true identity? I shouted my anger and slammed the head of my axe against the bars. The ore on the cells bent and groaned.

I'd never been skilled at controlling fury when emotions took hold.

I turned to the prisoner, gripped his bars, and bent them. He watched in a bit of horror and awe as I stepped into his cell. "Where was he taken?"

"I-I-I don't know. Some serfs came and . . . they broke him out. I've heard of you." He scanned my mask, glanced at the axe in hand. "Blood Wraith?"

"Tor." I ignored the man and turned out of the cell. "We find him. Now."

"Wait. Let me come with you, Wraith."

"No."

"I'm a good fighter. I'm good with fury. Please. I can help you."

I wheeled on him. "What is your name?"

"Stieg. I can fight with you." He looked again at the bent bars; no doubt filled with questions. "We all can."

There were only two more fae who answered with pleas to free them.

"We don't need more air folk," I said and stomped back to Tor.

Stieg followed.

"Not everyone has air fury. These two have different talents. Take us and we'd swear to you, Wraith. We might be in a hole, but we hear talk. We know how you torment these Timoran bastards."

"You're in bindings." He was, but the others weren't. "Why just you?"

Stieg shrugged. "Don't know."

"Because the woman and I are not air fae," another prisoner said. His arms were bloodied and bruised, but he grinned. "They think we're broken and not a threat."

"Are you saying you are a threat?"

"Absolutely."

"What do they call you."

"Casper."

I looked around at the cells. Casper had a ragged beard,

tattered clothes, and one eye had swelled shut. The woman looked like she wanted to slit a throat the way she glared.

Tor met my eye. He gave his head a subtle shake as if he already knew what I was going to do. "Fury will tell them too much."

True, but they had the same look of hate for ravens as I did. "If you join us, you call me Blood Wraith or Legion Grey. What you will see may cause you to think things, but don't. If you call me anything but these names, I will kill you. Agreed?"

"I'll call you any name you like if you get my sorry ass out of here," said Casper.

This was a risk, but we could use extra hands now that we'd be fighting our way to Halvar. I lowered to a crouch, pressed my hand against the stone floor. As a boy the burn of fury drew tears to my eyes. Sol teased me relentlessly, and I learned to crave it instead.

My fingertips heated on the stone. The cells trembled as the ore, rock, and soil bent against my magic. The prisoners gasped and scrambled back when slowly the bars creaked. They bent at different angles. Some cracked.

I closed my eyes, pressure growing on my shoulders. Fury was taxing and this was more than I'd exerted since the curse lifted.

"Three hells," Stieg said in a breathless gasp.

I cried out a final wave and watched as the bars on their cells widened and broke at last. Dust settled. The prisoners stared at me, still in their cells, as if I might break them much the same.

I wiped sweat off my brow with the back of my hand and

stood, retrieving my axe. "We're leaving. Stay and gawk if you like."

I didn't wait for any of them before sprinting toward a drain at the back of the cell block.

"No, no," Stieg said, laughing. "We're coming, Wraith. My lot is cast with the Earth Bender."

"They will slow us down," Tor grumbled.

"Do you all know how to fight?" I asked.

"Night Folk learn to hold a blade in Timoran or we die," said Casper.

"You said you were not Night Folk."

"When?" Casper asked. "It's not my fault if ravens don't understand there are more talents than air and pyre and illusion. My talent is with water. Different, like you, Wraith. You bend the earth, and it makes me wonder if you—"

"What did I say?" I snapped. "Know me by two names or I cut your throat."

"Give us a blade or get out of the way. All men want to do is talk." The woman shoved her way through. Her hair was dark and cut in jagged layers. Beneath the grime and dirt on her face two silver piercings gleamed in her cheeks. Her skin was soft brown, but her eyes were nearly gold, and her wrists were absent of the silver binders.

"Are you Night Folk?"

"No," she said. "I was traded here to be used for your king, then I heard he died."

I narrowed my eyes. "Used in what way?"

"I am what is called an Alver."

My stomach flipped. "From the East? We know an Elixist."

The woman grinned viciously. "They are my favorite Kind. I am called a Profetik."

"What the hells is an Alver?" Stieg whispered to Casper. He simply shrugged.

"As a Profetik Kind my senses are impossible to match," said the woman. "But taste is my greatest talent. I was here to be a poison taster for your king."

"He is not my king," I snarled.

"I don't care. You get me out of here, I will be indebted, and I will stand with you until it is repaid."

"You do not return home?"

She winced, a bit of her hardened shell breaking. "I will repay this debt, but I will return. I have a husband who searches for me. An Elixist with more skill than I've ever seen. He will tear the world apart to find me, and I rather like these smelly boys. I'd hate to watch them get caught in the crossfire of his rage."

I grinned beneath my mask. "Your name? If we are to bleed together, we ought to know what to call each other."

The woman lifted her chin. "Junius of Skítkast. I prefer Junie."

The name of her homeland was familiar. Bevan—he'd mentioned it before. If it was as wild and untamed as Bevan said, then we could count on Junius knowing her way around a blade.

"Tor, give them the means to defend themselves." With a grunt, Tor handed out three of his knives. I took out the second axe. "We don't know who is attacking, but we are not here for that fight. We came to retrieve our guild member. Help us, and you're free."

"We're yours, Blood Wraith," Stieg said. He bowed his head, almost as if he suspected something else.

Let him. He'd done as I asked and did not question, did not use another name.

"Casper," I said. "Your fury connects with water?"

"A strangeling, that's what my maj always called me. Not quite typical Night Folk. More like a water nyk."

"There are canals under these cells. Can you clear the water enough for us to pass?"

"Depends on how much, but I could likely get it so we don't drown, at least."

I kicked dirt and rancid straw away from one of the iron grates in the floor. Together, Tor and I lifted the grate away and stared into musty blackness. "Down there. What do you need?"

"Nothing." Casper stroked his wiry beard, then cracked his neck side to side. "All I need to do is swim."

"Careful," I warned. "There is likely a current."

"I'm a good swimmer, Wraith. Touching, though, how close we've become so quickly that you're worried for me. They call you the Bane of Timoran, but you're a bleeding lover under all that aren't you?"

"All right," Tor said, shoving Casper's shoulder. "Get on with it."

Casper snickered and leveraged his legs into the hole. I was glad for the red mask tonight. They didn't need to see any hint of the smile underneath. This reminded me too much of life before the raids. When Night Folk and Ettans teased, laughed, and lived together in peace.

It made me want to fight for a crown I didn't desire. One I didn't deserve.

I had no plans to wear it, but I had grand plans to burn it.

Before he disappeared, Casper faced me. "I'll call you when it's clear."

Then, he was gone.

Silence thickened like smoke, choking breath, and stilling the senses until all we could do was stand still and wait.

A cry of pain echoed from the bottom.

"Casper!" Stieg shouted.

Nothing.

Sweat slickened my hold on the axes. He had little time before we would need to abandon him and take a different route. If water talented fury could not clear the canals, we didn't stand a chance.

Perhaps fate brought us here with Casper, an unbound water fae. A warning that my original plan was futile. I would've gotten us killed.

"Clear!" Casper's voice called up to us.

I let out a long breath, shoulders slumped. My relief lasted a single moment. "Go," I told Junie. "Go."

She was brave, this foreign Alver woman. I'd give her that. She did not question, did not hesitate, before following Casper into the darkness. Tor and Stieg went one after the other. I slipped into the chill of the hole, uncertain how far the drop went, but a boom outside left me no choice.

We needed to leave. Soon.

Cold air whipped at my face for a few heartbeats before I slammed into soaked, muddy earth. Decay soiled the air. The walls were covered in flowing water. Casper grunted; his hands clenched in fists. The water had divided and flowed upward across the curved tunnel and ceiling, like moving walls over the stone.

"Would be nice if we could hurry," Casper said, his face flushed and red.

I nodded and followed a gleam of light in the distance. At the first gate blocking the canals from the streams that led into the forest, I took the bars in hand. My own fury was weakened from the cells. The bars gave a little, but not enough to fit someone of Casper's size.

"Let me through," Junie insisted. "I'm smallest and can pick the lock from the outside."

"And who says you won't abandon us?" Tor snapped.

"No one. I suppose you'll need to trust that I keep my oaths."

"Go," I said through my teeth, fighting the ore to bend and break.

Junie turned sideways and slid through the opening I'd already shaped. She fumbled, and for a moment I thought she might run. If she had a family, a husband, why wouldn't she?

But she turned back, studying the gate. "It's a simple enough lock." Using the tip of the knife, she manipulated the keyhole for what seemed an eternity. Casper kept drawing in sharp breaths. More water pooled around my knees.

"*Junius*," I said.

"Shut it." She bit the tip of her tongue, cursing the blade.

I tried to urge the bars more. They gave a little, but my arms trembled. Fury burned like it might break through my skin any moment.

"I can't hold it," Casper said.

Stieg gripped his arm. "Well, you must hold it!"

Water splashed to my waist, then my chest. At my shoulders, I tilted my chin, ready to hold my breath.

Then, the gate clicked.

Junius tossed the lock aside and ripped open the bars. We spilled into the streambed with the rushing current, grappling for the edge.

Stieg laughed and pounded Casper on his back a few times. "Well done, water nyk. Well done."

Casper waved his hand, then flopped onto the bank to catch his breath, but Tor nudged his shoulder with his boot. "Get up. We can't stay here."

We had escaped a distance from the fighting but staying out in the open was foolish. For a moment I forgot others had joined us and pulled down the red mask.

"I almost expected fangs," Stieg murmured to Casper.

I ignored them and took in our surroundings. "Stieg, you said our man was taken by serfs."

"Yes." Stieg came to my side. "But I doubt they were truly serfs. They had a powder that dissolved the damn hinges."

"Why come for Halvar?" I asked Tor.

"Someone must've connected him to the Blood Wraith. We ought to expect a ransom."

True, someone might've known Halvar was a member of the Guild of Shade. But the more likely scenario was someone knew he was Halvar Atra, first knight to the restored Valen Ferus.

More than a ransom would be paid. We'd be forced to do the bidding of the one responsible until we bartered for Halvar's freedom or bought silence. The darker parts that called to me preferred to slaughter whoever had taken him and be done with it.

Maybe I would.

"Make to the trees," I said after a pause. "We'll decide our next move out of sight."

Casper, Stieg, and Junius gathered their knives and ran after Tor toward the gates. The attack at least gave us a clear path. Every guard was at the front, shoving the invaders back.

Of course, we'd need to discover who attacked tonight. They might be the ones who took Halvar, and I needed to know who was responsible for stirring discontent amongst Ettans and Night Folk.

They would be one to watch, support, or kill if they interfered with my plans again.

"Legion!" Tor shouted, careful to hide my name. "Get down."

Behind us, in the shadows of the back drive, a prison coach parked aside a back entrance. I dropped behind one of the berms of mud and straw dotting the yard.

Four ravens burst out the door; someone struggled between them. The driver of the coach hopped off the front and unshackled the backdoor.

"Ari! Ari!" a woman screamed. She kicked and thrashed and put up a fight.

"*Kvinna*! No!" Another voice shouted from the front gates.

My heart stuttered. No. No, it wasn't . . .

The men who attacked pointed their shields at the coach. They were trying to reach her, trying to save her, but kept getting stopped by more ravens.

"Bring her to the king," a guard said. "He's missed her."

"All gods," I said under my breath.

"*Valen.*" Tor whispered and dropped to my side. "Valen, no, think about—"

I didn't wait for him to finish. Elise was here and they were taking her to Ravenspire.

I drew my axes and sprinted for her as fast as my legs would go.

CHAPTER 11
ROGUE PRINCESS

"I t's *Kvinna* Elise," the guard said once he pulled back my hair and studied my face. His grin sent a shudder dancing up my arms. "The little traitorous princess. There can be no doubt what side you've taken now." He spit on my boot. "You stand against your folk. I'd do the king a service by slitting your throat now."

He whistled and three guards surrounded me, all placed their hands on my arms, holding me with unyielding strength.

I dropped. They dragged me. I kicked. A guard slapped me.

Outside smoke from the battle burned my throat. In the corner of my eye some of the Agitators fought. I didn't know who, but they would be my chance. Halvar and Siv were likely deep in the trees by now. By the time my absence drew them back, I'd be on my way to Castle Ravenspire.

There, Calder would humiliate me. Runa would torture me. Then, they'd kill me.

"Ari!" I screamed, desperate for anyone to hear me. "Ari!"

"Shut your mouth," a guard snapped. He hit the back of my head with his fist.

"*Kvinna*! No!"

I let out a rattling breath. *Ari*. He saw me. He sounded distressed. But would he take the risk and come after me? Halvar, maybe. Siv and Mattis, yes. But what could they do against the whole of Ravenspire?

The guard tried to shove me in the back of the coach. I struggled against him, earning another strike to my mouth.

"Get inside you stupid—" The guard let out a sick grunt. At once his grip loosened and his fellow ravens scattered.

A scream caught in the back of my throat.

In the center of his forehead a black battle axe split his skull. I stumbled against the coach when another person leapt from the top and splattered the blood of another guard.

My throat tightened. He was here.

Hells, I wanted to reach for him, to fight with him. The Blood Wraith ripped his axe out of the guard's head and turned on the driver and two remaining guards. They slashed bronze swords at him, but he sliced their legs at the thighs, or the weak points under their arms.

The driver weaseled his way out of the bloodshed after taking a strike to the arm. He crawled on hands and knees toward the front of the coach.

I took a raven's blade off the ground and met the driver at the front, jabbing the point against his throat.

"Get up," I said, dark and low.

With his hands overhead, the driver came from under the coach, but in another breath, he shoved me and tried to take the sword from my grip. I kicked at his ankle. He fell forward, but took me down with him.

The driver tried to roll on top of me, but I managed to leverage the sword between us. I thrust the blade up until a strangled gasp ripped from his throat. Out the back of him, the point of the sword gleamed bloody and wet in the dim light. I'd skewered the man over me; his blood dripped on my face. My grip on the sword faltered and dropped his dead weight on me.

Until different hands tore him off.

Valen, masked beneath his hood, pulled me to my feet.

"Valen," I whispered. Three hells, it felt as if turns had gone by since seeing those dark eyes. "You're here."

I didn't know what to expect. His eyes gave away his anger. He might turn away and disappear. Would he ask about Halvar?

All at once, I forgot to breathe when he dropped one of his axes and pressed his palm to my cheek.

Blood and bone surrounded us. But for a moment, I could be still.

"Elise." His voice was soft, a hint of desperation underneath it all. Then, he stiffened. "What have you done? Why are you here?"

Ari needed the Blood Wraith. And I agreed. But, no doubt, he'd be coerced. Ari and his folk wanted this fight badly enough he would threaten and use me against him. Perhaps he'd use Halvar, too, now that I'd delivered the Shade into the Agitators' hands.

I gripped his arms. "Valen, the Agitators attacked, but they came for you. They knew of Halvar, so they planned to break him out, but only to get to you."

His eyes narrowed. My heart sunk in my chest when he stepped back. "You told them of me."

"I cannot. You made it so."

"You will not stop until I stand in a fight I do not want."

"No, I am telling you so you may go before they see you. Halvar is safe, Siv and I got him out. Leave, Valen. I see it in your eyes that you do not want to stay here. Go, then. We will take back this land without you."

So many words were being left unsaid. I wanted to plead for him to stay, to fight, to be here with me. All gods, I was furious with him. My heart ached for him.

I turned away. By the cheers ringing from the clans, I guessed the battle was ending. They'd been victorious and it would be over soon.

"Elise."

I winced but didn't turn around. If I looked at him again, I would not leave him a second time.

"Elise! Down!" Valen's hands gripped my arms and yanked me to the mud. His body covered mine. Shouts broke out, something about an archer on eaves.

I stopped listening when Valen didn't get off.

His breaths were ragged, sharp, and shallow. I adjusted, so I could sit up. "What hap—no! Valen, no!"

He met my eye, blinking rapidly. In his lower back an arrow had pierced deep into his body. Blood pooled around the wound.

"You need . . . need to pull it out."

"Hold still," I whispered and gingerly touched the arrow.

Sweat coated his brow. I tore his tunic and tried to hide my horror. Too much blood bloomed across his skin. Acid rose in

99

my throat as I snapped the arrow, then gripped the remaining shaft. Valen slumped, but stilled, bracing. On a count of three, I ripped the arrow free. He groaned and fell onto his shoulder. More blood bubbled from the wound. In a frenzy, I stripped my tunic to my undershirt and pressed the fabric to his skin.

"Valen, look at me." Tears blurred in my eyes. His gaze went glassy, the same as the moment he died in my arms at the Black Tomb. When, like now, he'd stood in front of me and took a blade in my stead. "Please stay awake."

"Elise." His voice was soft. His fingertips touched my lips. His eyes fluttered closed.

"Valen? Valen!" I shook his shoulders, resting my ear over his heart. He was alive but fading. Each breath came uneven, and his pulse unsteady.

"What the hells happened?"

I whipped around. Ari, Mattis, Ulf, and a dozen Agitators darted to us.

"The Blood Wraith," Mattis said, breathless.

"Help me," I pleaded. "He's taken an arrow and is losing too much blood."

Ari kneeled at my side and helped me roll Valen onto his shoulder.

"Leave him!" Tor and others I didn't recognize rushed at us; blades drawn.

"The Guild of Shade, I presume?" Ari asked, still helping me with Valen. I nodded and added pressure to the wound. Ari lifted his chin to Ulf and Frey. "Stop them."

The two guards signaled to their unit and turned on Tor. They outnumbered Valen's guild three to one, but I knew Tor was formidable.

"Tor," I shouted. "Stop! We've got him."

"Who?" Mattis asked, but he shook it away and faced the oncoming attack.

Tor wasn't listening. He dropped his blades, and for the first time since the curse lifted, I witnessed what Tor was capable of. His palms burst into icy blue flames.

"Bleeding Hells," Ulf grunted, dodging a stream of fire. "A pyre fae!"

I didn't know the others with Tor and Halvar, but they raised blades against the Agitators. They didn't move with as strong a step as Tor, were dressed in rags, but they fought despite it all.

I turned away. Valen needed help, and quickly.

Ari helped prop him up but kept glancing back at the skirmish between blade and fire. He cursed under his breath and rested a hand on my shoulder. "Keep him alive, Elise."

Ari left my side. I knew the stand-in king had strong fury, and after a few moments Tor cursed them. Ari held out a hand and Tor clutched his head. So did the others. Illusions, no doubt. By the way they struggled, terrifying ones.

Frey, Ulf, and Mattis moved swiftly and snapped silver bands around the wrists of the Guild of Shade.

My insides hardened. "No! What are you doing?"

"Elise, it is necessary," Ari said.

"Those are painful."

"I'm aware." Ari rose after clamping them on a woman's wrists. She didn't flinch but glared the same as others. Ari came to my side, another set of bindings in his hands. "Understand, they are needed."

"You're forcing them, Ari! This is what Ravenspire does."

"We are not Ravenspire!" he shouted. It was troubling to hear his playful demeanor shift into something harsh and angry. "They are Night Folk. They are Ettan. If they do not stand with us, then they are against our people, and are enemies." Ari closed his eyes and softened his voice. "I swear to you, this is merely to get them to hear us. I will give them a chance to listen, and to join us."

"And if they do not? What will you do, lock them in chains? Kill them?"

He didn't answer and flicked his gaze back to Valen. The Night Prince was still breathing, but it was weak and labored.

"He needs our healers. We'll use the prison coach." Ari snapped his fingers again. "Ulf, Frey, help get him up."

Mattis joined them. Ulf kneeled by Valen's head, grinning. "Let's see who lives behind the Wraith's mask, shall we?"

"No!" I shouted. "Ulf, he—"

He pulled down the red cloth. Mattis jolted back, his mouth open.

"That's . . . he's . . ." He pointed his stun at me. "Elise, that's Legion Grey."

Ari lifted one brow. "I've heard that name." His grin widened. "Dear *Kvinna*, I know where. Did you not have a man by that name in charge of your dowry negotiations?"

"Dammit." Mattis scrambled to his feet. "Does no one speak true anymore? He lied to you. The Blood Wraith was in your chambers all that time."

"Stop it," I snapped, exhausted from listening to them speak of Valen like he was a prize to be won or killed. "I have already accepted his name, Mattis. I have, so if I am able then everyone else should accept it."

"Why should we?"

"Because there is more to this man than you know. And I assure you he will not take kindly to being bound."

"Then it is a good thing these decisions lie with me and not you who clearly cannot see through emotions." Ari was short tempered. He'd battled, he was covered in blood. We all were on edge.

Ari was not wicked like Calder, but he would not win favor with Valen by forcing him to act outside his will. After being a slave to a curse for so long, Valen would never listen to the stand-in king like this. And what irked me most was I could not give Ari the full truth. I could not explain why the Blood Wraith would never stand with him.

I pinched my lips and turned away. "Forget his face for a moment and help me save him."

"Do not touch him!" Tor shouted. Ulf pressed him against the ground now that the bindings were on his wrists.

"Tor," Mattis said. "The attendant who was with Legion? Who was inside the prison, Elise? Who is the other Shade?"

"Halvar," I said, helping Frey and Ari lift Valen into the back of the coach. I climbed in beside him and kept my hand on his wound. Already my tunic was soaked in blood.

"Halvar." Mattis chuckled bitterly. "Of course it was."

The Agitators led Tor and those bound with him to the rear of the coach. Though Tor's mask was still in place, his eyes gave away his fear when he saw Valen unconscious in the back.

Ulf slammed the door on them and took a place on the driver's bench with Frey. A whip cracked and the mare pulled forward.

"Tor," I whispered until he lifted his eyes. "I did not want this. He . . . he jumped in front of me."

"He always will," Tor snarled. "You will either be his rise or his downfall. And neither of you sees it."

A tear dropped onto my cheek. "I will convince them to release you. All of you."

"I care little about me, Elise Lysander," Tor said. "But be warned. Save him, or not even bindings will stop me from killing every last one of you."

CHAPTER 12
NIGHT PRINCE

*For so long the wind had beat against us in the iron cages. Harsh
frosts coated the land, and the false king took a great deal of pleasure
leaving Arvad's sons in the elements. I tugged the thin, wool blanket
around my shoulders.*

"Sol, are you ever afraid?"

*Sol lifted his head. The strands of his hair and the ends of the dark
beard were covered in frosty crystals. Doubtless I looked much the
same.*

*He coughed. The sound of it ripped from his chest in deep, raspy
draws. When it passed, my brother slumped against his side of the
cage, and closed his eyes. "Yes. I am always afraid."*
*Sol never showed it. He stood stalwart, never bending to the Timoran
raiders. He even took a guard's eye—the reason we were in the cages.*

"More now," he went on. "Because they know how to break me. They have found my weaknesses, little brother."

"You speak of Tor?"

Sol grimaced and hugged his own pathetic blanket around his body. I did not know if Torsten lived. The moment the raiders discovered him to be Sol's consort, he'd been dragged away. Sol attacked and blinded the guard.

For a night we listened to the screams. The next morning, we were bound and tossed in our cage.

"I speak of him," Sol admitted. "But my weakness goes beyond him. They know to hurt me with those I love. They've taken Herja. Maj. They tortured Daj in front of us. They lock you in here with me, so I may see you grow weaker." He hung his head, his voice cracked. "I cannot sleep. I cannot close my eyes for I fear if I do, you will not wake."

"Sol," I said, an angry burn in my eyes. "I am nothing. Do not let them use me against you. If I die, then I die. You are the hope of Etta. Fate determined your birthright long ago and you will take it back. But do not weaken your resilience because of me. Turn your heart to stone if you must."

"Turn my heart to stone? What a miserable existence."

"Look around, brother. We are living in misery."

Sol scoffed; one side of his mouth curled. He looked more like our father than me. More proof he was born to be king. "Let them hurt me. At least then I know I still have a heart. I am unashamed to say if you die, then a piece of me dies with you. I love, and they use it against me, true. But I will never regret loving. Not even you, stupid as you are."

I laughed. Well, it was a sound somewhere between a laugh and hack.

Even still, I could not remember the last time laughter had even been a thought.

The memory startled me awake. A chill on the wind brought back the burn of the frosted winter nights. Someone had placed a heavy fur over my body. I pulled it around me as if the frigid nights of the past would break me once again, tried to sit up, but the world started to spin.

"Lie back." A soft voice commanded me. Familiar and gentle. "You lost a great deal of blood."

"Do not speak like he is not a killer, Elise. How many folk has he slaughtered?"

I rubbed my head, unsteady even in a bed. When had I found a bed? Who was speaking of me?

"Hush. You're only angry because you liked him and feel betrayed. But that is enough."

"And you are defending a man who has lied to you and put you at great risk."

"He saved us, Mattis."

Mattis? I knew the name. The haze in my skull would not allow me to place it.

"You are blinded because you found him appealing, admit it."

"Mattis, if you cannot find anything useful to do in here, perhaps you should go elsewhere. Maybe speak with Siverie since wallowing in anger does not seem to be suiting you well."

Not long after the click of a door broke through my fog. Something cool and wet touched my brow. I tried to swat it away, but someone else took my hand.

"You have a fever," she said. "Let me help."

I cracked my eyes. Pale light filled a room. Dawn's light, and a few candles on a bedside table. Her blue eyes came into focus next; her icy hair was loose and long over her shoulders. I studied her for a moment, ignoring the tightening in my chest, ignoring how her touch healed better than anything.

"Elise." My voice was dry as sand.

"I'm right here, Valen," she whispered.

The sweetest sound was my true name from her mouth. We were alone if she spoke it out loud. "What happened?"

She dabbed a cloth over my brow again and sighed. "You insisted on being a hero again and allowed your body to be impaled. It is a habit of yours I rather hate."

The fog still gathered, but in a moment of weakness I reached out a hand, searching for her. She obliged and took my hand, resting her brow to mine. Hazy as she was, my fingers found her jaw, her lips.

Madness took hold of my tongue, and I admitted the truth before I could stop it. "I have missed you."

A hot drop splashed on my face. Hells, I'd made her cry. I

never claimed to be skilled with women, and clearly, I remained out of practice. But she surprised me. A jolt to my senses when her warm palms took either side of my face and Elise pressed a gentle kiss to my lips.

I'd dreamed of her kiss.

A kiss that unraveled every piece of me. A kiss I ought to run from.

If I had learned anything from the past, it was better to hide a heart than give away the ones you loved most.

So, I would run. For her sake.

But I kissed her back. Gently. Weakly.

I would run tomorrow.

Elise brushed her fingers over my forehead and pulled away. Thick black took hold again. My body shivered but boiled. Her face faded into nothing, and I fell back into a fitful sleep.

I DIDN'T KNOW how long I slept. When I woke again, wretched thirst afflicted my throat. I groaned and stumbled out of bed, disoriented. The flicker of candles was enough to know I was in a strange room and in a strange house made of mossy branches. And I was without a shirt.

My fist curled around the seer stone around my neck. Its power was gone, but it had become an odd comfort.

I needed to find water. My lips cracked at the slightest twitch. A clay bowl sat on the bedside table. No doubt the water used to soothe my fever. I hardly cared and tipped it into my mouth. The taste was awful and gritty, but it served the purpose well enough.

A stitch in my side drew my gaze to a dingy linen bandaged around my waist. A harsh fetid smell burned my nose from the wound. Gingerly, I peeled the bandage away. Dried blood surrounded a wound covered in a putrid, brown paste.

I flipped through thoughts and memories. The prison and the arrow. Gentle hands. A soft kiss.

Elise was here; she'd been at the prison and now brought me here. Wherever here was.

Once the bandage was back in place, I turned to my lower half. My trousers reeked of blood and sweat. I'd like to wash or change into something clean at least. Being in one position for so long, the dirt clung to my skin like a new layer.

I unbuckled the belt at my waist, but stopped at a new voice.

"Oh, hells, please stop. There are things I do not wish to see."

Blood rushed to my head, chasing away the last of the haze. I looked over my shoulder. Junius sipped from a drinking horn, smirking.

She wasn't alone. Casper, Stieg, Tor, and . . . Halvar sat against the wall.

"Good to see you out of bed," Halvar said with a wink. "We were beginning to think you'd resigned to get fat and lazy."

I crossed the room; the wound pulled when I reached for Halvar, but I didn't care. I embraced him tightly, laughing. "You're alive. I wasn't sure if the ravens would kill you because of fury or because you talked to them so much that it drove them to murder."

Halvar grinned. Dark circles were under his eyes, but he seemed healthy. "I charmed them. Alas, you were rather slow in your pathetic excuse for a rescue, so I did begin to wonder if I'd be leaving headless."

Stieg snorted. "They did not rescue you. The girl did."

"Ah, yes. My guild was too late," Halvar said. "I nearly forgot a disgraced *Kvinna* and her Agitator companion did the saving. Perhaps I ought to go embrace them. We know it would be a most enjoyable experience for them."

I scoffed and shoved him in the chest. "Keep talking, my friend, and you shall find yourself in the prison again. How long have I been asleep?"

"Days," Tor said. He had yet to smile or show any kind of relief. "They have us in Ruskig."

I had not been to Ruskig since the raids. The shore here had always been a favorite place of my mother's, but when the fury walls went up it fell to ruin.

Tor wrung his hands together. He wouldn't look at me.

"You're troubled," I said. "What is it?"

Tor leaned over his knees. "We have, it seems, three new members of our guild. At least in the eyes of those in charge here. I think they should know the truth if they are to serve you."

"They do not need to stay," I said. "We have found Halvar. Our agreement is at an end."

Casper clicked his tongue. "If it's all the same, I'd rather stay. Where am I to go? Ravenspire has taken everything from me. My lands, my family."

"We're blood bonded now," Stieg said. "We fought together, and bleeding won. That is not something I forget."

I shook my head and looked to Junius. "You didn't run."

"I keep my promises," she said with a sly grin.

"And your promise is fulfilled."

"True, but these are dangerous times. Here, I am a fugitive as well as back home. I need to be cautious. You and your lot seem to be the type that know how to be cautious *and* deadly. I am yours. For now."

"And what of your husband who will watch the world burn to find you?"

She chuckled and played with the ends of her dark hair. "He will, I assure you. But Niklas is a good ally to have should you ever need one. A guild who protected his wife will not go unnoticed. He is the guild lead of our folk, you see."

"Will you send word to him?"

Junius dragged her lower lip between her teeth. "I want to. More than anything, but it is dangerous. I fear what will happen if he acts rashly. *I* will go to him when the time is right."

I respected the value she held for her husband. Doubtless it was painful to remain separated. "Then we will do all we can to help you return in one piece when the time is right."

She grinned. "We have a deal. Help me return to my homeland, and I shall help you in the interim."

"We've had these conversations already," Tor said in a growl. "If they vow devotion, then it is my advice that they know."

"Of course, if we tell them, and they try to run after learning the truth, we will need to kill them," Halvar said.

Stieg's eyes widened, until Halvar barked a laugh and slapped him on the back.

There would be consequences of bringing three strangers into our guild, into the truth. Their lives, or ours, could be put at risk. Even more—trust was hard won. I had some trust for them, but more needed to be proved.

Casper yawned and scratched his trimmed chin. "If you're going to tell us you're the Night Prince, we already know."

"Is that all?" Stieg asked. "Now I'm disappointed. I was hoping for a new secret."

I gaped at Tor and Halvar. Tor appeared ready to slaughter. Halvar took on a more delighted and entertained look.

Junius cleared her throat. "Pardon, but who is the Night Prince?"

Casper gestured at me. "Valen Ferus. A Bender. One who can break the earth, my foreign lovely. The last one on record if I'm correct. Centuries ago, this land belonged to his line. Do your Alver folk live long lifetimes?"

Junie nodded.

"As do Night Folk. I wish we could say we simply outlive the tyrants of Timoran, but they keep breeding more. But he is the true heir to the throne."

I held up a hand for silence. "How . . . how did you know?"

"Your fury," Stieg said as if it should've been obvious.

"I told you it would give away too much," Tor insisted.

"I do have a question," Casper said. "Where have you been, Prince Valen? Why leave us to suffer so long?"

I hated that they thought we had abandoned them. They knew the truth, so they deserved an answer. With the help of Tor and Halvar we told them everything. The curse. The journey to be free of it. What became of my family. Tales of Elise Lysander, the rogue Timoran princess.

"Why keep the truth?" Stieg asked. "Tell folk who you are, and they will stand with you."

"I must avenge my family. To do it, Ravenspire must not find out, or they will send all their forces to end my line for good. So, you will continue to call me Legion, understood?"

Casper and Stieg shared a look, but in the end they both agreed. Junie studied me in a new light.

"What is it?"

"You have no need of my opinions, but keep in mind I come from a land with four regions, each with their own brutality against Alvers. It seems much the same here. If you are ever able to do more, I hope you will. You and your people seem to have suffered enough."

"I am not standing idly by. I plan to turn Calder's people against him. Watch them tear themselves apart. I do not need a crown to do it, and the people are rising without me. I will merely open a window of opportunity. Perhaps it is fate that another takes the crown at long last."

Stieg wrinkled his nose but didn't argue.

"So that woman you took the arrow for freed you?" Junius asked after a long pause.

"She did," I admitted. "We parted ways because she does not need to take part in my revenge."

"I understand that, but I'm confused what has changed? She fought and lost it all to free you, so why trap you now?"

"Trap me?"

"The wound in your back must be painful if you have not even noticed," Halvar said. He rolled up his sleeves. Two silver bands were on his wrists. Tor revealed his. Stieg. Casper.

Junius chuckled and lifted her hands. "I've told them time

and again these do nothing against mesmer—my magic. But they are rather pretty, so I'll keep them."

My eyes fell to my wrists. Bindings locked on each wrist.

My blood was heavy with the pulse of magic keeping my fury blocked. Halvar was right, I hadn't noticed. The fever had burned so harshly, I'd not realized the ache likely stemmed from my fetters.

I stumbled back, heart racing. Wretched, violent memories of being bound and trapped in Ravenspire, in the quarries, turned my stomach until I leaned over the water basin and retched.

My mind spun in suffocating panic, anger, in a need to survive.

Trapped.

Blood pounded in my skull. I leaned over the bedside table, my lungs burning in harsh breaths.

Tor gripped my shoulder. "They will not keep us here. I swear to you."

I despised my weakness. "Tor . . . I can't—"

"They will never take you. Not again." He leaned into me. "But I would ask you something. If they were to . . . take me back, be the man to end me, Valen. Before they get a chance."

The horror of the request makes me want to retch again, but I nod. "If you promise the same. I wish to die with honor, not in a cage."

"All right, enough. Hells, before we leap to killing pacts," Halvar began, "I think we need to keep our heads here. I was with Elise, and she did not seem pleased about these bindings. I don't believe it is her idea."

"Yet we are bound. She knows more than anyone what

being a prisoner would mean to us," I said in a kind of growl. I'd long forgotten my skin was clammy and dirty, was passed caring I wore nothing above my waist. I stomped to the doorway and ripped it open to a busy, moving town.

She'd soothed me in my illness, while keeping me hostage.

I hated her.

I hated her so much I thought I might love her. And I hated that even more.

"Valen." Halvar hurried to his feet. "Where are you going? We don't know who's out there."

I narrowed my eyes. "I'm going to our captor. Elise Lysander will soon know what a mistake she has made."

CHAPTER 13
ROGUE PRINCESS

The hall was packed with people. Ettan and Night Folk. Men and Women. Some danced to lyres and drums. Others laughed, ate, and drank at Ari's long table in the center. The eaves arched and were decked in glossy ribbons and banners bearing a raven emblem for the old Etta.

I bit the tip of my thumbnail, unable to eat anything, and stood in a circle around Ari's seat. Mattis and Frey laughed with the new king of Night Folk, reveling in the success at the prisons all these days later.

Ploys and schemes were being made, and I could not focus on any of it.

Valen was recovering, but the healers kept him doused in nightelm, a potent herb to bring sleep.

I needed to speak with him, warn him that he was not entirely free here.

When Ari ordered that his guild, including the new prisoners who'd followed the Blood Wraith, be placed in the binding bands, Tor and Halvar looked at me as if I'd stabbed them between the shoulders. A shot from behind. A coward's way.

"I suppose it is fair, dear *Kvinna*," Halvar said. Like usual he had smiled, but there was menace in his voice. "We did take you when you did not wish to come with us."

Tor was more dangerous in his silence. He'd make good on his threat should we hurt his prince and his guild.

They were bad enough, but when Valen realized it . . .

I closed my eyes and hugged my middle, looking for an opportunity to speak again with Ari.

"They accepted food," Siv said at my side. Being scrubbed and dressed in a gown now no one would suspect she'd infiltrated the fury quarries only two days before. I'd borrowed a long dress, too, but kept my dagger on my belt.

"An improvement," I said. For most of the day, the Guild of Shade had refused anything and walled themselves behind doors with Valen. "Did they threaten you?"

Siv grinned. "No. It was one of the new men. He thanked me, told me he had to return to speaking ill of us, then closed the door."

"Any word on . . . Legion?" I could hardly think of his true name in the presence of so many. Not with fury guarding my tongue.

Siv shook her head. "I didn't see or hear anything. But if they are taking food, perhaps he is beginning to wake."

My chest bloomed with the heat of anticipation. "Then I need to speak with Ari."

Siv followed me, shoving through Ari's circle. Frey was in the middle of telling a tale. He'd cleaned his russet scruff from his face, and his earthy eyes gleamed with laughter. Not the serious, hot-tempered man I'd grown accustomed to. But like most here, when trust grew, defenses became thin and true natures shone through.

Mattis eyed Siv. For once he did not look at her like she was river rot. More sadness, a longing in his gaze. If he would put aside his stubbornness, he would relieve the tension always clenched in his body.

"Ari," I said.

The king didn't hear me and laughed as Frey finished his tale.

"Ari." I tapped his arm.

"Ah, Elise," he said, grinning. "You look well and lovely tonight. What do you think of this hall? Perhaps not as grand as you're accustomed to, but I think we are on our way to taking the great hall of Ravenspire. There we will have room for true revels and dancing and feasting."

"Sounds delightful," I said. "But I don't want to speak of the size of halls. We need to discuss the treatment of the Blood Wraith."

"Yes, the healers say he is on the mend. Thank the gods. We fought so hard to bring him here, it would be a shame if he were to die."

"Ari you sound like a callous king, if you'd like to know."

He chuckled and took a drink from his horn. "I've been practicing." He glanced at me and let out a sigh. "Elise, don't fret over this."

"You don't know him. He will take offense at being forced."

"The bindings are for our safety against his fury."

"Did you see him use fury?"

"I did not. Call it an educated guess." Ari tapped the points of his own ears.

"Yes," Mattis said. "How did he conceal he was Night Folk when he posed as negotiator? I've never seen such a thing."

"It is a mystery," Ari said. "But even without the defining Night Folk characteristics of the Wraith, you, Elise, have never given me a straight answer regarding his power. His guild is made up of rare fae. He is the leader. It does not take a brilliant mind to believe he must be the strongest among them."

Ari faced me, leaning over the arm of his chair. His eyes were bright with intrigue. I liked the man, despite my better judgment. He had an insatiable curiosity, and I believed he did want the best for Etta. But he was wrong here. Valen would not take kindly to his plan.

"Elise, would you tell me more about your relationship with the Wraith now? I admit I was surprised to learn he had served as your negotiator under guise. Did you know his true identity the entire time; did you always plan to fight against your family? What separated you? The Shade you rescued from the prison is almost as vague as you. He talks but says nothing all at once."

I scoffed. "That is Halvar for you."

"See." Ari pointed at me. "Right there. You call them by their given names like you are the closest of friends."

"It is because they infiltrated her life. They *were* friends. To all of us," Mattis said. "Isn't that right, Elise?"

I gave him a look. He was still angry, and I hated that I could not tell him everything. "It's true. Halvar had been on our lands for nearly a turn before Legion arrived."

"But why?" Ari asked. "Why did they want to enter your life?"

"They needed my connections," I said. "That is all. Something my family stole from them. It was nothing but a valuable medallion. I helped them retrieve it."

It was not a lie. Not entirely.

Ari laughed and rested his head against the back of his chair. "Very well, Elise. I'll believe they plotted to overtake your life for a family heirloom. They must've been terribly bored with a great deal of time on their hands for such an intricate plan."

"I'm not lying. Plans became hastier after my sister's coup, and I'm not saying I was happy to learn I'd been deceived, but I realized the error of my family. Realized the Blood Wraith was not a demon, and when it was finished, we parted ways."

"Not a demon?" Mattis said with a huff. "He kills mercilessly."

I smiled sadly. "No, Mattis. He kills when necessary."

Ari tapped his lips, eyes narrowed. "You hide things for him. Interesting. I would love to know how such a man has achieved such loyalty from others. Even the prisoners from the quarries have chosen him over living freely with us."

"The Guild of Shade rescued them. That sort of thing brings loyalty," Siv said.

Ari bobbed his head, agreeing without saying it.

"You want his loyalty, Ari?" I asked softly.

"Naturally."

"You won't get it. Not if you force him to be here."

Ari fiddled with a silver ring on his finger. His jaw twitched. "Then he should listen to our plans and join with us."

"He won't," I said, frustration bubbling to the surface.

The hall wasn't boisterous, almost hushed, as I held Ari's gaze. His eyes went over my head. "If he will listen to anyone, I assume it will be you."

"I would not assume that."

"I suppose we're about to find out." Ari rose from his chair, lips parted as if about to speak.

I followed his gaze and my insides turned to knots. Valen parted the crowds without a word. All he did was walk forward. Shirtless, a scowl on his face.

I licked my lips. I didn't blink.

He looked nowhere but me as he stormed forward.

"Blood Wraith," Ari tried. "We've been waiting to speak—"

"Elise," Valen snapped, his voice low and raw. "What have you done?"

He shoved through the circle. At once Ulf and Frey stepped in front of Ari, their swords half removed from sheaths. But the Wraith did not aim at the king. He turned on me, backed me against the wall.

His hand went to my shoulder, the tips of his fingers on my neck. It was meant to be threatening, judging by his countenance, but Valen's touch had never been anything but gentle.

"Step back from her." Mattis held a blade to Valen's throat.

For the first time, the Night Prince seemed to realize we were not alone. He studied Mattis, head to foot, then swatted the sword away. "Leave us, Carpenter."

"I will not, *Legion Grey*," he said snidely.

"Mattis," I hissed. "Please. He won't hurt me." I turned my stare in a sort of challenge back to Valen. "Will you?"

He held up his wrists with the silver bands. "Why?"

Ari cleared his throat. "It was a decision made by me. Necessary, seeing as we don't know you, but would be glad to speak with you."

Valen didn't look to Ari. "You would bind me? After everything."

His name wouldn't form on my tongue, not his true name at least. "Legion, let us speak elsewhere."

"As I said, Elise was not the one who bound you, Wraith," Ari said. "But sit, eat. We have a proposition for you."

Valen's thumb traced my jaw. His body trembled in anger. It was a clash of opposites, as though he wanted to touch me, but hated that he did.

"I will not be *enslaved* again," he said, not to Ari. He spoke to me. "There is nothing more to say."

"Enslaved?" Mattis made a noise of disgust. "You lived the life of a wealthy merchant in Mellanstrad. Had position. You know nothing of these people here. Know nothing of what suffering is like in Timoran."

"Mattis," I warned.

"Bold claim, Carpenter," a rough voice joined the dispute. All eyes turned to the back of the hall. Tor, Halvar, and the three others joined the crowd. As expected, Tor had a blade in hand, and Halvar reached for a horn of ale. Tor stepped forward, his gaze on Mattis. "You speak in such a way when you lived the life of a tradesman with the protection and favor of a *Kvinna*. Perhaps it is you who does not understand suffering."

"Leave it be, Tor," Valen said. "We have nothing more to say to these people."

He turned to leave, a final glare at me, but stopped when Ari stepped out, blocking his retreat.

"Move."

Ari grinned wickedly. "I don't think I will."

My tongue stuck to the top of my mouth. Siv was the only one who shared my worry, but she was also the only one apart from his guild who knew whom they disrespected. I thought I might retch if the tension grew any thicker.

Valen clenched his fists and butted his chest against Ari. "Get out of my way. I am not afraid of bloodshed."

"Duly noted," Ari said. "But I will not move. Not until you hear me. We are the ones who saved you, after all."

"You are the fools who got in our way. You took my Shade, started a battle with Ravenspire with what? A pathetic army of refugees and the exiled. Get out of my way."

"You have no power here, Wraith. You are bound, weapon-less, and weak from your injury. What harm will it be to hear us?"

"I don't like the way you speak. Is that enough?"

Ari laughed dryly. "I could command it. I'd rather not. I'd rather us be allies."

"Command?" Valen laughed and looked to his guild. "He could command me. And tell me, fae, who are you to command me?"

"Your king."

I closed my eyes against the ripple of murmurs in the room. Frey and Ulf looked at Valen like he was an insect, one who'd be squashed beneath Ari's boots.

Fools. Gods-awful fools.

Valen's expression changed. The hint of the creature he was once cursed with faded, and his eyes brightened. In a taunting way. "My king?" He beamed and looked back to the Guild of

Shade again. "Do you hear this? A king has been restored. What bloodline are you from?"

"The land chose him," Frey said. "He brought back life that was dead here."

"Ah, I see. Yes, Etta chooses who will rule, but what life did you restore?"

"Look around Wraith," Ulf said. "There is power returning here."

Valen studied Ulf. "I know you. You were the fool at the caravan."

"You should not have let them go."

"This is your fault," Valen said, jutting a finger toward Ulf. He looked ready to throttle the man.

"Legion, please," I said under my breath.

He glanced at me. "You support this king? You support his claim?"

"Ari is a good leader. He has protected these people and inspired them. It wouldn't hurt you to listen to his plans. You could have a role here."

He chased the space between us again. "That is not what I asked you. Do you support *this* king?"

I swallowed with effort, my voice hardly more than a whisper. "I see no one else willing to take his place. No one else to support."

Ari snorted. "Thank you, Elise. Your enthusiastic devotion is overwhelming."

Valen's eyes drank me in. He didn't blink until Ari returned to his chair and cleared his throat.

"Whether you believe I have been chosen as king or not, Wraith, I don't care. The truth is we have begun an uprising. An infantile call to war, true, but a call, nonetheless. As most wars, there are sides to choose. In this, there are two. Either you stand with your people—the Night Folk—or you turn a blind eye to what they endure at the hands of Timorans.

"In that case, you are our enemy. So, you will remain bound until your loyalties are made known." Ari rolled the ring around his finger again. His demeanor was calm, unruffled, but there was a threat in his tone. "I see the murder in your eyes, but I assure you, if you kill me, you'll never remove those fetters. I alone have the key to them. It is hidden well."

Valen's face paled slightly. He reached for his waist, as if searching for his axes, but came up empty. "You force our hands. How very Timoran of you."

Ari clicked his tongue. "There is too much at stake to play friendly games."

"What do you want with me, King?"

"I want your fealty, your sword, your reputation. I know you can plan and plot, clearly if you fooled all of Mellanstrad and a royal house. You broke into the quarries with you and one man. Be that man for me. You are one of the few who brings a degree of fear to the false royals. Help us, fight for us, and you shall be free among us."

Valen folded his arms across his chest. "And if I refuse?"

"You stay fettered. Our prisoner."

"I think I'd prefer to kill you. I'd do it while you slept. No pain. Quick and swift."

"I don't seem to be getting through to you." Ari paused, then grinned. "Here is what will happen, Blood Wraith. You will be under guard, as will your guild. If you resist us, if you harm us, if there is even a whisper of you plotting to undo what we have started here, one person will pay."

My heart stilled when Ari looked to me.

It didn't go unnoticed from Valen. "Speak plainly, King."

Ari laced his fingers over his body. "Your anger gives away the hurt you feel for Elise's role in your capture. That hurt proves you care for her deeper than you'd like to let on."

"You'd bring harm to a woman to get what you want?" Valen lifted a brow in disbelief. "What a bold man you are."

"Kings are often forced to make difficult choices."

"Ari?" My face pebbled with sick heat. This couldn't be happening.

"Elise Lysander will be the cost, Wraith."

"I'll kill you first," Valen grumbled.

"And you've proven my point. I've found a soft spot in your armor. She will pay the price by being offered as a Timoran royal and enemy to our court and our people—"

I stepped to the front of the hall. "I have proven my loyalty more than once."

Ari held up a hand. Words were lost to me anyway.

"Or, like the Queen Lilianna of old, Elise will serve as the bridge between peoples. I will take her as my consort and queen."

Valen blanched at the mention of his mother, then reddened when Ari suggested he'd make me his Queen Consort.

"You're rather sly," Halvar called out. "Usually I respect that, but I like my little *Kvinna,* and I don't like how you're speaking of her."

"It is not my concern if you like it or not," Ari said. "This is your choice, Blood Wraith. Comply. Hear us, or Elise is the cost."

Valen spared me a look. I lifted my chin and met his gaze. "I do not stand for this. I refuse to be a pawn. Speak your desires and think nothing of me."

"That is impossible," he whispered, low so only those closest could hear. Valen faced Ari. "I do not serve you. I will not accept you as king until you have proven you are worthy of Etta. But I will not slaughter you either. Yet."

"Will you hear us? Join us? I will remove the bindings."

"Remove them and the temptation to end you will take hold."

Ari sighed. "And you will face the consequences."

"I suggest you keep me bound, then. I will not join you, but neither will I resist you. You're right, you've found a soft spot in my armor. You have my guild bound like dogs. And you threaten Elise. A woman who saved my life, who I am indebted to. Any action I take in your name will not be because I join you, not because I serve you. But because you forced compliance. You have set the stage for the sort of ruler you will be, *King*."

Valen tipped his chin in a vindictive bow and stormed from the hall. The Guild of Shade remained, glaring at those nearest them, then followed.

CHAPTER 14
ROGUE PRINCESS

"You're angry with me."

I turned from the peace of the pale moon to find Ari standing in my doorway. His hands clasped, and two guards at his back. When he stepped into my small shanty, the guards remained outside and closed the door on us.

I didn't reply and faced the moon again.

"I don't blame you. Those types of conversations are never pleasant."

"Forgive me, Majesty, but I'm quite tired tonight."

Ari came to my side, a cautious smile on his lips. He'd allowed a bit of dark scruff to coat his chin. Gold rings pierced his ears, and more kohl lined his eyes. Someone had braided his hair on the sides and pulled it half up. He looked regal and handsome, and I wanted to scream.

"Elise, I would not put you on trial as a traitor."

"Why say it then?"

"Because I needed him to understand the gravity of our plight."

I shook my head. "I know being a ruler and leader is never simple. It is not one way or another. There are wretched choices the leaders of this land have made, brutal ones even. But I will not be a piece in the game."

Ari's eyes soaked up the moonlight. He nodded. "I did not mean the first threat, but the second . . . it is not such a bad idea. In fact, it's a rather good one."

"What?" My brow furrowed. "The part about me being your queen?"

"Why not? I'm fond of you, and you tolerate me."

"Hardly."

He chuckled and leaned over the windowsill. "More importantly, you are Timoran royalty and have favor with people from both sides. I came here to tell you it is my intention, after I am officially coronated, to ask you to be my queen."

"Why wait? You could force me now."

"Elise, I have no need to force lovers." He tilted his head. "And I have not been coronated yet because I wish to earn the throne. You know Etta chooses its rulers. I have . . . I have been unable to bring life back like I did when I touched the moonvane all those weeks ago. I want to be certain I am the king this land needs."

I held a bit of sympathy for Ari. He wore a look of distress. It wasn't power he sought, but he truly believed the coincidence of the moonvane blooming under his hand had come from his fury. He took the responsibility as a duty, not an aspiration.

I could only pray he would receive the opportunity to hear the truth. That the Night Prince returned. That Valen Ferus restored life. And he was simply a stubborn mule at the moment who refused to take up the same duty.

"Ari . . ." My thoughts jumped in my head. "You don't want me as your queen."

"I do."

"You do not love me."

"It's no secret this is a strategic match, but over time emotions strengthen, affection grows. We both care for this land, for fairness, for all people. We would do well together."

I turned from the window, so he would meet my eye. "Ari, I would challenge you on nearly everything. I'd drive you mad. It is not my nature to remain silent."

"I never liked silence."

I snickered and rested a hand against his chest. He was young and ambitious. He was sincere in what he was asking. I could see it in his eyes. "My purpose as a second *Kvinna* was to produce an advantageous match in Mellanstrad. When I escaped it, I promised myself if I were to ever take vows, it would be done for love. Not rank. Not strategy."

Ari looked down and covered my hand with his. "It's a wonderous thought, Elise. But I don't think your quick refusal is because you do not yet love me, more that your heart was given to another already."

A flush teased my skin. I eased away and returned to the moon. I didn't want to talk of this. It was a confession I'd avoided; one I'd feared since Valen Ferus was taken into Ruskig.

Ari ran his fingers through the ends of my hair. A touch so gentle it was hardly there. "You keep secrets from us about Legion Grey and what truly happened between you two. You know why he is the Blood Wraith. Why he despises Ravenspire but will not stand with us."

"Please don't ask me. I cannot tell you."

"I won't ask. I hope in time you'll simply tell me on your volition because you trust me." Ari took a step back. "I'll leave you now. But you should know, Elise, I will ask you to be my queen. I hope you'll give it thought. I understand you gave your heart away before, but I am not certain it will be possible for him to return the gesture. Even if he wanted to. You and I may never love each other like the true romantics, truth be told, I am not sure I have a heart capable of it, but I would not turn from you. I would never silence you."

I hugged my middle. Blood pounded in my ears.

"Well, I've said enough," he said when I remained silent. "Sleep well, Elise."

Only once he was gone, did I let a tear fall.

DAWN BROUGHT COOL MIST. Ribbons of damp curled around the trees and shanties when I emerged from my own shack. Frosts weren't far off, and it would be trying to keep people in Ruskig fed if we did not work on storing food.

I draped my shoulders in a fox fur stole and took a woven basket into the shadows of the trees. Ruskig was surrounded by hedgerow, wood, and walls of brambles and moonvane. Its own world.

The grass turned vibrant green with morning dew, and midnight purple at dusk. Green and yellow moss speckled black trees. Creeks and streams were clear blue with white stones on the bed. Deer grazed. Ravens watched in the treetops. Blue, magenta, and glossy black flowers blew in a breeze in a nearby meadow.

Ruskig held magic. This is what the land could be. What it should be.

I kneeled next to a sprawling cloudberry bush. The golden berries were plump and in need of plucking. By the time the sun chased away the mist, half the basket was filled with cloudberries, rowanberries, herbs, and spices.

I reached for a shrub with strange purple fruit. In all my dull lessons from tutors, I couldn't recall an image or name.

"I wouldn't touch those if I were you." I jumped back, startled. She laughed at my surprise. The prisoner who followed Valen. The woman opened her mouth, leaned toward the bush, and breathed deeply. "Yes. Toxic, to be sure."

My brow furrowed. "How do you know? What did you do?"

"I can taste the poison in them."

"But you did not eat them."

"Observant."

I scoffed. "I hear you are an Alver. I've only recently become acquainted with the term. My old steward called himself an Alver."

"Yes, so I've been told. Alvers classify themselves into Kinds. Each Kind has a different sort of magic that utilizes some part of the body and mind. Me, I am called a Profetik, so my senses are heightened. Usually someone like me would see impossible distances, or in pitch night. Or hear better than a wolf. Some even see visions, or warnings. I taste. And those—" she pointed to the berries, "are very much poisonous."

I recoiled from the bush. "I'll take your word for it."

The woman gave me a small nod and turned to a plain shrub with leaves as large as my head. "These, though, help with a cough. There is a scent released when crushed down that soothes."

I grinned and plucked several of the leaves. "Your magic is a useful trick to have."

"A coveted one. Profetiks are used across the kingdoms."

I didn't know what to say to that. It was unfair to be used for her gifts, but kings and the powerful had been placing themselves above common folk for centuries. This woman was taken and used the same as Calista had been for her twists of fate.

I propped the basket on my hip and watched the woman cup water from the stream and drink. She was lovely. Exotic in a way. Her skin was soft brown, and she kept her black hair in intricate braids.

"I'm Elise."

"I know." She wiped her mouth with her sleeve. "I'm Junius. You may call me Junie."

"Where are you from?"

"A slum called Skítkast. In the East."

"Oh, my steward, Bevan, said he planned to sail to Skítkast. To live among a smuggling ring for Alvers."

A shadow passed over Junie's face. "Then he goes to Niklas. He will be well watched over."

Her chin quivered. She turned away and began washing dirt from beneath her fingernails. I hesitated, but after a moment I kneeled beside her.

"I didn't mean to upset you. Who is Niklas?"

Junie's cheek twitched. She swatted at a tear on her cheek. "My husband."

I didn't know the woman, still my hand went to her shoulder. "How long have you been parted?"

"Nearly a turn," she said, scrubbing her fingers with more vigor. "We were together the day it happened, simply buying supplies, and I was snatched while he haggled with a merchant. Right off the street, the instant his back was turned. The sea is vast, there are numerous kingdoms, and regions. If I had not been freed, I am certain he would never find me."

"But now?"

She met my eye. "Now, I have new friends who will help me find him again. In the meantime, I will serve here."

"The Blood Wraith," I whisper.

"The king. It will be a fine connection to have in the future."

"Ari is the one keeping you—"

She snickered, bringing me to a quiet. "Come now, we both know I'm not speaking of Ari."

My mouth parted. "All gods, he told you?"

"His guild felt we ought to know whom we served. He has my loyalty, and in turn he has promised to help me return home."

"I am grateful you're loyal, but I fear serving . . . L-Legion . . . will put you in a fight that is not your own."

She offered a bemused look. "Why do you not call him his true name?"

"I can't. Not around you, at least," I said in a huff. "The fool has fury locking my bleeding tongue. I can't speak of anything."

Junie laughed and stood, helping me to my feet. "Now it

makes sense. After discovering all you risked to free him, I didn't understand why you kept what you know a secret."

"I'm not sure I would speak his name even if I could. Clearly, he does not want the role of king, and he has been trapped for so long—why punish him by forcing him to take such a mantle as the crown when he does not want it?"

Junie stayed with me as I gathered the basket. Together we began the walk back into the township.

"Tell me," I said on the edge of the wood. "Are toxins all you can taste? Or is everything heightened?"

She glanced over her shoulder, then lowered her voice. "There is another tricky talent I have. I've not told anyone yet, but I sense you are good and only wish to help Valen."

I lifted a brow. "I don't want anything to harm him."

Junie grinned. "I taste lies."

"*Lies*? Impossible."

She snickered. "Not exactly. Mesmer is magic of the body, unlike your earth magic. When folk lie, there is a reaction in their bodies. A rush of blood, perhaps. A quickened pulse. Sweat. I taste the difference."

"That's amazing."

"Yes. Another reason kings seek me out. Bastards. As if I would tell them if they had a traitor in their midst. I'd pray they were assassinated."

My grip tightened around the basket. "Is that your plan with Legion?"

She beamed. "And that, Elise, is why I told you. You are perhaps the most loyal to him. No, I have not told him my talent, not because I don't trust him or am plotting against him. It's more I'm accustomed to keeping it a secret, but I've been using it subtly. So far folk here seem quite loyal to Ari and his plans. Will you tell anyone?"

"I suppose you'd know if I lie?"

"Oh, I will."

"I feel I should tell Legion."

She grinned again. "I will tell him. Understand the reasons, though, why I do not tell everyone."

"I won't give you up. I can't deny it will be useful. Very useful."

Junie bobbed her head in a kind of agreement and helped me take the other side of the basket.

"I think he should take his throne," she said after a moment. "Truth be told, I think he will realize it himself. I've seen the grimiest of folk amongst my guild. But I've also seen what happens when honorable folk realize their fate. He will find his reason to take his place. And as I said, a king shall be a delightful friend to have."

She stole a cloudberry from the basket, and popped it onto her tongue, grinning.

"There you are, foreign lovely." The bulky prisoner sat on a cask with the other man, Tor, and Halvar.

Junie rolled her eyes. "Casper, I have told you my name."

"But foreign lovely is more mysterious."

Tor caught my eye, held it for a breath, then walked away. My heart sunk deep in my chest. Halvar grinned and patted the empty space on the cask.

I obliged and sat beside him.

"You are troubled, *Kvinna*. Tell me what I must do to brighten your spirits."

I nudged his shoulder with my own. "I'm afraid you are the only one who seems to want me around lately."

Halvar looked in the direction Tor had gone. "You ought to know by now he was born with an abhorrent temperament. No fun at all."

"And you are his opposite."

"I take that as the highest of compliments." Halvar wrapped an arm around my shoulders. "In truth, don't mistake him, Elise. He is not angry at you. How can he be? You freed us. It is worry you see from him. Worry of what could happen, what likely will happen, and how we are not in control here. Tor cannot stand being out of control."

I patted Halvar's knee. "I swear to you, I will continue to fight for your freedom from the bindings."

"Hells, we'll never be free of them," Halvar said. "Not if *my liege* does not stop fighting with everyone in this bleeding camp."

I stood. "Where is he now?"

"*Fighting.*" Halvar pointed toward the stable. "I believe it has only just begun if you'd like to stop it. Unless you'd like to watch. They are rather entertaining."

Irritation burned in my blood. Valen's anger was going to be the death of me. These were *his people*.

I pinched my lips into a tight line and stomped toward the small stable.

The nearer I came the clearer came the shouting.

"Tell me and I'll consider it."

"Give them to me." Valen's voice was low and dark.

"How did you hide that you were Night Folk? What is the harm in telling me?"

I groaned. This is what we'd become. Bickering children.

With my shoulder I shoved open the door. Mattis leaned against one of the carts, a smug expression on his face. Valen stood five paces away. He'd pulled his hair back and was dressed in a black tunic. For a moment I was drawn back to the nights he'd been assigned as my guard before the coup at Ravenspire.

When he'd kissed and touched me in the old schoolhouse.

How things had changed.

I caught sight at the reason behind Valen's frustration. Mattis had one of the black axes in his hand. The way he kept flipping it in his grip and inspecting it like a treasure, I had few doubts Mattis was doing it to irritate Valen intentionally.

"I liked you better as a carpenter. You're rather annoying and I'm in no mood."

"Well, I liked you better before I learned you were a liar and a thief and a killer." Mattis laughed softly. "What will you do, Blood Wraith? You are bound, you have no weapon, and if you touch me, Elise will be the one harmed."

Valen's fists clenched. "It will not always be this way, and I don't forget those who offend me."

Mattis dragged a finger down the back edge of the axe. "These are incredible. Such craftsmanship. A true battle axe. I think I might take it. Give it some use for good instead of needless bloodshed."

Valen took a harsh step toward the carpenter.

"Enough," I shouted.

They both turned. Mattis's face flushed pink and Valen smirked—like he once did as Legion Grey. Always composed, always scheming.

"Elise," he said. "There is nothing wrong here, but I feel I should tell you if your friend the carpenter suddenly goes missing, I had nothing to do with it."

"You are not going to make him disappear." I frowned and went to Mattis, taking the axe from his hand. "You—stop it."

"He can't use them anyway. It'd be a pity letting them go to waste."

"They are not to be touched," Valen said.

I held out an arm, blocking him from hitting Mattis.

"Mattis, I'm sorry you feel betrayed," I said. "But turn your anger to Castle Ravenspire. They have harmed us all; they have given Legion reasons to hide who he is. They were the ones who tortured you, not Legion, not Siv."

"It is not that he betrayed me—he came to harm you."

"I would not have harmed her," Valen insisted. "You know nothing."

"He doesn't, does he?" I gave the Night Prince a pointed look until he turned away. Shaking my head, I faced my friend. "Can it be enough to know that he saved me, I saved him, and we trust each other even if you do not understand it?"

Mattis stared at the straw on the ground, jaw tight. "It is enough that I believe he will not slit your throat. But I don't trust him, and I believe he should be bound indefinitely. He's dangerous, I see it in his eyes. Like he can't wait to kill again."

With that, Mattis turned and left out a different door.

Silence surrounded us. My heart ached; it raced. I glanced at Valen. He didn't look at me. Instead, he leaned one shoulder against a post, staring at two cross-eyed goats.

"He's not wrong," he said, voice soft.

"About?"

"The bloodlust. It remains."

I pressed a hand against my stomach as it flipped upside down. "You're still cursed?"

"No," he said, glancing at me. "I no longer change, but it's as if the call to slaughter is still there. Pulling me to do unspeakable things."

I had wanted to touch him for so long. Not as I did when he fevered, not with anger, but in a moment where it was us, calm and alone.

I placed my hand on his arm. He didn't pull away.

Valen turned into me. We'd become so close. His fingertips touched my cheek, cautiously, as if he fought against the urge to pull back. When he gave in and cupped one side of my face, I leaned against the warmth of his hand, the rough calluses on his skin.

He opened his mouth, then closed it again, reconsidering what he was going to say. The Night Prince pressed a gentle kiss to my forehead. "I cannot lead here as you want, Elise. Not when darkness still lives inside me."

"You are not darkness, Valen."

He was slipping away again. Too soon his hands left my skin. "I'll leave you now."

"How surprising. You've done nothing but avoid me."

His dark eyes drew me in, like a starless night. "And that is for the best."

My barely healed heart shattered. Valen refused to see himself as worthy of anything but blood and death.

He once told me his heart beat for me. Mine did the same for him.

As I watched him leave the stables, watched him put

distance between us, I broke for wanting him.

I would do all I could to get the Night Prince to see he could be more. He could rise as the man Etta needed, but I would not keep wounding my heart for a man who would not take it for his own.

CHAPTER 15
NIGHT PRINCE

Ari's faithful, massive guard took up the entire doorway of the shanty. Ulf. The wretch who'd started this madness by his interference.

His beard was braided in two strands, beaded with bone and silver. Ulf was a formidable Ettan, but looked at us with a pinched scowl when we did not move at his presence. Did he wish me to bow? Stand alert? It was a laughable and entertaining thought all in one.

Ulf cleared his throat for a second time. "The king has summoned you."

"I'm sure he has," I said, and poured another horn of the watery ale of Ruskig.

"You will come to him."

"Will I?"

Halvar and Stieg snickered. Junius gave me a weary look. She did not agree with me keeping my name a secret. Hells, she was almost as bad as Elise. It didn't help the two of them got on like old friends.

The second *Kvinna* had, once more, won over my entire guild. Sneaking them sweet cakes, or extra ale, or furs for their beds. Speaking on their behalf in front of the pretend king, Ari. She was infuriating.

In the weeks since being tethered like an animal, unable to touch steel, unable to satisfy the burn of fury, I'd fought to keep a distance.

But like the call to blood, I was drawn to her.

Against all my judgment I would steal glances at Elise Lysander. I'd stand close, imagining her skin against mine. All it would take to make it true was claiming the throne and revealing my true name. My shoulders slumped. No. She could not be tied to me even then.

I knew firsthand what became of queens of the Ettan throne.

Not that Elise would even want to be my queen.

I didn't want her as queen. I did not want to be the bleeding king. I simply wanted to purge Etta of the Timoran rule. Another problem between us—those I planned to tear to pieces were part of her blood.

She did not know it yet, but even terrible as her family was, it would be a grave challenge for her to watch them die.

Ulf shifted in the doorway, drawing his knife, and drawing my thoughts away from Elise's blue eyes. The man stabbed the point of his blade into the small table. Casper scoffed. Tor was ready to leap into a battle. His anger was much like mine, always boiling beneath the surface.

Ulf clicked his tongue, then sat on one of the chairs, and

robbed Stieg of his ale horn. "Stay here if you please, Blood Wraith. I prefer it."

"What is the threat if he refuses today?" Halvar asked. He leaned back in his chair; his ankles crossed over the table. "I enjoy the creativity."

"No threat," Ulf said, popping a roasted nut onto his tongue. "But if you don't go to hear the plan of our king, I fear Elise will be left to carry it out on her own."

I let out a long groan, but it sounded more like a growl. "Apologies, Halvar. The threat is wholly unoriginal."

"It is," Halvar murmured. "You ought to use Tor, or Stieg against him this time. Not me, for we've been cramped in here too long and I think by now he would gladly give me over to you."

"I would."

"Hells, I would've yesterday," Casper said. "Do your mind and mouth ever stop?"

Halvar laughed and hit Casper in the shoulder, hard enough he nearly toppled out of his chair. They brawled, grinning, and challenging the other. Tor grumbled, and Junius abandoned the shanty when they nearly knocked her drinking horn out of her hands.

We were all growing a little restless.

Ulf chuckled bitterly. "You mistake me. King Ari does not send her in your place as a threat. No, this is Elise's choice. She will have a greater chance at surviving, though, if Legion Grey were to accompany her."

He'd already won. Then again, Ulf knew he'd won before he ever stepped inside the shanty. Ari knew how to drive the knife deeper inside my back. Knew how to break me down.

He was cunning.

A good quality for a king.

Still, I wished I had my axes. Maybe I'd take an ear from Ulf. An eye? He was haughty and I didn't like him. In truth, I liked Ari more than Ulf. Hard to believe, but it was true, and I planned to watch this sod carefully.

"Tell your king we'll be along," Tor answered for me. He would know the same as the others, I would respond if it kept a bit of peace for Elise.

Ulf stood, taking another drink for himself. He exaggerated a gasp and wiped his mouth with his sleeve. "I will tell him. But he is your king too. You'd do well to remember who has power here."

Once the door was closed, Tor narrowed his gaze at me. "Yes, I would love to remember who has power here."

"Speak plainly, Tor. Don't mince your words."

"Plainly? All right. They have you by your bleeding balls, Valen. Demanding your attention and service like some indentured servant. You, the Night Prince. I cannot stand to watch it."

"You would do the same were Sol being used as bait," I said under my breath.

Tor's fingers twitched. He didn't dispute the claim.

"At last, you admit she is your *hjärta*," Halvar said. "I will tell you I told you so shortly."

"She is not," I insisted and stomped toward the door. "But she will not suffer because of me."

True enough. I fought mightily hard to convince those around me that I complied because Elise was the one who freed us of the curse. No other reason than the debt was vast and would take a lifetime to repay.

I fought mightily hard to convince myself of the same.

Ari gathered his council around a fire pit in the center of the township. Not a large gathering. His guard, Elise, Mattis, Siv, and my guild once we arrived.

"Good of you to join us, Blood Wraith." Ari sat at the head. Someone had fashioned a circlet of rowan leaves for the king.

The sight of it tugged at my chest.

My parents rarely wore crowns unless they were on official business, but the ones they wore resembled Ari's.

I was consumed with vengeance and rarely allowed myself time to think of them. The way they laughed and teased. The way my father taught me to fight. How my mother taught me about herbs and healing.

I blinked my stare from the circlet and settled on the edge of the fire.

"As I was saying," Ari went on. "There is a caravan of refugees across the fjord. They are exposed and weakened. But their messenger assured us they have something of worth if we will come to their aid. Out in the open as they are, soon Castle Ravenspire will find them and destroy them. I need men, and the Guild of Shade, to accompany our rescue party on their journey."

A sick twist tightened in my stomach when Ari gestured at Elise, Mattis, and Siv. They were the rescue party?

"And how do you expect to travel to these refugees unde-tected, then smuggle them across the fjord, and back into Ruskig?" Halvar said, petulance in his tone.

Ari stood, opened a fur sack, and removed a scroll of parchment. "We use the land." The king sprawled the parchment—a map of hills and landmarks—across a boulder near the flames. He pointed to a cliffside near the southern shores. "Here is where they are waiting for us."

It was a half a day's ride from Sven's alehouse, but there were sea caves and coves. A treacherous, but cunning place to take cover.

When Halvar joined Ari at the table, a forgotten memory took shape in my mind.

We lifted the hem of the tablecloth. Too many of us crouched beneath the back table. My knees ached, but I bit my cheek to keep from thinking of them.

Across the room, my father rubbed his forehead and closed his eyes.

"Hells, Daj looks tired."

Sol elbowed me. "Don't swear, Val. Herja will tell Maj like she always does."

He stuck out his tongue at my older sister. She glared at him, curled her fingernails she'd sharpened into claws like her ugly, flat-faced cat, and hissed.

Sol leaned away from her.

I snickered behind my hand. He'd never admit that Herja was tougher than him, but . . . she was.

"Shut it," Halvar whispered. He gnawed on a dried strip of herring. It smelled terrible, but I think he did it to bother us. "I want to hear."

"We're going to get in trouble," said Tor, the smallest among us. He was four turns older than me, but I'd surpassed him in height just this turn, right after I'd reached ten.

Sol slapped Tor on the back, the gold in his eyes bright like bits of sunrise. "Do not forget why we're here. The reward will be great, my friend. Hal—strategy."

Halvar shifted. He was the one who'd gained the most muscle this turn. Then again, now that he was fourteen, he'd begun training with the knights. "We use the pillars. Valen is the skinniest—"

"No!" I protested. "Tor is—" I grunted when Tor punched my arm. "Stop it. I outrank you."

"Don't be a sod, little brother," Sol told me.

"Val is the weakest," Halvar went on, making it worse. "So, he'll be bait. You pretend to be sly, my littlest prince, but you won't be. While you're being caught and reprimanded, we'll make our way to the honey cakes."

"But then I won't get one!" I whined.

Herja rolled her eyes. "By the gods, we'll save you one."

"I'm telling Maj you swore," Sol said as he shifted on his knees.

"It's a solid plan, Hal."

"Just remember me when it comes time to pick your first knight,"
Halvar said, brushing his long curls out of his face.

"Ready? And . . ."

The tablecloth lifted. We all let out screeches of surprise. Dagar,
Halvar's father, and the true first knight frowned at us.

"Ah, we have sneaks about the castle." Dagar reached for Halvar
first, gripping his tunic by the collar and pulling him from beneath
the table. "Well, out you go."

None of us tasted a honey cake until the next full moon.

I GRINNED, watching Halvar huddled over the map, thinking on
his feet, strategizing on a whim. He reminded me a great deal of
Dagar. A fair man, who was cunning, and strategic in every
move he made. Without Dagar, there would be no Ruskig. He'd
evacuated most of our folk during the raids. He'd helped build
the fury walls. No one here even understood who Halvar was,
and what value he brought.

I had half a mind to confess the truth, if only to give Halvar
the credit he deserved.

"You will lose time traveling only by night," Ari argued.

"Yes, but we will conserve lives. Ravens rarely patrol in the
deep wood after dark." Halvar laughed bitterly. "They fear
Night Folk and tales of nyks and wolvyn. We shall make them
believe those myths wholeheartedly."

Ari grinned. "So, you agree to go?"

Halvar must've realized his slip of the tongue and lifted his eyes to me.

I frowned. There was no part of me that wanted to follow any command given by Ari or his guard, but Elise was dressed in dark clothing. She had a dagger on her waist. She was going and she wouldn't look at me.

All gods, the woman would be the death of me.

She already had been once.

Never did I anticipate such an infuriating, foolhardy, beautiful creature to take command of my every decision. I tried to keep a fair distance, tried to keep aloof, and I still cracked at the slightest thought of harm befalling her.

She did not have fury, but she might as well have. Elise Lysander cast a spell over me. One I could not break.

"We will go," I said as I stepped to the edge of the fire. "But you will release our bindings."

"Absolutely not," Ari said without looking at me. "I cannot risk you out there with my people and guards when I do not know what you will do."

"All respect, Ari," Elise said, still without looking at me. "It would be to your benefit to allow them their fury."

I opened my arms, smirking, as if to demand he agree with her. Truth be told, with my memories returned of days when my word reigned, it was growing difficult to play the submissive to a king who was not truly chosen by the land.

"Thank you for your insight, Elise," Ari said. "However, the Blood Wraith and his guild have hardly shown their faces. We don't know them even after weeks. The bindings remain." Ari returned his attention to the map. "If that changes your resolve to assist in our rescue, then I suppose we shall excuse you to return to your dwellings."

Blood raged in my head. What a pompous, arrogant . . .

"Hells," I hissed under my breath. "We'll go, but we will be armed, and your guards, *everyone*, will do as Halvar directs. No one matches his skill in strategy."

One corner of Ari's mouth curled into a grin. He'd won and he held no qualms in letting me know it. "Agreed. Rest up, Wraith. You leave at dark."

CHAPTER 16
ROGUE PRINCESS

Halvar insisted we break from Ruskig before the highest moon. The moment right before the final light of day faded behind the hills. A cold trill of exhilaration surged through my veins. This night was tense and dangerous, but even more than the fury quarries this felt like a step forward.

The missive received from the refugees' scout said the camp held something of value. Something that could hurt Ravenspire.

I flicked my fingers when we left the gates. In truth, it was more likely my excitement bloomed from restlessness. Days in Ruskig were filled with battling Ari and his stubbornness about Valen, or avoiding Valen because it ached like a thorn in my heart to be so near, yet he behaved as if I were no one of significance.

We'd said little to each other.

I mostly spoke with Halvar, Stieg, or Junius. Tor was always on edge, and Casper spent most of his time with Valen.

But tonight, this, *this* was something I could do to shed a bit of usefulness. I could assure folk running from my sister that they had an ally in Timoran. Even if only my name were used, at least I was doing *something*.

At Halvar's word, we kept a steady pace through the wood and thickets nearest the coastal cliffs. Too far to rest eyes on the sea, but near enough the air grew heady with brine and mists. We only rested to drink a few sips of our waterskins and rub out any aches in our feet.

The roads were uneven. Rocks and edges cut into boots and caused more than one stumble. Even Mattis had stopped trying to keep an unyielding pace and strode beside me, watching each step he took as we climbed a steep forest trail.

My knees burned. Dirt gathered beneath my fingernails.

But I never asked why we strayed off easier roads. Halvar was impressive to watch. Occasionally, he'd pause to lift his head to the sky, inspect leaves, bark, or soil, then tell us which curve to take, which hill to climb.

Besides, he had enough arguments from Ulf and Frey. He did not need mine.

"Do you think they will ever realize he's ignoring them?" Mattis murmured. He used his chin to gesture to the front. Ulf—again—was insisting Halvar lead us closer to water. For softer ground and drink.

His response? Halvar rolled a worn battle axe in his hand and slung it over his shoulder, blade up. One swing and he'd be perfectly aligned to slash Ulf's neck.

A muscle pulsed in the royal guard's jaw. He shook his head and stepped back.

I grinned. "I think it's irritating to Ulf that Ari agreed to put one of his prisoners in charge."

Mattis flicked his eyes to the front. His smile faded. "They don't need to be prisoners if they'd abandon the Wraith."

Mattis took any form of deceit personally. I wished he wouldn't. In truth, if he could not trust them, his grudge might get him killed.

"Halvar will never abandon him, and nor should you." My eyes fell to Valen. Positioned a step behind Halvar, next to Tor. He was the Blood Wraith tonight. Red mask, black hood. The only missing piece were his black steel axes.

He was formidable and threatening to look at.

I missed him.

"Why do you stand by him when he hardly looks at you?"

I winced, his words cut, swift and harsh. "When someone trusts you so much that they reveal their broken, splintered pieces, you cannot unsee them. You help them mend. You share yours."

"And you trust he showed you what was truly broken? Not simply what he knew you'd want to see and believe?" Mattis took my hand and helped me balance on a jagged part of the trail.

"Yes. I saw every wretched piece. Pieces he could not hide even if he wanted. He may never speak to me again, but it would not change that I trust he would never harm me." On instinct, I rubbed the missing tips of my fingers. "Intentionally."

Mattis regarded me with a frown. "Then help me understand, Elise. When I was taken to the prisons, one of the only consolations I had was knowing you and Siv and . . . Mavs had escaped with Legion Grey. I've come to realize I give my trust away too easily. Still, since you are so unrelenting, I wish to understand."

"Mattis, I can't tell you more. I can't tell you why he is the Blood Wraith. I can't tell you the depth of his reason for infiltrating my life. I can't tell you about his fury."

"Why?" He quickened his step to keep my pace when I took a slope faster. "Don't you see how it will help us all understand him and trust him better?"

I laughed bitterly. "Oh, yes. I see how it would help a great deal."

"Then open those royal lips and tell me."

I wheeled on him, a grin of frustration on my face. "Mattis, don't you think I would if I could? At least to you because, like him, I *trust* you."

"I don't understand. Why—"

"All gods!" Siv's voice broke behind us. She did not go out of her way to speak to Mattis. I took a guess that her silence was to avoid angering him further, but tonight she glared at him. "How many times does she need to say she would if she *could*? Meaning she *cannot*. He has forbidden us to speak of it. Fury in a strong enough fae can compel."

She shook her head and shoved through us. Mattis's lips parted. He stared after her for a few heartbeats before his understanding hit.

"Hells." He glanced to me. "You *can't* tell me."

I huffed. "As I said."

"He's a bleeding sod. Siverie can know and not me?" Mattis said. Not exactly angry, more like he was envious.

I chuckled. "She was there. She witnessed the same as me. She is fury locked, too, so don't try."

Mattis snorted. "He compels you into silence, avoids you, and you remain loyal. He must be quite the lover."

My chest tightened. I struck his shoulder. "He is not . . . my lover."

Mattis grinned for the first time. "Right. Either way, you no longer need to defend him. He wants out and the first chance he gets he will be gone. Guard yourself, Elise. He does not want to be here."

He didn't need to tell me. I knew exactly why Valen Ferus wanted to leave. I knew whatever we had once was not enough to turn him away from his call to blood. But my wall against the pain he'd bring was brittle and weak.

"I know," I managed to say. "I do not agree with him, but I think in his mind distance will keep us all safer."

"I wouldn't know. Apparently, only you and Siv do. Are we safer away from him?"

I shook my head. "No. I think he is needed here. But only if he sees it for himself. He has lived a lonely life and has few people he can trust." I nudged Mattis in the ribs with my elbow. "Funny, sounds like you have a great deal in common with your lack of trust."

Before he could respond, Halvar called for a pause.

We'd reached a flat part in the wood. Trees surrounded us on all sides. Shadows were thick as new ink.

"We'll sleep here," Halvar said. "No flames. Tor and Legion will take the first watch."

A few groans went through the line of guards. With the sea so near, the night winds would cut to the bone. Dawn was approaching, but the moments before the sun rose were cold-est. I tugged two rolled wool pieces from a satchel and curled in tightly with Mattis and Siv. He relented, silently, that she could keep close. No one needed to freeze tonight.

I pulled the wool beneath my nose. My eyes burned from fatigue. But before they gave in to sleep, I caught the eye of Valen as he crossed the camp for the first watch.

He paused for the slightest moment, as if studying me. Memorizing me.

For a few steady breaths all his broken pieces were on the surface. He battled against himself. Indifferent? I didn't believe it.

He tried to make himself believe it.

I grinned. Doubtless, the Night Prince would fail miserably.

Sol spoke with Arvad this evening. He left their meeting with a new smile. One of contentment.

When did my firstborn come of age to take a consort? His choice comes as no surprise, and I am overjoyed. Torsten has been his second half since boyhood. Still, I cannot see the Sun Prince as anything more than a cheerful, clumsy child darting through the corridors.

Now, I am penning a declaration of his hjärta *for all to know.*

Herja has no interest in consorts or vows or love. She is focused on the blade. Fine. I have no wish to share another child anytime soon.

Although, as usual, to be like his brother, Valen now casts his eyes at the courtiers and gentry daughters, as if seeking out the one who will take his heart.

The Night Prince had no desire to hear my reminders that he has only just turned twelve . . .

I LIFTED my eyes from the pages and blinked at the pale light of morning. Tears blurred the soft writing. I didn't know why the scene dug so deep, but I kept my back toward camp, praying no one saw me.

I had no luck.

"Must be a terrible thing you're reading if it draws tears."

Halvar leaned against a tree, grinning. My stomach lurched. Behind him Tor and Valen appeared, returning from the first watch. Stieg, Mattis, and Frey disappeared into the trees to take the next.

"No," I said. "Not terrible."

"What is it?" Halvar sat beside me on the boulder.

I avoided Valen's gaze, though I felt it on the back of my neck. "Lilianna's journal."

"Ah," Halvar said with a chuckle. "All those turns we teased our dear prince for scouring those pages, now we know they are written of us, and I've a new interest in them. What is the entry today?"

Tor wore his sour expression and said less than Valen. Still, maybe he'd like to know. "Uh, I read about when the Sun Prince selected his consort."

Halvar's grin twitched, and a shadow crossed his eyes. Together, we cautiously glanced at Tor.

The pinched, bitter glare was gone. His face was softer, his eyes dark as pitch. He licked his lips and took a step to me. "May I . . . see it?"

I handed him the journal and cracked a few knuckles, watching him scan the page. My heart lightened when a smile curved over his lips. A weary, distant smile, but one was there all the same.

"I remember this," he said, then handed it back to me with a nod of thanks. He nudged Valen's arm. "And I do remember you asking every girl from our lessons if she could handle loving a prince."

"He was so disappointed when no one was interested," Halvar said.

I clapped a hand over my mouth at a rogue, chirp of a laugh. Valen glared at them, but the way his lips tightened I took a guess that he was trying hard not to smile. This moment felt too real, too easy. We'd lived behind walls for so long, catching a glimpse of what life was like when the Night Prince was still Legion Grey to me was unsettling.

The moment passed too soon.

"You ought to try to rest," Valen said, eyes on me. "We'll be leaving soon."

"I thought we were traveling at night?" I looked to Halvar for explanation.

"We were," he said. "Until we discovered one of those bleeding caravans is heading to Castle Ravenspire. They're too close. We need to get a move on it and get to these refugees before they try to travel in the open."

"What sort of caravan?"

Halvar shrugged. "Probably for the upcoming vows."

I grimaced. Runa and Calder spent the coffers of this land to create an extravagant vow ceremony. For weeks wagons and carts had traveled from all townships delivering goods to Ravenspire.

I knew the Blood Wraith and Guild of Shade had attacked several.

"You're going to let them pass?" I asked.

"We are to focus elsewhere," Valen said. He took a step away, then softened his expression. "You really ought to rest."

I tried, but sleep refused to come. When Halvar signaled we were to move deeper into the wood, my eyes burned from fatigue.

The route lost any hint of a path the nearer we came to the wild, untamed cliffs by the shore. Rocky, slate stone broke underfoot. The clean air of the sea invigorated the senses. Trees grew sparse and turned to black pebbled beaches with jagged coves and caves.

Wise and dangerous for the people to hide here. On one hand, Castle Ravenspire would likely not risk their patrols to hunt them down. They'd simply starve them out. On the other side, these ledges were notorious for strange tides and harsh winds.

Halvar drew our rescue party to a halt. His brow furrowed as he scanned the empty shoreline. Nothing but smoke from dead fires and sea mist met us here. A prickle of unease climbed the back of my arms. At my side, Siv snapped the tether keeping her knife to her waist.

My blood heated. We were too late. It was the only explanation. They'd already fled, or worse. Castle Ravenspire could've taken them.

I was wrong on all accounts.

Before the thought of their fate finished, cries and shouts ambushed those of us in the back. From the darkness of the caves, figures dressed in shabby cloaks and caps pounced. Someone had a knife pressed to my throat in the next breath. My mind whirled in the ways I'd need to twist or strike to break free.

The voices near me gave away, Siv, Frey, Casper, and possibly Mattis had been caught the same as me.

Hot breath raked over my neck. "Stand still, and—"

The man holding me didn't get to finish. A small, fixed blade knife whistled past my ear. The man cursed and narrowly dodged the strike. Two more breaths and he cried out. Valen and the others free of the ambush surrounded the shadows.

The Night Prince held another knife—I wasn't sure where he'd gotten one—and narrowed his eyes at the man with his hand around my throat and blade to my nape.

"Take your hands off her," Valen warned.

The man hunched, using me as a human shield. "Don't come closer or I cut her."

"You won't get the chance."

A whistle broke the night. At the mouth of one sea cave a man made of harsh joints and loose skin, as if it simply draped over his bones, stepped into the sunset. "That'll do. Unless I am wrong, these visitors are not from Ravenspire. Look, they bring with them Hans."

A breath of relief went through our captors when the scout pushed around Ulf's body, hands raised.

"They've come for us," he said. "Crispin, they've come for us."

Crispin—the bony man I assumed—grinned. With a wave of his hand, the knife abandoned my throat, followed by a mumbled 'sorry'. Valen took a harsh step forward, and the man who'd caught me fumbled over the pebbles, cursing.

"You missed," I whispered with a glance at the knife on the ground.

The Night Prince curled a grip around my wrist, pulling me back. I wasn't sure he even realized he'd done it. The barest hint of a grin played on his face. "I do not miss."

"You're welcome here. We are in your debt," Crispin called out. He waved us toward the caves. "Come inside and see what we have won for the new king of Night Folk."

CHAPTER 17
NIGHT PRINCE

The caves were damp and cold and packed with shivering people. No one had been properly fed in a long while, and most had sores or chapped skin from elements and old beatings.

I did all I could not to look at them.

Crispin must've been a sort of elder for the refugees. His hair was thin and grey as dawn. His beard was hardly a beard. Patchy and jagged. Stained cloth wrapped his feet, keeping slabs of leather on the soles in makeshift boots. When the frosts came, dressed as they were, most here wouldn't survive if they did not return with us.

"This way," Crispin said, guiding us into a cavern.

The stones and bottom were slick and wet from sprays of sea, but the mouth faced the water. Natural light broke apart the dimness, enough to have a clear view of the two battered Ravenspire guards, tethered on their knees.

Crispin grinned with a touch of madness. "We told you lot

the trip would be worth it."

Ulf and Frey muttered to each other; Ulf, satisfied with the pathetic sight. Frey seemed more unsettled. Movement in the corner drew my attention to Elise. Her expression was heated and broken all at once. I resisted the urge to go to her, clenched my jaw, and turned away. Ravenspire was my enemy. They were hers, but I could not forget they were also her people.

These guards—for all I knew she might've known them.

I wanted to shield her from what would come should she continue with Ari's plans. She'd watch familiar faces die. Or she would fall at the hands of those she once loved. The demon inside cursed her for being such a fool. For placing herself in this position. The call for blood and battle begged me to be indifferent to the banished *Kvinna*.

But the greater part wanted to take the conflict away and touch her until she melted into me like times before.

Halvar chuckled and stepped toward the bound guards. "What are we supposed to do with these sods? They look like they haven't eaten in a week."

"Exactly," Crispin said.

"You've been starving them?" Elise asked, disgusted.

"It'd be us or them," Crispin said and stepped toward one of the guards. "They want to be free, they want food is truer, so they said they'd be willing to talk and give up the plans of the false king."

Halvar bent at the waist, meeting the eye of one raven. The guard's face was chapped and scabbed. His eyes were rimmed in red, and he reeked of vomit.

"They could easily lie."

"Won't," the guard muttered. The Otherworld was inches

from the man, no doubt.

"That hungry?"

The guard closed his eyes. His breaths became harsh and labored. "We . . . know plans."

"But you might slither back to your camp and tell what you know of us."

"They wouldn't make it over the ridge," Elise said and frowned.

"Does the woman sympathize with these bastards?" Crispin whispered to Tor. He thought he whispered, but we all heard.

Elise narrowed her gaze. "I sympathize with humanity."

"It is nothing less than what Castle Ravenspire would do. What they have done," I said before I could think better of it.

Elise schooled her glare at me, a pain she didn't hold for anyone else hidden in the flashing blue of her eyes. "Forgive me," she said with a tremble of anger. "But I do not wish to become like Castle Ravenspire."

Crispin snorted. "Then you ought to stay out of things like war, *de hän*. It's bound to get messy."

One of the guards began to cough. The sound echoed in the cavern. Elise lifted her chin, ignoring us all, and went to him. She inspected his skin, his pulse, then faced Crispin. "The least you could do is get them some clean water. You wish them to speak—then wet their bleeding mouths."

Crispin flushed, but I didn't think from anger, more embarrassment he hadn't realized it first. He glanced at one of his fellow refugees and nodded. It took a few moments before the boy returned with a pail and spoon. Elise took the bucket and carefully ladled water into the ravens' mouths.

One gagged and nearly spewed his empty stomach. Against my better judgment, I went to her side and took the spoon. This moment was too familiar. "You go too fast," I said, voice low.

She leveled her scrutiny on my hands as I spoon fed both guards small amounts of water. She wrung her fingers in her lap and whispered, "You say it as if you have experience."

I paused. Dark memories choked my breath. Nights when hunger gnawed on me from the inside out. When thirst burned until I could not speak.

"Because you *do* have experience," she said more to herself. Her eyes fell to the rocky cave floor, a look of wretched pain carved in her soft features.

What was she thinking? I wanted to ask, but turned away, barring her out instead. I finished spooning two more swallows for the guards, then stood. "What is Calder planning?"

One raven, the strongest, lifted his eyes and took me in. "Spare my sister's life . . . before I say a word."

Sister? The second raven hunched over. She was bound in such thick furs, hair matted over her face, I hadn't given it a thought that she was a woman. Her eye was swollen shut; her fingers bruised as if they'd been broken more than once.

"We didn't do it," Crispin hurried to say, as if he knew I was about to ask. "They fell, right off the cliff and onto the shore. S'how we caught them."

"They fell off the cliff?" Tor pressed.

Crispin nodded vigorously. "When night falls it's bleeding hard to see, what with the stone being damp and dark. That's not to say I don't think ravens are stupid in the head, but I suppose anyone could've tumbled if they got too close."

I faced the two haggard guards again. "You talk, she receives care."

"You can't make promises, Wraith," Ulf grumbled. "You're not in charge here."

"But I am, big bear," Halvar bit back. "If you want information from anyone, the Blood Wraith can do it."

The raven's eyes widened when I lowered to one knee.

"Blood Wraith." His words came in a breathless whisper. "All gods."

"What is your name?"

"Brant. She's Kari," he choked out.

"Where is the rest of your unit?"

Brant shuffled on his knees and winced. "We . . . were separated. Our patrol took the south shores and towns."

"Separated. Seems unlikely."

The raven looked away from us. His nostrils flared.

"Lying will do you no good," Elise said. She gave me a knowing look. She probably thought the same as me—we could use Junius's gift, but they didn't need to know. Elise cleared her throat and pressed harder as if she had the ability to taste lies. "You are not being truthful, and we've traveled for some time. Our tempers are short, and our patience runs dry."

A bit of pride burned in my chest. Clever *Kvinna*. She knew the signs of untruths as well as any warrior here. She'd always been different than other Timoran nobles, and as much as I tried, I could not get my fill of her. I had memories of turns gone by, and I did not recollect meeting any woman, even in Old Etta's gentry, who stirred me, challenged me, shackled me like Elise Lysander.

Brant pointed his worry at his sister. "One of . . . one of the captains in our unit, I . . . I caught him forcing himself on Kari. I . . . I attacked him."

"Water," Halvar ordered when Brant's tale was lost in a coughing spell.

Junius was the one who stepped forward and wet the raven's lips.

"Thank you," he whispered.

I tapped his cheek, so he'd continue. "You attacked your officer? That's a death sentence."

"Do you have a sister, Wraith? Maybe a brother?"

Elise drew in a sharp breath, unintentional by the way she pinched her lips. Hot steel pierced my chest, digging and carving.

"I did."

Brant nodded. "Then you know. It could be a bleeding king and I'd tear him apart. It is rare for women of Timoran to serve as warriors, they are often taunted, raped, or even killed. But we had no one else, nowhere for her to go once I joined. She proved her strength and was accepted under the condition that she remain with me. As my responsibility. Spare her, and I talk."

I believed him. The agony of being unable to protect Herja and my mother still ached. Countless nightmares were burned in my brain of all the things I could've done, should've tried to do to save them.

"You have my word she will live. What do you know?"

Brant seemed appeased, or perhaps too tired to argue. He cleared his throat and spoke slowly. "The king—Calder—he hunts Night Folk. He believes their blood can . . . create elixirs and poisons and magic that can be used by Timoran folk. He wishes to use them as weapons. Already he has poisoned Night Folk. Manipulated them with dark, twisted fury, then those who are too weak to serve him, he drains them. He takes their blood to study and experiment with."

"That's impossible," I said.

"Is it?" Brant scoffed. "I've seen it. They have Night Folk who serve them. Strong ones. Already they've been able to recreate strange elixirs that grow the earth like fury, some can poison."

"How do they manipulate Night Folk?"

Brant closed his eyes for a few breaths. "It is strange fury. Not from Night Folk, at least I don't think so. There is a witch that lives in the castle. There are stories that her kind can grant any desire, any wish. All she must do is write it and the fates will change the path. Even change the loyalties of Night Folk."

I stiffened when Elise's hand rested on my shoulder. Her eyes were wide in what looked like horror.

"Calista," she whispered. "The enchantress."

Blood drained from my face. Were they cursing more Night Folk?

"What enchantress?" Ulf shoved to the front. "What are you talking about?"

Elise blinked through her stun. "Um, Queen Annika, she had a witch—as she called her. She could . . . write stories of fate."

Brant tried to smile. "Yes. Yes, that sounds like the one we've heard about. As I understand, Castle Ravenspire has been keeping these witches since the beginning. Who knows how many they have."

One. Elise looked at me. We both knew they had one. The

others, the one who'd cursed me, was long dead. But one remained, forced to do their bidding. Although, the girl saved me in a strange way. Writing a tale that would summon me to the Black Tomb. But how long could she fight against them before she met the Otherworld?

"More than hunting Night Folk," Brant went on, "every unit was given orders to find the new queen's sister."

A nervous tremor flooded the cavern. Feet shuffled on stone. Hatred clogged my senses. I'd take a great deal of pleasure killing the boy king should he try to touch Elise.

"Why do they want her?" I asked, voice harsh and entirely the Wraith's.

Brant shrugged. "Their witch said she can't be killed, or she was needed. Something. I don't know everything. All I know is we were to find her and take her. Alive."

So, the fate witch was still protecting Elise in a way. Brave of her. And, no mistake, whatever plans Runa and Calder had, we'd ruin them.

I stood and looked to Crispin. "As you promised, you provided something useful. Now, they've held up their bargain. Release them and get them some bleeding food."

"Who are you to command?" Ulf said. "You hardly speak to King Ari, now you demand us to follow your every order."

"Shut up, bear," Halvar said condescendingly.

"You are bound," Ulf said. "All of you. Frey and I are the royal appointed guards. What we say is for our king. You have not even picked a side. We don't need to nurture ravens."

"They are fugitives," Elise said. "They won't return to their unit."

"I don't care," Ulf said. "They are enemies."

"And even war has decorum," Halvar said, sounding a great deal like his father. "Quit pissing and moaning that your king put a bunch of Night Folk in chains in charge. You feed us, so treat the ravens as your prisoners if you'd like. I've found it quite tolerable. They might be swayed to your side."

"I do not want them," Ulf grumbled.

"Enough," Frey said, shoving his fellow guard behind him. "Ari is a fair king. Even with enemies. Take them from this damn puddle and give them what you might have to eat."

"It isn't much," Crispin said.

"We have a few provisions from Ruskig for all of you," said Siv.

Crispin nodded and refugees stepped forward and cut the leather bindings on the two ravens. Weak as he was, Brant hurried to Kari's side when his sister slumped forward. Once he brushed her hair off her face, her femininity became clear. She was slim, with a splatter of freckles over her nose, and long eyelashes.

Halvar gathered her in his arms. Her eyes fluttered open before her head slumped back. Frey and Mattis helped Brant stagger from the cave, leaving the rest of us in silence.

After a few moments, Crispin clapped his hands. "Well, I suppose we should prepare to leave."

When I went to follow, Ulf shoved his finger in my face. "You watch yourself, Wraith. You have plans in that dark head, and I don't trust you."

"Likewise." I grinned wickedly, a lust to gut the guard throttled my logic.

Ulf stormed out. Junius tapped my elbow, a worried furrow between her eyes. "His anger tastes sour."

"And that means?"

She shook her head. "Not sure, yet. But it usually means I will soon lose trust for him. I will keep him in my sights."

As would I.

The others filtered into the main cave. Elise staggered over the rocks, avoiding my gaze.

Say something. She'd been spoken of, she was part of her sister's plot, and deserved some kind of thought. No one else had said a word.

I needed to speak to her, to forget for a moment I'd shoved her away. Forget revenge and blood and remember moments when we snuck into alcoves, and all was right in the world.

"Your cousin will not find you." Empty words, and not what I should've said by half.

Elise paused, eyes bright and so alive. So near. "He might."

I took a nearer step. "No, he won't."

"If he should—" She hesitated, biting nerves into her lip. "Then kill me before he takes me."

"Elise—"

"I'm going to see to the ravens," she interrupted. "Thank you for doing your part in sparing their lives. I'm sure it wasn't easy when you despise Timorans so much."

She left. Without another word. Not even a glance. Usually, she looked at me with longing, anger, or frustration. I'd take any of them to *nothing*.

Why was I surprised? Had I not wanted her to write me out of her life? I'd succeeded, and she would be safer no longer connected with a vengeful prince.

Then why did her empty gaze hurt like a fist to my heart?

CHAPTER 18
ROGUE PRINCESS

We didn't remain in the sea caves long. A bit of rest, half a hard honey roll, and a bit of watered-down wine, and Halvar insisted we make for Ruskig.

With the refugees in tow, the journey would be slower, and we'd need to be strategic on the roads we took. If we complained about the rocky paths before, they were nothing compared to the sludge and slick mud in marshes and swamps close to the fury quarries. We'd take a route that would add an extra day and lead us around the back of Castle Ravenspire.

Ulf had more than once told Halvar he was a fool and likely wished us dead to lead us on such paths.

By the morning after leaving the caves, more than one in our party believed him. Some even muttered that Halvar and the Blood Wraith plotted against us, and would abandon us close to the castle for the ravens to pick clean.

I grew weary of their grumbling, but didn't want to stand

near Valen, either. He was aggravating, and beautiful, and I didn't wish to be bothered by any of it.

My steps slowed until I wound up at the back of the line where Brant was tied at the wrists behind a cart that held his sister, who'd only regained consciousness last night, then fell back into a troubled sleep.

Brant's face was clean, and his beard had been cleared of sweat and debris. He wasn't much older than me, maybe a few turns were all. Handsome, with sharp icy eyes, and a curve to his shoulders as if the world crushed his back.

I kicked a pebble. It struck the wheel of the cart. Brant followed it, then lifted his gaze to me, studying my profile.

"You are Timoran," he said in a rasp.

"I am."

The corner of his mouth twitched. "If I had to guess, I'd say you are not just any Timoran."

"I am no one."

He chuckled. "Yes, and I am not being dragged to my death."

"You're not," I said.

"Really? Because the Blood Wraith said so? He is a killer himself; I do not take much stock in his word, *Kvinna*." I flinched and Brant scoffed. "As I said, not just any Timoran."

"How did you know?"

"When I mentioned Ravenspire sought you out, you reacted. So did half your people. I was too muddled to notice then, but clearly you are among them. Why did you turn from your family?"

"Because my sister and Calder are preparing to slaughter innocent people. They stole the throne through a coup. This land did not choose them." I tugged on my braid and sighed. "This land didn't choose anyone in my line."

"Treasonous talk, *Kvinna*," he said. Not threatening, more playful, like he'd expected I'd say nothing less.

I shot him a sly grin. "Do you disagree?"

"No," Brant said. He peeked over the edge of the cart when Kari shuddered in her sleep. "No, I don't disagree. Timorans are raiders. Our ancestors stole most things, then we fight to keep it."

"What if we didn't have to? Fight, I mean. What if we could all be united? It was what King Arvad and Queen Lilianna tried to do."

"The Night Folk king?"

"His queen was Timoran."

Brant regarded me with a lifted brow. After a moment he nodded. "You're right. I'd nearly forgotten, but I had an amma who told us the story of how the ice land joined with magic by their union. Amma Pjoke always indulged Kari with romantic tales and said at their union the gods parted the skies and shook the earth to show their approval." He chuckled and looked to the skies. "I don't know if peace is possible. You don't know the strength Calder is gaining. He has support from the eastern kingdoms, and some from the western kingdom. He does manipulate Night Folk to serve him."

My stomach turned sour. Doubtless Calder would gather a formidable army, one that would be difficult for even Valen to stand against. If only Ari would free him from his bindings. If only the Night Prince would quit being so damn stubborn and take his place.

I shook away thoughts of him. Not now. Not yet. With a

cautious grin, I sidestepped, so I stood shoulder to shoulder with Brant. "Are you well? Do you need to rest? Halvar will listen if you do."

"He is the one who leads?" Brant asked before cursing when his foot was swallowed into a thick, grimy mud pocket.

"Yes, he is of the Guild of Shade."

"Another surprise. The Blood Wraith and his guild have humanity."

"They do."

Brant let out a long sigh. "I'm fine. And this Shade, this Halvar, he has inquired of Kari several times. Even found an old woman who knew something of herbs to help fend off infection in some of her wounds."

My heart warmed. Halvar was a good man. They all were. Simply . . . lost.

"They are prisoners, though?" Brant asked.

"It's complicated," I said. "The Blood Wraith wishes to fight against Ravenspire alone, and King Ari wants him as an ally. They are bound from using fury, but were given leave to help find the refugees."

I didn't see a need to tell him I was the bait Ari dangled in front of Valen. That would only raise more questions.

Brant snorted, stretching aches from his neck. "I've decided I do not understand men like the Blood Wraith."

"Better not to try," I said, grinning.

A whistle signaled us to a stop. I'd not realized we'd come so close to the ledges of Lyx and the royal townships.

"Now comes the fun part," Brant murmured.

My fingernails dug into the pads of my palms as Halvar and Tor traveled down the line giving instructions on our next move. Tor—who'd brightened, slightly, since he read Lilianna's entry—stopped at us.

"We're about to go on the backroads through the old tombs." Tor gave me a knowing look.

The Black Tomb. My breath shook when I released it. We'd cross through the place where Valen Ferus died, then was reborn.

I touched Tor's arm and lowered my voice. "Is he . . . all right?"

His jaw flinched. "He survives. As always. Keep your eyes open, Elise. I do not trust the place."

I took out my dagger and looked to Brant. "*I'm* trusting you."

He groaned in relief when the leather bands fell away. I handed him a switchblade Mattis had taken from Ari's supply. Worth it to see the relief on the raven's face.

The land of the Black Tomb hadn't changed much. Knolls caked in mud and long grass straight ahead. The space remained marked by thick vines of moonvane at either corner. Between the walls of shrubs were pitiful, defaced towers which turned the entire enchanted area into a large square, a kill zone should ravens perch at the tops of those towers and fill the space with their arrows.

Or, by the gods, if those shadow guardians returned.

Moonvane carved across the Black Tomb. Around the moonvane were crests of the Lysander line. I shuddered. It was haunting to see our family runes and symbols in the open. They were not there before. Had Runa come here? Did Calder know what I had done? Bleeding hells! Did they know of Valen?

I turned from the ghostly crests to the rounded sod burial

chambers. Around the chambers were new totems of the gods, and around the totems were spikes with heads. Not just any heads—ravens.

My stomach turned harsh enough I covered my mouth to keep from retching. I was a bit ashamed that my first thought was of Valen. Had he done this? He'd pushed me out because Ravenspire was sending guards. Or were these the misgivings of poor warriors who had failed their new king?

I had the chance to ask. Valen wove his way through the cautious line of folk passing through the thick shrubs and into the Black Tomb, his eyes dark and sorrowful. Once again, the red mask covered his nose and chin.

At my side, he turned forward and walked, saying nothing.

I slowed my pace. Sure enough, so did the Night Prince. When Brant and the cart were ten paces ahead, I faced him, eyes narrowed. "Are you behind the slaughter here?"

The pause he gave unsettled me, but after a moment Valen leaned in and said, "No. But our friends sadly departed from their bodies are why I will cross with you."

"Oh, now you care so much." Petty perhaps, but I was angry enough I could scream. Words came on their own volition.

To irritate me further, Valen chuckled. "Is that your way of saying you have missed me?"

He was the Night Prince. He was the heir to the Ettan throne. He'd been cursed, used, beaten, starved. He lied to me. But there would always be that witty, arrogant, *infuriating* tongue of his that drew a smile against my will.

"I have hardly noticed your absence."

The corners of his eyes wrinkled. Hells, I wish I could see

the grin for myself. He withdrew two narrow swords as I turned away.

"I see they've trusted the Wraith with weapons," I said. "What a proud thing for you."

"Oh, no, *Kvinna*. There is no trust for me here. I stole them."

Valen ushered me forward, holding back a branch of moonvane, a look of longing in his eyes when he studied a blossom.

"Why do you think my family crest is here?"

"I don't know," Valen admitted. "But it's either a taunt that your sister is on to what this place means, and she expected you to return, or it's simpler, and Calder gifted the lands to his future queen."

"Let us hope it's the second option," I said.

Valen dipped his chin. "Let us hope."

It was not helpful knowing the Night Prince was on edge. He buried it in light tones and easy conversation, but Valen's gaze hadn't stopped sweeping over the space. We shoved through the moonvane carefully. On the edge of the boundaries, I smashed into Brant's back. The raven hadn't moved past the moonvane hedge and stared at the expanse of the Black Tomb.

"Brant?"

"This place brings blood," he whispered. "I've studied sagas. It is cursed."

Valen and I shared a look. The raven had no idea the secrets of this land, nor how right he really was.

"I think it once was cursed," I tried, "but now it is nothing but a burial site."

"No," Brant said. "There is something in this soil. I know it. King Calder did things to this place. It calls for blood."

"What do you know?" Valen asked, sharply.

"Nothing, only that this place traps people and Castle Ravenspire came here not long ago. They've done something here, I'm sure of it. I *feel* it."

"Brant," I said, trying to soothe while trying to push him onward. I'd heard of mind stun, and even if Brant was a raven, he'd gone through an ordeal. No mistake, his mind must've been whirling. "Let's go slow. See, Kari is in the cart, and they've crossed into the tomb. Nothing has happened."

"Call it a gut feeling."

"Perhaps you have a bit of Night Folk in you," Valen said, rolling a sword in his grip.

Valen had been taunting the guard, but Brant nodded his head, voice flat. "I think I do. I've always felt things others didn't, sort of like I know what to do in situations, or I know when bad things are about to happen. And bad things are going to happen."

My skin prickled. He tried to hide it, but Valen stiffened. I didn't miss how he took out his second sword.

"*Kvinna*," Brant said. "Take care."

I didn't say anything. The way Brant looked at me, as if he knew my connection with this place, was unnerving. The guard closed his eyes and stepped into the open.

Nothing happened.

"He's losing his wits," Valen muttered.

Maybe. It was possible the mind stun had settled in. But there was a chill rolling up my arms. Brant's warning, the admission his instincts were not typical, had me on edge.

"Ready?" Valen asked.

"Are you?"

He stared ahead. "No, but what choice do we have?"

I didn't know why, but his honest response left me feeling better. If the Night Prince hesitated—perhaps out of a bit of fear—then maybe I wasn't such a coward. Valen held out his hand. I took it, holding fast.

Together, we crossed once more into the lands of the Black Tomb.

The stars glimmered overhead; the breeze teased my hair. Nothing changed.

I chuckled nervously, embarrassed for being such a fool and so afraid. The curse had lifted. Like I told Brant, it was nothing but a burial site now.

Two more paces and the ground shuddered. Valen stopped. His grip tightened on my hand. My body stilled as the breeze faded. Black blotted out the stars.

I couldn't scream, couldn't move.

The wall of shadows broke into individual apparitions. The gold gleam of fiery blades burned against the dark.

The fury guardians screeched. They surrounded us. Then, they attacked.

CHAPTER 19
NIGHT PRINCE

The guardians came so quickly. I hardly had time to lift a blade and gut the shadowy gizzard of one before another was at our backs. Elise struggled to take out her blade, the pommel snagged on the leather sheath. I maneuvered so her back was to mine and cut down the guardians before they came close to her.

"What are you doing?" the bleeding idiot of a carpenter shouted. Mattis stared at us like we'd lost our minds.

"What the hells does it look like?" I snarled back. "Pick up a blade and fight them."

"Fight who?"

All gods, there was no time to deal with Mattis and his constant questions. Elise straightened at my back, weapon at last in hand, and let out a cry of rage when a fury guardian flew at her heart.

"There are too many!" she screamed.

I cursed under my breath. The shadows fought me. Those

cursed fiery swords drew wretched heat across my face. But after a moment it was clear who the guardians really wanted. My insides curled in a bit of cold terror. Elise. They were aiming their strikes at her.

Once I made the connection it was clearer than anything. Somehow these bastards were aiming all their focus on her. I was merely in their way.

We swung and jabbed. Some of the refugees stared at us like we'd lost our minds. The dark remnants of the creature inside wanted to slit their throats to get them to stop staring and bleeding help us.

Tor and Halvar sprinted back to us, blades raised.

"What is it?" Tor shouted. "What is it?"

"What . . ." I grunted through a swing against a guardian. An otherworldly shriek rattled my blood when it turned into cold mist at my strike.

Tor and Halvar held weapons. They stood off at least twenty paces but acted like they didn't know where to strike.

"Can you not see them?" I shouted. Cut. Dodge. Jab. Elise screamed at my back. She thrust her dagger through a guardian, and if it had a throat, it would be shredded.

"No!" Halvar shouted. Stieg, Casper, and Junie had joined them, just as bewildered.

"It's the damn guardians!"

Tor came closer, swinging a sword aimlessly. He hit one guardian by chance. "Tell us where! Why the hells can't we see them?"

"They're . . ." I faded and focused on two guardians coming at my flanks. Each sword burned in my grip. I cursed Ari. Fury would slaughter these shadows, no mistake, and the fool of a king and his wretched bindings were keeping me from protecting us. From protecting *her.*

"They're everywhere!" Elise finished.

Tor and Halvar stepped in. So did the others. Junie closed her eyes. But after a moment she started turning to guardians and striking with near perfect aim. Could she *taste* them?

Frey and Ulf stared at us in bewilderment. They were bleeding worthless. Siv rushed for Elise, but a guardian shoved her back. She screamed in surprise, no doubt, unable to see what force had stopped her. Mattis had ceased with his stupid questions, raised a battle axe, but no one knew where to strike.

"I think it's blood," the lunatic of a guard shouted at us.

I hardly heard him. My arms ached. Elise breathed heavily. More guardians rose. They'd soon swallow us whole. I nearly watched her die here, I refused to do so again.

"It's blood!" the raven shouted again. He was smiling, the fool. "Wraith, they want her blood."

"What the hells are you—" I couldn't finish. I needed to save breath.

"It was marked for a Lysander!" Brant said again. "This land is cursed for her. It wants her blood!"

"Then how can he see them!" Halvar shouted.

It didn't matter. Call it instinct, call it desperation, I had an idea, and it wouldn't leave me. This place had demanded blood to lift a curse once. The guardians would spill it anywhere, but we'd spilled blood in a specific point to break the bonds of fury.

It was the only chance I had.

Without warning her, I snagged Elise's wrist and sprinted up a slope.

"Valen . . ." She must've realized where we were running and quickened her step.

At our backs, wails and shrieks, like phantoms in the trees, gained. We clawed our way over a raised lip of the stone symbol at the top of the hill. A sphere of briars and coiled serpents on the hilt of a blade. I dragged Elise to the center. The crest that broke my curse remained part of the stone.

"Your hand!" I shouted.

Elise held out her palm. In a breath I slashed a wide gash across her fair skin and forced the blood on the stone.

Nothing.

Bleeding hells. Nothing.

The guardians rushed at us. At her. There were too many and I had no more plans. With nothing more to do, I wrapped Elise in my arms, smashed her to my chest, and pulled her down to the stone. With my body, I covered hers. She clung to me, and I closed my eyes. Elise buried her face in my chest. I curled one hand around her head, holding her tightly, waiting for the strike of those fiery blades.

Light glared through my clenched eyes. Hisses and growls faded like smoke on the wind. In another moment, all I heard were our own gasps and the thud of my pulse in my head.

"What is that?"

I think it was Frey who asked. I cracked an eye. A faint dome of light surrounded us, then dissolved into mist.

Another moment and Halvar skidded to my side. "Are they gone?"

I nodded, still clinging to Elise. She trembled. Or maybe I was the one trembling.

"It was the same as that night," Halvar whispered, so only we could hear. "The blood glowed, then the light came."

"Get the raven." I had questions for Brant. We'd adjusted into sitting, but I hadn't released Elise, and she hadn't released me by the time Brant was dropped to his knees. I glared at him. "You said it was cursed for her. How did you know?"

"I told you," he murmured. "I get these feelings and I know enough about fury curses to know most require blood to end them. If this land is truly cursed, I assumed blood would be required. The Lysander crests, they told me it was likely *Kvinna* Elise's blood it was after. I used no great magic, I am not hiding anything from you, I simply deduced the feeling."

"But if it wanted Elise," Frey said, "why did the Blood Wraith see them and no one else?"

Brant squared his scrutiny against me. "I don't know. The only conclusion I have is this land knows the Blood Wraith. It could not hide from him."

My blood stained this land in sacrifice. I wouldn't say it out loud, but if Brant was right, it made a bit of sense. Unfortunately, his assumption drew everyone's eye. Frey and Ulf regarded me like a new enemy. Siv bit her bottom lip, but she knew as well as us why this land knew me. Mattis tilted his head, studying me, then Elise.

Tor stepped forward. "We can all take guesses into understanding fury curses later. I say we get the hells off this bleeding land and out of the open."

The Guild of Shade guided the others away from the stone, back to the refugees below. Elise and I followed, but once we crossed into the shadows of the trees, I took her hand.

After the guardians, I could not keep my hands from her if I tried. At least, not for the next few moments.

Alone, I faced Elise. She leaned into me when my hand traveled up the length of her arm. "I hate this place."

She laughed and pressed her forehead to mine. "All gods, so do I. And I hate how you insist on continually using your body as my personal shield."

Elise rested a hand over my heart. I covered it with mine. "You are smaller than me. It makes sense I should be the shield."

"No, size has nothing to do with it. You have a sick need to play my hero."

"Am I your hero?"

She hit my chest. I laughed and curled my arm around her waist, keeping our heads together.

Elise's fingertips stroked the side of my face as her smile faded. "I'd rather you keep breathing than be any kind of foolish hero."

"I'd never be a foolish hero. I'd be a grand one."

"I think I hate you."

I laughed, and before I could think better of it, pressed my lips to hers. She drew in a sharp breath, but it was short lived. Elise kissed me back. Our breaths tangled until we breathed as one. My grip tightened in her braid, urging her body to mine.

I grinned. "If this is hating, I rather like it."

She hit my arm and curled her fingers into the neck of my tunic.

"I think of you too much," she said, breathless. Her teeth scraped my lip.

A groan hummed between us—from her or me I didn't care —it rumbled through my veins.

"Oh?" The smooth skin of her neck grew too enticing, too tempting, to ignore. She bared her throat when I kissed her there. "Tell me what you think about."

Why was I allowing this to go on? I should stop and walk away. My logic, my fears, all screamed at me to release her at once. But my logic fled into the deepest parts of my mind. Practically forgotten. I'd longed for this. It was wrong and weak. I'd bring nothing but discontent in her life, likely death.

"I think," Elise said, her gentle touch tracing the stubble on my jaw, "of what a fool you are."

"Hmm." I smiled against her mouth. "How romantic."

"About how you lied to me. Tricked me." Her fingers raked through the sweat and grime of my hair as if it were nothing. "About the night in the schoolhouse."

Elise dragged her hand down my stomach to my belt.

A dark, sensual need to spread her out beneath me, the same as that night, churned inside when she pulled on the buckle. Her fingertips slipped just below it. She grinned a little viciously when she realized how her simple touch drew out unmistakable need for her skin against mine.

Gods, all I wanted was to taste every piece of her.

"Elise," I said through a deep groan when she stroked her palm over my length straining against my trousers. Fire sparked across my skin, and I could not think beyond the wondrous sensation of her touch.

I nipped at her ear and pulled on the laces of her tunic until it split over her chest. I cupped one of her bare breasts, drawing my lips around the peak.

Elise gasped, rough and needy. She arched her back, as if desperate for me to devour every piece of her at once.

"I think," she whispered, "of how I would do it all again if it brought me you."

I did not deserve the crown of Etta. For a logical, reasonable king would keep his mind on what mattered most instead of indulging in baser instincts, instead of taking what he selfishly wanted.

I kissed up her throat, one hand still drawing out short, sensual gasps as I tugged and pinched on her breast.

I kissed her lips, hard and needy, wanting all of this to return to those dark, private nights.

My hands claimed the curves of her body, her taste, her tongue on mine. I wanted time to turn back. Before I was the Blood Wraith to her; before I was the Night Prince. When we were simply Legion and Elise.

This would not end how we wanted; of that I was certain. I had every plan to destroy Castle Ravenspire and had few hopes I would walk away still breathing.

She deserved more than a man who wallowed in blood. Elise ought to live a long, quiet life. And after this, if Ari succeeded, she might be able to have a love of her choosing.

Not someone dark and lost as me.

I dipped my chin and broke away. I didn't look at her but kept her close.

"Valen," she whispered. Her breaths were rough, but her touch was gentle as she rubbed her thumb over the furrow between my brows. "You do not need to turn away from me."

"You don't understand," I admitted, cracking my ribs a bit, and letting her in. "The memories I have—what they would do to you—Elise, it would be worse than the most wretched memory."

"I am at risk with or without you."

I knew it, on some level, I knew she was hunted for her name, not me. But add the truth that *Kvinna* Elise freed the Night Prince—she would be a greater prize for Ravenspire than me. A true traitor. I knew what Ravenspire did to traitors.

I remained silent.

Elise sighed and adjusted her tunic, hiding her skin away.

She pressed a kiss to the side of my head. "I cannot understand the horrors that haunt you, Valen Ferus. I wish you would burden them on me sometimes; ease your own. But you should know, I have never, nor will I ever stop believing you are more than vengeance. You are the power to heal this place."

She touched the point of one ear gently, then eased from my arms. Elise left me alone with nothing but my thoughts and an unquenchable longing I could not satisfy.

CHAPTER 20

ROGUE PRINCESS

Tonight, the pungent stink of Sven's alehouse was a comfort. Halvar led us from the Black Tomb, shaken, and decided the thickets around the alehouse were clear enough to camp. Sven didn't mind the added shim in his coffers when Ari's guard took up refuge in his drinking hall. The old aleman greeted Valen as Legion, asked when he'd be returning to their business, then busied about adding charges for silly things like opening a window, or kicking feet up on his tables.

I stoked a fire on the edge of the trees, listening to the laughter from the guards and some of Crispin's folk as they played and drank at Sven's tables.

"Is she well?" I asked Halvar. He dabbed Kari's forehead with a cool towel.

"Her fever burns," he says. "But she is fighting."

"You've taken an interest in caring for her," I said. "Why?"

Halvar shrugged. "I don't know. She is a fighter but has

been forced to do things against her will. She has been mistreated, and even if she is Timoran, she did not deserve it."

I smiled at him when he turned back to sopping her hot skin. What he meant was—she was like him. Valen had suffered, but so had Tor and Halvar. All had been trapped in the quarries, all had seen and witnessed atrocities against their people and families.

Curse them.

They claimed vengeance, but all three of the Ferus court had too big of hearts. They'd never succeed in their plans. They cared too much.

"Elise." Mattis materialized from the trees, dragging Brant behind him. My friend tossed the raven down.

"Mattis, what are you doing?"

"I want answers," he said, jaw tight. "This sod knew something about that place. You and the Blood Wraith saw something we could not see. What I want to know is how this raven knew the same things."

"Mattis, you heard his reasons the same as I did," I said. "He guessed."

"I'd like to think it was a bit more skilled than that," Brant said, but went quiet when Mattis glared at him.

"Do you know him?" Mattis narrowed his eyes.

"No." I furrowed my brow. "I've never met him before the sea caves."

Mattis looked as if he might break through his own skin. "Who is the Blood Wraith? Why did something attack you two at that gods-awful place? These secrets are driving me mad. I care about you, Elise, but I don't know how to protect you and S . . ." He trailed off, shaking his head.

"Calm down." Junius stepped into the firelight. "I think I can answer at least a bit about our little guard here." Brant straightened, intrigued as Junius kneeled beside him. She took out a small knife. "Hold out your hand."

Brant didn't question but winced when she made a little cut over the pad of his palm. I wrinkled my nose when Junius leaned over the bubble of blood and sniffed.

Brant pulled his hand away. "Uh, what are you doing?"

Junius lifted her head, grinning. "You're not Night Folk. You're part Alver."

"Really?" I lifted my brows and scooted closer. A new scent hung in the air. Harsh and tangy, like a sickly-sweet rot.

"Have you never smelled your blood?" Junius asked. "It's not a scent most can ignore."

Brant's face heated in red. "My family always believed I had weak blood, or some type of ailment. What is an Alver?"

"Me," she said. "I am an Alver. Like your Night Folk, we have magic. You say you get feelings?"

He nodded. "I can't shake them."

"Yes. There are Alver Folk who have incredible senses. Sight, feelings, instincts. Even to the point of being visionaries. You are my Kind. A type of Profetik—that's what we call folk with strange senses."

"A Profetik?"

"Yes, I know many who have senses like you. It's an impressive gift. I wouldn't say you have the strongest mesmer—"

"Mesmer?"

"It's what they call their fury," I told Brant.

Junie tapped her chin. "Are your parents from this land?"

Brant shifted; his fingers tangled in his lap. "My father's

wife could not have children, so he took many consorts. Some were once serfs. But we were never told who our mothers were and were raised by his wife as if she were our mother. She was, in the ways that mattered, I suppose."

"Ah, but one of those consorts might've come from a foreign land."

Brant simply shrugged.

Junius folded her arms and grinned smugly. "The good news is you're definitely an Alver. The bad news is now folk will hunt you like a wolf in the night. Welcome to the world of magic."

Ulf and Frey joined our circle. Ulf crouched in front of Junius, glaring. "How do you know he has your twisted fury?"

"Mesmer," she corrected. "And I know because his blood is potent."

"And he was the one who saved us at the Black Tomb," I said.

"I still don't understand how," Mattis pouted.

"Magic, Carpenter." Junie laughed. "Can't you leave it at that? He likely saw a vision in his head and wrote it off as his own thoughts."

"This is . . ." Brant shook his head and looked to where his sister slept. "Kari, wouldn't she be an Alver?"

"No," Junie said. "Not necessarily. Sometimes two Alvers don't produce Alver littles. It comes to whomever fate chooses I suppose."

Ulf pointed his frustration at the bindings on Junius's wrists. "Can you still use your magic?"

"Oh, yes. I told you all this. To me, these are nothing but pretty bracelets."

With a dangerous, cruel grin, Ulf took out a boot knife. "Then I say we cut out your throat. Who is to say you won't turn on us? You first, then the raven."

"Step back, Ulf." Valen, and the rest of his guild broke through the trees. "You won't touch her."

Ulf barked a laugh. His breath was like sour ale. "And what can you do to stop me, Blood Wraith? You've got those pretty bindings on. We've got your lover—" He gestured to me. I didn't flinch. "You're nothing but Ari's mutt."

"*Legion*," I warned.

I wasn't fast enough, or he didn't care, it was hard to tell.

Before the name finished leaving my mouth, Valen threw a straight blade knife (where he kept getting his weapons I didn't know) and the point narrowly missed Ulf's neck. It thudded into the corner post of the alehouse.

Ulf was stunned into drunken silence. Valen crossed the space between them, the cool, collected, sly grin on his face.

"I tire of you." He took a deep breath and patted Ulf's cheek. Hard. "I may be the mutt, but I wonder what your precious king will think when he learns at every turn you have threatened to kill or disobey those he put in charge. We are here at his word, are we not? Leave the raven, leave my guild alone, and—" Valen tilted his face near Ulf's, close enough he could kiss his cheek if he wished. "Stop threatening *Kvinna* Elise in front of me."

The thick guard tensed. Veins bulged in his arms. He was barely holding his rage in place as Valen disappeared, his guild at his back. Frey went to Ulf, only to be shoved back before the burly guard stormed off in the opposite direction as the Guild of Shade.

The Night Prince said nothing to me, and I wanted to

strangle him. Last night I drifted to sleep to thoughts of his mouth on mine. His hands claiming my body. His desire for me that he resisted. Gods, I resisted him, too, but continued to fail miserably.

I tried to be sympathetic. I didn't know what wretched memories lived in his head now, but I saw the fear in his eyes. Heard the pain in his voice when he admitted nightmares haunted him of what Ravenspire would do to me.

What he did not realize was I shared the same nightmares.

More than once, I had laid awake imagining what Calder might do if he learned the Night Prince had returned. The sort of torture Valen would endure should he ever be captured again.

Fear, though, did not numb the pain of my longing for him. While we walked free—all I wanted were moments with him. *It won't last.* I tried to shake the cold, intruding thought away and failed. *Even if you survive, he is a prince. You are nothing.*

I jolted when someone touched my arm. "Oh, Siv," I said, holding my chest. "You startled me."

"How are you?"

I flicked my eyes over her shoulder. Mattis pouted with his back against a tree near Brant, but they weren't close enough to hear us. Frey had followed Ulf with a defeated curve to his spine. Still, I kept my voice soft. "How much longer do we go on serving a king when we know the true heir is among us, angering everyone he speaks with?"

Siv's face twitched. Ah, she thought it was funny. I found no humor in any of it.

"Elise," she said when I turned away. "We cannot force him. I have faith that when the time is right, he will realize he can do more, be more, if he accepts the path fate has chosen for him."

"I wish I shared your optimism."

"Come with me. There *is* something I wanted to speak to you about." Siv pulled me into the shadows of a large white aspen. "The Black Tomb was cursed again, and I think it was done by the same girl witch you met."

I shake my head. "No, Calista wanted to be free."

"I'm not saying she did it by choice, I'm simply saying Ravenspire might understand better what she can do."

"Do you think they know the truth about Valen?"

Siv shrugged. "I don't know, but Elise, if they are using this girl to alter fate, if the raven spoke true, what other dark magic are they using?"

Possibilities scraped across my brain until my head throbbed. "We ought to be prepared for anything. Calista is sly, though. She hates them. I don't think she'll sabotage us—at least not intentionally."

"Who is this witch?" Mattis stepped between us. He'd moved so silently I hadn't heard him approach.

Siv looked at him, a heavy shadow in her gaze. A thousand things unspoken between them. "She is a prisoner we met before the coup. A slave to entertain the royals with her magic. But she can predict fate, even alter it. It's a gift that could prove dangerous to us."

"Then we should send an assassin to kill her," Mattis said. "Maybe the Blood Wraith, since he is so fond of killing."

"Stop being so sour," I said with a glare. "We're not killing the girl. She is not free there. But I would not turn away a plan to rescue her."

Siv nodded her agreement.

"I'm not sure if it matters," Mattis said, "but I have an idea of when we might get a chance at finding the witch."

"Really?" Siv said. "When?"

"It will be risky, and it will take us into Ravenspire again."

"This fight will inevitably end up at Castle Ravenspire," I said.

Mattis smirked. "True enough. I'm talking about the vows. In a short time, Calder and your sister will take their royal vows. Already there are caravans moving across the land, filling the docks with the finest things for their bleeding ceremony. We go in then."

"How? There will be countless ravens on guard."

"We must be creative." Mattis stroked his chin. This moment made me long for carefree days when we would spar at the bell tower, when we'd mock the traditions of nobility, and eat milk cakes as if there were no ranks between us.

"We'll need Ari's support and his command," Siv said. "But I see the logic. We find a way to go in undetected and cut them at the knees. Lift their skirts and see what they're hiding underneath."

For the first time in weeks, Mattis grinned at Siv. He tipped his chin in a deep nod. "Exactly, my bloodthirsty Siverie. Exactly."

CHAPTER 21
NIGHT PRINCE

"Valen," Stieg said, breathless. He slapped the lintel post on my doorway. "You're going to want to come. Quickly."

I shot from the lumpy bed; half dressed. Since we returned from retrieving the refugees two days ago, I'd hardly stepped into the sun. In part because Ulf tried to cause trouble whenever we met. Another reason was to keep from falling into the stormy sea of Elise's eyes. If I saw them again, I would not be able to let go.

I was already trapped enough.

With a fresh tunic over my shoulders, I hurried after Stieg. Tor and Casper already waited outside. Last I saw Halvar and Junius they were tending to the ill raven guard. The woman had come to, but the healers of Ruskig kept her in and out of sleep the same as they had with me.

Fresh rain during the night sparkled over the vibrant grass but caked thick mud on our boots as we climbed the slope to the royal longhouse. A blast of boiled fish and wild vegetables struck when we stepped inside. The fire blazed. Folk drank from wooden ewers and bone cups. Around the fur lined dais, once again, a crowd huddled, deep in conversation with Ari.

His dark eyes found me over the heads of his loyalists. "Ah, the Blood Wraith. I thought you might come if you heard the news."

I narrowed my eyes and took a step toward the dais. By his side, Elise studied me. New rowan leaves were braided in her frosty hair, painted bone decorated her bare neck. Thoughts of her fast pulse, the feverish heat of her skin under my lips came when I stared too long at the slender curve of her throat.

I was a fool. Hiding away in my tiny room, as if my very being did not demand I be near this woman. As if my distance was any kind of protection for her. Truth be told, I was starting to think I was more interested in protecting myself. Too many loved ones had been ripped from my life, and I could not stomach losing another.

"Come. Join us," Ari said, beaming.

"What is this?" I asked.

"We're discussing the arrangements."

He was goading me into asking, and it worked. "What arrangements?"

"For the royal vows. The ceremony will be soon!"

My hands clenched into tight fists. I shot my gaze to Elise. "You did not agree to this."

She lifted a brow, confused.

"Oh. Oh, I see. You've misunderstood," Ari said, with a chuckle. "Although, I am confident Elise will come to adore me soon enough, this ceremony is not ours. The false king and the *Kvinna* Runa will be vowed at the next high moon."

"Apologies," Stieg whispered, patting my shoulder. "He made it seem like the royal vow would most definitely be here."

Ari chuckled. "I found it rather clever and had an inkling the Blood Wraith might come running at that rumor."

"Ari," Elise said through her teeth. "You play dangerous games."

"I play entertaining games."

"By the gods, tell us why the vows matter?" Tor snapped.

"They matter a great deal," Ari said as if we should be keen to whatever stirred in his mind. "This ceremony will be attended by nobles across the land. No doubt even those from different lands. Countless Ettan serfs will be forced to be there. It is our opportunity to show the world there is a new claim to the throne. And as my friends have pointed out—" he gestured to Mattis and Siv, "it is our opportunity to see what fury Castle Ravenspire is hiding. We're going to take their Night Folk and their witch."

"Their witch?" I looked to Elise. With a subtle nod she confirmed it—they wanted the fate enchantress.

"It will be a show of strength, but if we take their fury," Ari said, "it will ensure Calder's reign is short and we take back what was stolen from us."

Murmurs hissed around the fire. Ari bore a wild sort of madness in his gaze. I wanted to mock him, tell him his plan was reckless, but by the hells it made a bit of sense. Royal vows would be attended by every noble household. If Ari wished to weaken Calder's forces by killing off his high-ranking blood and taking any fae he had in his control, then it would be a perfect opportunity.

Ari adjusted the fur cloak over his shoulders and faced the circle once again. "There is work to be done before the vows. We need to alert common folk, serfs, and many of those we've called friends in the past to our intentions. We need numbers. There is no other way to say it. The false king has over a thousand ravens at Castle Ravenspire alone. Throughout the kingdom, the number will triple."

"At least," Halvar said. He teased a great deal, but no one would understand the strength and strategy of an army more than him. "But do not disregard alliances that have been made in distant kingdoms. We don't know the true forces Ravenspire holds."

Ari nodded his concern, one fist in front of his mouth as he stared at the flames. "A fair point, and another reason we must assemble our own."

"But we must also get inside," Mattis said.

"Yes. I think our best chance is using a bard and minstrel cover," Ari said. "There are many jesters and fools called in to entertain such an event."

Frey blew out his lips. "It will take planning and bribing."

"Yes, and again, we will need numbers. So." Ari clapped his hands. "We start where we know there are loyal folk. Elise and Mattis have already agreed."

"Agreed to what?" I asked, my gaze drifting to Elise. She met my eye but turned back to Ari after a breath.

"To returning to Mellanstrad and recruiting those left behind since the coup. There are those loyal to Elise, not her family. Mattis has friends in the tradesmen. But so did Legion Grey, the merchant, as I understand it."

Ah, the true reason Ari wished for me to join. He wasn't wrong. While I built Legion's reputation in Mellanstrad, I'd acquainted myself with wealthy folk, serfs, dock men, gamblers. All manner of the population. I'd wanted—needed— to be popular to be selected as the vow negotiator.

But would they stand with us? They were miserly, unskilled, and accustomed to serving others. I couldn't say.

"How will they trust him when they discover all he's done?" Mattis said.

"They will not know him as the Blood Wraith," Ari said. "He will return as Legion Grey, the loyal protector of their kind *Kvinna*."

Siv cleared her throat. She never said much, and often avoided my gaze. In this moment, though, she stared unblinking at me. "I think it is a good plan, however, Legion appears . . . different than when he left. He is clearly Night Folk. We must come up with a reason."

"Another fair point, dear Siverie," Ari said. The king tilted his head. "Wraith, what do we tell them? If you agree to return, that is."

"I will not be forced?" I asked. "Odd."

Ari's grin gave away his annoyance. "I have set my terms for your compliance. You know the consequences. But let us pretend you decide to go along with our impressive plan instead of pouting like a child. What do we tell them? Or would you rather I cut off the tips of your ears?"

"There is no great secret how I concealed my lineage," I said, biting back a rush of anger. "Fury is how it was done, so that is what I would tell them. It would not be so hard to believe Night Folk would want to remain concealed in Mellanstrad."

"It is strange fury."

"Not my problem."

Ari scratched his chin. "Are you saying you'll go, or not? I don't wish to stay here all night and there are plans to make."

My gaze drifted back to Elise. This time she stood, returning a narrowed glare, and said, "Make your choice independent of me. I do this with or without you. I do not need your protection. Not any longer."

Be honest with her, for once in your bleeding life. No mistake, I'd become a coward to the truth, resisting it until I pushed her away again and again. Affection and love led to leverage enemies could use. It led to pain. Elise was my *agony*.

If the beast, the unfeeling monster inside, were ever needed, now was the moment.

At my silence, Elise turned and abandoned the longhouse.

To those around us, they might not have caught the underlying meaning in her words. She'd released me from any debt I might have for her part in breaking the curse. She'd chosen this fight, independent of me. I'd promised her I would always protect her, even if I was not with her.

But she no longer wanted it.

Strange, but the idea of her no longer needing me, no longer wanting me, ached more than the arrow I took to the back.

Over the nights in Ruskig, vengeance had simmered to an annoyance.

The longer I remained here, the more my drive to battle

against Ravenspire stemmed from Elise. A desire—a need—to protect her from it all. Ari was wrong. Elise was not a soft spot in my armor, she was the bleeding destruction of it.

I spared a glance at Tor and Halvar. They revealed nothing on their faces. They would follow whatever choice.

I lifted my eyes to the king's throne, voice dark and low. "When do we leave?"

CHAPTER 22
NIGHT PRINCE

ater slapped against the boards of the narrow
longship. The black laths disappeared in the shadows
of the river. Each row was made with care not to stir too many
waves, or too much noise.

Ari surprised me. I didn't know how he came by the vessel,
but it gave us the way into Mellanstrad. We slowly rowed our
way through the fjord and into the river that ran through lower
Mellanstrad.

It was not a warship, not even a vessel worthy of nobility. A
dozen oars, a tattered sail, a raven head instead of
Jörmungandr as the figurehead. Still, it saved time and gave us
a means to escape without running on foot if Castle Ravenspire
had a foothold in Mellanstrad. Scouts reported what few ravens
remained spent their time at alehouses or sleeping in abandoned homes.

I didn't trust it and would be on my guard.

Tor added a knife to his belt. He, Halvar, and Frey disembarked first, checking the surrounding trees. At their clear, Ari directed the rest of us to leave the boat. Junius and Casper were to remain with the longship since Casper was a water fae and Junius was a skilled blade.

Pointless for Casper, since Ari would not remove his bindings. I pointed out the hypocrisy and the fool simply laughed.

Elise left the ship with Mattis and Siv. She had said nothing to me on the journey upriver. What was there to say? I had too many words and none ever shaped into anything worthwhile. I hated that she'd come. Hated that she'd face her home again. She'd see it scorched and ruined, like the night that bastard had tried to touch her.

I should've killed him

My fists clenched, and I hadn't noticed until Elise shot a bemused look at my hands, then met my gaze as if silently beseeching me to share what bothered me. At my silence, she chose to stand by Ari instead.

"We'll go to the game halls first," Stieg said at my back. "Will he send Elise to her lands?"

"I don't know, but if he does it will put her at too great a risk."

As if on cue, Ari pushed his way between us. "*Herr* Grey," he said with a touch of mirth. "We follow you into the slums of Mellanstrad. I pray to the gods you still have friends."

The new king seemed to enjoy my discontent. He refused to return my axes, an oversight on his part. Should we be attacked, I would be forced to sit idly by and watch.

Halvar nudged my shoulder, handing me a woven satchel. My friend winked. One glance inside drew a grin to my face. A red mask, black cowl, and a sheathed dagger, stolen from Ari's personal supply.

I'd be Legion Grey tonight, unless I needed to be someone else. Someone of the deadlier sort.

I shouldered the pack with the Blood Wraith's supplies and took the lead through the trees.

Lower Mellanstrad was changed. Tenements less lively. Most rooms had gone empty after Ravenspire tore through the streets. Where racks and lines of linens and trousers hung, now empty lines remained. A hot tang of blood hung in the air. Each step in the damp dirt roads released a bit more. No doubt, I was the only one who could taste it.

A familiar clawing to breathe it in, to embrace violence gnawed inside my chest.

I paused in front of a whitewashed old house, studying the scorched doorframe. The broken windows.

"What?" Ari shoved through the small crowd from Ruskig. "What is it?"

"This is where Legion traded," Halvar explained.

I turned away and aimed for the game hall. Whatever shim or notes of wealth I'd left behind in the small office belonged to Ravenspire and Calder by now. It was a strange thought, to miss such a time. Even cursed, there had been moments as Legion Grey where I found a bit of peace, belonging, and usefulness.

Now I knew my name, yet had little purpose but to kill and hate.

As we walked, a few people greeted us, some pleaded for shim or bread. A few women and men from Ari's court—they'd become self-proclaimed courtiers—offered refuge in Ruskig.

Most beggars looked at us like we'd gone mad, but some stepped in line.

I hid my awe and pleasure when Elise was among the first to offer ale and bread to the weary. A few gasped, bowed their heads. Some sent prayers for their *Kvinna's* return. Most were too lost in the haze of suffering to even notice.

The game hall was positioned near the docks. Before Ravenspire came against Mellanstrad, the house leaned to one side. Now there were missing slats on the roof, and the door didn't hang quite right on the hinges. A pungent breeze of brine, salt, and sweat always hovered near the peaks. It was no different now.

"It appears to be full," Ari said.

True enough, the windows of the hall glowed in candle-light, and a few barking laughs broke the night every few breaths. Outside, men staggered, drunk and satisfied. Some had women and men on their arms.

Women were never allowed before. Perhaps they'd stopped caring after their lives had been overturned.

Ari clapped me on the shoulder. "Well, let us get on with it then."

Ari, Frey, and the courtiers began to make their way down the muddy slope toward the house.

"They'll be desperate," Tor said. "Shouldn't be difficult to convince them."

If more folk did not join Ari's cause, I had few doubts he'd take Elise as his queen consort simply for her name. He was not wrong in believing the people of Mellanstrad favored the second *Kvinna*.

Her temperament and fairness were the qualities I'd

exploited when I needed a royal to break my curse. Doubtless if she aligned with the new king of Night Folk, others would then follow.

The thought turned my stomach.

"You do not need to do this." Elise came up behind me, tossed back her hood, frowning.

I wanted to reach out to her, to feel the softness of her skin. I wanted to run.

"I am bound to do as the king says."

She scoffed. "You care little what Ari says. Go back. This is not your fight."

"Elise . . ." My voice caught in my throat. She stared mutely as I tried to say something—anything—but I had nothing.

"I wish you would leave instead of torturing me with your indifference. Let me forget and just . . ." She shook her head and started to walk away.

I grabbed her hand and pulled her back. My gaze fell to the two missing fingertips. So many things had brought us together, so many were trying to drive us apart.

"What do you want?" she whispered. "Resist long enough and Ari will release you, for you will be of no use to him. And do not use his pathetic threats about taking vows with me as an excuse. I know how to stand on my own, and frankly, I don't think you care much anyway."

I cared. I cared too bleeding much.

"You are naïve," I said instead of all the kind, gentle words I could've chosen. I leaned my face alongside hers. "Ari is the recognized king, and this is war. If an alliance with you is what strengthens his forces, you will be given no choice."

"I will always give myself a choice."

I shook my head. "And that is why you're naïve. He befriends you now, but even you must admit if an alliance would benefit this land, then you would agree."

She lifted her chin, voice low. "I grow so weary of pretentious kings thinking they have a say in my life. Consider me no longer your burden to bear. My fate is mine."

Elise stomped down the hill without another word.

I'd wounded her. Her eyes gave away the truth. First, her uncle had demanded she take vows with fools of Timoran. Ari threatened her freedom and her heart. And me. I was the worst of them all. I ran from her when she begged me to stay. Invaded her peace. Stole her position. Thrust her into this fight, remained distant, drew her back in, then pushed her away again as if her sacrifice didn't matter.

I adjusted the pack on my shoulder. She wanted me to leave, but no mistake that would be wholly impossible.

At the game hall, Halvar, Tor, and I went in first. The room reeked of smoke and unwashed skin, but my body relaxed. Almost like we'd come home.

"By the bleeding hells! It's Legion Grey."

Korman, a night watchman who had a proclivity to overindulge on drink, raised a horn. He'd always been a ratty man, but his beard was missing patches of hair, two front teeth were gone, and a new scar carved his lip.

I grinned. "It has been a long time, my friend. You're much uglier now."

"And you three have damn fae ears."

"We do."

"Sit. You've got a story to tell, and I've got all the bleeding time in the world." Korman bellowed a laugh and slammed his horn on the table. He pulled out a chair next to him, grinning, and gestured for me to sit beside him. "Get this sod a drink."

The aleman nodded and busied behind the counter. Korman sniffed and leaned over onto his elbows. "Legion Grey. I thought the Norns plucked your string of life into oblivion long ago. First, I'd like to know how you hid you were Night Folk. There's a few underground fae who'd love to know."

I grinned and leaned back in the chair. "Complicated fury spells. The kind that requires blood sacrifices and eating your firstborn. Not worth it."

Korman snorted another laugh, rubbing his chin. "I'll pretend I believe that. Where the hells have you been? I've not heard talk of you since the siege at Ravenspire."

"I've been surviving the same as everyone. Tell me, what is Mellanstrad like now?"

Korman winced through a long gulp of ale. "Like the second hell. Cold, dreary, filled with too many men who love knives. They watch us like we're hiding bleeding royals here. They kill us through tax and fines. The only place that stays alive is this place. And only because the ravens like Hugo's ale."

"They think you hide the *Kvinna*?"

Korman snorted. "The bleeding queen thinks her sister will be the undoing of her stolen throne. Like she's a deity with the power to change fate. Tell me, *Herr* Grey, where is the little *Kvinna*? I heard she got her throat slit by the Wraith."

I fought to keep my expression neutral. Korman glared at his drinking horn for half a breath, then went on. "We've taken in the folk from the Lysander estates. What's left of them, at least. I say she's dead or she ran. Timoran royals never did have much of a backbone."

"You'd think differently if you knew *Kvinna* Elise."

Korman shrugged. "I suppose you'd know best. Do you know where she went? You were with her at the castle."

"I was, but we were separated and—"

"I'm right here, Korman."

I let out an annoyed groan as Elise shoved her way through the growing crowd. With a pointed look, I begged her to leave.

Korman stared, aghast. Murmurs rippled through the hall as she removed a hood from her pale hair and sat beside me at the table. Elise's shoulders didn't slouch, she didn't falter. No, she took a bleeding drink of the horn Hugo had brought for me.

"*Kvinna*," Korman said in a breathless whisper. "I . . . I heard the Blood Wraith took you for his own and devoured you."

She grinned. "Although I would've found that utterly enjoyable, I'm afraid he let me go."

Korman looked at her as if she'd slipped into a bit of madness. My face heated.

"What are you doing?" I asked through my teeth. "You were to stay back."

"I am not going to stand there and let the folk of my township believe I abandoned them." Elise looked back to the night watchman. "What have Runa and Calder been doing here? Why?"

Korman met my eyes. "I don't know why they do the things they do. They arrest folk. Execute them, all because they say they are aiding you. Why do they fear you?"

"Because Elise is a Timoran royal who stands with the new king of the Night Folk."

I rolled my eyes, again, when Ari came forward, haughty

and grinning like this was a game. Did no one know how to stick to a plan?

"Korman," I said. "This is Ari Sekundär. The accepted king of Ettans and Night Folk in Ruskig."

Korman's eyes widened. "All gods. You do have a story to tell."

Ari took the seat on the other side of Elise. He beamed at the table. "It was rather surprising; however, we know Etta chooses her kings and queens."

"King Ari brought back the moonvane. Saw it with my own eyes," said Frey. "He put his hand on a shrub and the blossoms bloomed."

I flicked my eyes to Elise. She met my stare for a moment. I could practically hear her telling me Etta *had* chosen her king, but he was ignoring the call.

A few men gathered around Korman and listened to Ari speak of their refuge in Ruskig. He spoke of the attack on the fury quarries, of the alliance with *Kvinna* Elise—the Timoran who had always been fair and kind to Ettan folk.

"We came here for you," Ari said, his voice steady and powerful. "We will not leave you without support a moment longer. *Kvinna* Elise insisted you were her people and I agree. We have your friends with us. Elise and Legion Grey. We have fury on our side. What we need are able-bodied folk willing to fight for this land. The fates tell us the time is now."

A hush settled over the game hall. Korman dragged his fingers through his greasy hair. Women prayed. Some people nodded, grinning a little viciously. Others seemed ready to bolt out the door.

Halvar set down his horn and clapped Korman on the

shoulder. "Come on, now. What is this silence? You are the folk from the pit of this land. Violent, capable, and without conscience."

"Stop," said a dock man named Harald. "Your flattery will get you nowhere."

Halvar chuckled. "This is our land. It was robbed from us through bone, and blood, and torture. Stand with us. Fight for your folk. There is life still in this soil and we cannot do it if our people are not united."

Korman let out a long sigh. "You really infiltrated the fury quarries?"

"We did," said Ari.

The night watchman glanced at Elise. "Your people will flay you. They'll carve you to pieces. How do we know you truly stand with us?"

"She does," I said. "No one here has seen the sacrifices *Kvinna* Elise has made for people who are not her own as much as me."

"She treated us kindly." A woman's small voice echoed over the heads.

Elise stood, scanning the back, until she grinned. "Arabella, you're here."

I rose from my seat as Elise weaved through the crowd to an Ettan woman with a raven tattoo on her throat. A mark of a serf.

With the smallest hesitation the serf embraced Elise and laughed. "I knew if they were so obsessed with you, then you were still alive."

"How are you? Where is Ellis?"

"He works for Hugo in his hog pen. He'll be in shortly. It is good to see you, *Kvinna*." Arabella faced the room again. "I served at the Lysander estates, like many of you. Elise never mistreated the serfs. She snuck us food, defended us against her father's wrath. Even against the old king, she would hide us if he arrived looking for serfs to trade."

Elise wiped her eyes and squeezed Arabella's hand. She looked at Korman. "I was born Timoran, but I have no land. I am not Ettan, and I am a traitor to my own folk. I *choose* to stand with those in Ruskig."

The night watchman said nothing. A few folk whispered. I tensed, ready to defend Elise should they turn on her. Foolish of Ari, of Elise, for jumping in. Anyone could use her as a ransom to find favor.

My chest burned from holding my breath by the time Korman chortled into his horn. "Ah, don't look so worried *Kvinna*. We'd take you without all the speeches. Consider yourself Ettan with a dash of raider in you."

The game hall laughed together. I almost relaxed. Almost grinned.

Until the door to the hall slammed open and Stieg shoved inside, breathless and flushed. "It's Castle Ravenspire! They're here!"

"What!" I was on my feet in half a breath.

People scattered. Korman flung open a door in the floor and shouted for women and young ones to get below.

"How'd they know?" He grumbled, then glanced at the counter. "Ah, cursed gods, Hugo!"

For the first time, I realized the aleman was nowhere to be found. My blood pounded in my head. "He sold you out?"

"Got scared. Probably when he saw the likes of her,"

Korman said with a gesture to Elise. "They keep a bleeding camp of ravens at the Lysander estate. Top guards, Legion. Top guards. Even spotted one of the royal hansoms a time or two. They want her. And badly."

"Elise," Ari said. "We need to go."

"There is no time," I snapped and dug into the satchel. "Everyone who can, run for the southern docks. There is a boat on the river."

Stieg glanced out the window. "Better hurry. A bleeding royal coach is heading this way."

Elise looked at me, eyes wide with horror. She removed a dagger from a sheath on her leg. Mattis and Siv came from the back of the game hall and stood at her shoulders. I held her gaze when I slipped the cowl over my head and masked my face in the red cloth.

"Bleeding hells," Korman said. "You're the Blood—" The night watchman pinched his lips, held up his hands, and shook his head. "No. Nope, I don't even want to know."

"Now would be a good time to give me my axes," I said to Ari.

"No such luck," Ari said, cautiously looking out the window. "They remain in Ruskig."

"Fool." I removed the dagger from the satchel. Ari saw it but ignored it as I turned to my Shade. "Stieg, take the people to the river."

He didn't hesitate and followed a group of women through the trap door. Korman sniffed and wiped a hand under his nose. He rocked on his heels at my side.

"You should go," I said.

"Rather not."

"They could kill you."

"Then make sure I have my sword in my hand when I die, Wraith." He winked and unsheathed a battered short blade from his belt. "I'd like to sup with the gods."

"Frey," Ari said, one hand on his blade. "Tell me what's happening."

Frey went to the window, he looked side to side. "They've at least two dozen ravens. There's a coach, My King. A fine one. Like the Shade said, it's either a royal or high noble. Oh, there is someone stepping out. Hells, it's the bleeding captain of the royal guard."

Elise paled. She looked to me. Without realizing, I'd worked my way over to her side. I took her hand, lacing our fingers, and whispered close to her ear. "Is it him?"

If Jarl Magnus, the bastard who'd nearly killed Elise, was outside, I'd slit him navel to nose without a second thought.

"I don't know." She shuddered and tightened her grip on my hand.

A voice from outside silenced the game hall. "We come in a truce. A moment of peace."

"It's Jarl," Elise said.

Fury I couldn't use boiled in my veins.

Jarl called out again. "We've come for a conference with *Kvinna* Elise Lysander. Tell her, if she is in there, that her sister, the queen of Timoran, wishes to speak with her."

CHAPTER 23
ROGUE PRINCESS

The game hall fell into discomfiting silence. The only sound was my pulse thudding in my ears.

"Elise," Jarl shouted. "Come outside and no harm will befall you or anyone here."

"Don't," Valen said in a dark voice. His hand still clasped mine and he tugged me back.

"Go with the Shade. Take people out," Ari commanded Frey.

The guard nodded and opened the floor hatch once more. The ravens were everywhere, and with Jarl here it would mean Calder and Runa sent their fiercest warriors.

Ulf stared out the window, his jaw tight like stone. "They have too many. They'll obliterate us."

"Fate is on our side, Ulf," Ari said in a steady voice.

The way the bulky guard closed his eyes, I doubted he had as much faith as his king.

Mattis and Siv both took out their own weapons. Siv a

dagger, Mattis an axe and knife. Siv looked to me, fear buried beneath bravery. Mattis glanced at her. An entirely different emotion in his eyes.

"Elise," Jarl called out again. "I didn't want it to come to this."

A new sound filled the night. A scream. A child's scream. Followed in another breath by Arabella's.

"Ellis!" She bolted to the door, but Tor caught her. Arabella kicked and thrashed and screamed for her son. Tor held her tightly against his body until she crumbled, sobbing in his arms.

He looked to me, then Valen. Even with his mask Valen's anger radiated like an open flame.

"Come outside and the boy lives," Jarl said. "Hide away like a coward and I'll send his head inside for his mother to bury."

Arabella choked out a strangled sob. She vomited, still cradled in Tor's arms.

I peeled my fingers free of Valen's grip.

"Elise," he snapped, reaching for me. "Don't you dare."

"I will not let him die for me. You've seen what Jarl can do —he will not hesitate to hurt a boy. Open the door, Ulf."

"Wait," Ari said. "It should be me."

"They want me," I said. "Ari, they don't know what you look like. It is still an advantage. They will not know who leads the Night Folk."

Ari looked as if he wanted to disagree, but he gave me a curt nod.

"You're not going out there," Valen said. "They are playing you."

I ignored him. "Open the door."

Twenty paces away, Jarl held onto Ellis's arm. The boy was crying but tried to stand firm.

"Release him," I called out.

Jarl's sneer turned my insides into hot acid. "I was beginning to wonder if you were really here."

"Release the boy, Jarl, or I will not take another step."

Jarl held up his hands, watching Ellis stumble. The boy sprinted into the game hall, into Arabella's arms. Even at a sturdy eleven, his mother rocked him, covered his cheeks in tearful kisses, and stroked his messy black hair.

"Get them," Ari said. "Go. Go."

Arabella gave me a watery look. Her chin trembled, then she disappeared through the hatch with another of Ari's guards.

Siv came to my side, she took my hand. "Don't do this."

"I don't have a choice."

Mattis came behind her. "Elise, please."

I took both their hands in mine. "Help take folk away from here. Please, I need you to help. I do not think they will harm me. Not yet. There is something they want from us first."

"I'm not letting you go out there," Mattis insisted.

"Mattis, this is battle. Negotiations and moments of truce are part of it. But the people of Mellanstrad are unarmed, and you both know how to use a blade. Fight for them."

I turned away at once. Behind me some of Ari's guard gave instructions to my friends on the path they needed to take to help the dock men, the fishermen, the women, and young ones toward safety.

I couldn't think of them. Not right now.

Valen crossed the room in three strides. "I'm going with her."

Halvar, Tor, and Stieg jumped to attention, ready to fight, or protest. Probably both.

"No," I said, embarrassed how my voice quivered. I rested a hand on Valen's chest. "No, you can't. You are *needed*."

Valen's face dipped close. Through the mask, his lips brushed my cheek. "Try to stop me."

"Go," Ari said, his eyes like black stone. "Scare the piss out of them, Wraith."

More than the Blood Wraith followed me into the night. The Guild of Shade had masked and armed themselves. They surrounded me like a dark circle, ready to leap in front at the first threat.

Truth be told, their nearness helped me stand a little straighter.

Jarl wore thick pelts on his shoulders. A blade on each hip and the hilt of another rose over one shoulder from a sheath on his back. Since seeing him last—the night he tethered me to a bed and tried to force vows—he'd grown a golden beard and allowed his hair to meet his shoulders.

His pale eyes narrowed. "Stop there. Not another step Blood Wraith. She comes alone."

Valen laughed, his voice no longer the Night Prince, but the low, gravelly rasp of the Wraith. "Afraid I'll finish the job I started last we met?"

Jarl winced but pointed his glare at me. "You come alone, Elise, or—"

"Or what, Jarl?" I said, snidely. "What will you do? You have returned your hostage. You have men, but you know how the Guild of Shade fights."

"It is a truce."

"And we will not lift a blade unless needed. But you must think me mad if you believe I'll go anywhere with you unaccompanied."

He clenched his grip around the bronze pommel of his broadsword. We were outnumbered, but I found a bit of gladness at the notable fear Jarl kept for the Guild of Shade and the Blood Wraith.

"Follow me," he said after a painful silence.

Jarl led us to a white canopy tucked behind the coaches and line of Ravenspire warriors. Seated on a plush cushion, dressed in a long gown, Runa stared us down like we were no better than the dirt on her feet.

My sister wore a gold circlet. Her hair had been braided, as a symbol for her upcoming vows. Gold rings lined her ears and fingers, and runes were tattooed on the tops of her hands.

I hated my sister. But in the same thought, I did not want to fight her.

"I had no idea you'd garnered such violent connections, sister," Runa said. "The Blood Wraith. I'd be impressed if you were not being such a fool."

"There are many things you do not know, *sister*."

A figure emerged from the back of the canopy, and I swallowed a gasp.

"Daj," I whispered. My father stood tall and broad. His skin no longer pallid and sunken. His hair had thickened, and his beard was braided and beaded in silver. Leif Lysander looked every bit the prince consort he'd once been.

Calista's story of sickly fate against my father had faded with Valen's curse, no doubt.

My father's jaw tensed. There was a fleeting shadow of pain in his eyes before his gaze hardened. "Daughter. I'm ashamed of the company you keep."

"Or terrified," Halvar said behind his mask.

Of course, he'd find a reason to tease even now.

"Runa," I said. "What do you want?"

My sister regarded me for a moment. "I want this quarrel between us to end, Eli. We are blood. We are sisters. You belong with your people and family."

"My family tried to have me killed," I said dryly.

"No, you're mistaken. We sought you out to keep you safe."

"After you killed our uncle? Safe from your actions?"

Runa frowned. "I don't expect you to understand, Elise. Our uncle was leading Timoran into the frigid wasteland our ancestors fled. We will save it. We've brought life back."

I snorted. Everyone claimed to be the one responsible for returning life to Timoran. If only they knew the man at my side was the one who had the magic to save this place, to heal the scars that ran so deep.

"Elise, the king has arranged a comfortable life for you should you come to your senses and return with us," my sister said. She gestured to Jarl. "You and Jarl will take vows—"

"No," Valen interjected.

My sister startled at his voice. It took a moment for her to peel her eyes away from the Blood Wraith and continue. "Together you shall be granted lands in Lyx, grander than even those of our parents. You will help us ensure peace with the

Ettans. They trust you; they value you. Together we can make Timoran what it is destined to become."

"I will not stand for your plans with Night Folk," I said. "I know you are trying to take fury for yourself. You torture Ettans, Night Folk, and our own people to further your ambitions. If you vow to cease these things, vow to step down from the throne, then yes, our quarrel will end."

Runa sneered. "You're a fool, Elise. So many people will be harmed if you do not stop."

My blood heated. I saw red. Laughter and memories as young girls faded into something like hate—it was a strange tangle of emotion. Disdain, agony, regret, sadness. I leaned over the narrow table that held a silver crusted horn for the future queen, drawing our faces a hairsbreadth apart.

"You are threatened, sister, or you would not have called me here. Perhaps it is you who is the fool."

Runa shot to her feet. "We will kill Legion Grey."

I lifted a brow. "What?"

Runa smiled, smug and wicked. "Yes. After you fled, we found your vow negotiator. As I recall, you fancied him. I will see to it every inch of his skin is peeled from his bones. His screams will haunt this land until your last breath."

Runa's breaths heaved. It took a great deal not to laugh.

Halvar took the liberty for me. "Such brutal description."

When I snickered, my sister seethed at me. "You think I won't?"

She was grappling and desperate to appear as the dark, formidable queen of the land. She would fail.

"I think you're lying," I said.

"I'm surprised. I thought you had more affection for the man." She turned to Jarl. "See it done."

Jarl bowed his head in agreement. I bit the inside of my lip. "Is that all you have to threaten me with?"

"I will take his eyes first," Runa said. "Perhaps you can keep them as a token of your callousness."

"This is tiring, and frankly disappointing. I expected better from the likes of Ravenspire," Valen said. "You lie, we know you do, and we shall never stand with your false, stolen throne."

"Your mistake," Runa said through gritted teeth. "He'll die to—"

"Enough." Valen let out an exasperated sigh and before I could protest, he pulled down the red mask. "Your threats are childish, and clearly Legion Grey is not in your grasp."

I took a great deal of satisfaction watching Jarl's face pale, watching Runa stammer. My father was the only one who appeared nothing but irritated.

"*Herr* Grey is . . . *he* was in my house all this time!"

"Strange, isn't it?" Valen said.

Jarl's eyes flicked between the two of us. I could only guess what sort of thoughts rampaged in his brain. How he'd kill Legion? How he'd hide from him. I hoped he'd lose sleep knowing Legion Grey fooled the entire kingdom.

He was still fooling them.

Runa, after composing herself, shoved a nearby guard. "Take an eye."

Valen reached for his blade, but to my horror she did not point at the Night Prince.

Runa directed the guard toward our father.

"Runa," he said, stunned.

My sister wheeled on me. "This is your doing, Elise."

Two guards gripped my father's arms. He struggled and shouted as they forced him to his knees. The guard my sister had directed removed a vial from his tunic. I'd expected a knife but imagined the murky liquid to be a kind of poison.

"Have you lost your mind?" I screamed at her. Valen unsheathed the dagger. Tor, Halvar, and Stieg did the same.

"Daughter, no." My father fought against the ravens. He clamped his eyes closed when the vial was lifted over his head.

Runa held up one hand, holding the guard in place. "His fate is in your hands, Elise. Come with us and save our father from suffering. Or perhaps my sister is truly dead."

An arm wrapped around my waist and pulled me back. Valen dragged me toward the flap in the tent.

"No!" I cried. Runa's grin faded. She lowered her hand and nodded. My heart stuttered. "No! Stop!"

Valen held me against his chest as the guard tipped the vial into my father's right eye. The potion hissed. Deep, black veins cracked from my father's eye, down his face and neck.

I desperately wished to look away. I didn't blink.

Whatever it was seemed to be rotting his eye from the inside out. His screams rattled in my head. How could she do this? What had happened to my sister to twist her into something so cruel and ugly?

She turned her dark, wretched gaze to me. "Kill them."

The next moments blurred. Valen pulled me out of the canopy. Tor and Halvar threw knives straightaway, almost as one, killing the two guards who'd held my father. Stieg faced Jarl. The clash of steel on steel burned through the night.

"I can't leave him." I struggled against Valen. My head spun.

"They will kill you," he said. "It is blight, Elise. Dark fury. He cannot be helped now."

I barely registered a line of Night Folk stood outside the door of the game hall, Ari in the center, swords drawn.

"Ready!" Ari shouted. He acknowledged Valen, hardly spared me a glance. It wouldn't take much to know something had gone wrong and the Blood Wraith was saving my life. Ari's guards raised blades; Night Folk lifted their palms. From the canopy, Runa shrieked for guards to attack—to slaughter us all.

Valen whistled, and in another breath, Stieg, Halvar, and Tor raced back to the game hall.

"Show them the fury of this land," Ari roared. "Show them what they will *never* have!"

His voice soaked deep into my blood, stirring something alive inside. Ari was not the true king. Someday he would realize it, but there could be no doubt that he was a leader. And a chilling one.

Night Folk moved as one. Their hands open, some kneeled. Fury called to the earth. Not in the way Valen could bend and break the soil, but thorns, branches, and shrubs reached out like sharp fingers and surrounded the Ravenspire canopy.

A shimmer of magic surrounded the game hall, doubtless some kind of illusion barred the ravens from seeing clearly.

Some of the guards cried out angrily as brambles coiled around their ankles, dragging them to the ground. Like snakes in the grass, shrubs entombed the guards in the ground.

"We hold!" Ari shouted. "Break away in units. Run to the river!"

Ulf stared blankly at the new rush of guards from my sister's camp. We had fury for now, but more ravens kept coming, like a scourge.

"What the hells is that?" Stieg shouted.

Valen's arm tightened around my waist, but once my eyes focused, I froze. Something dark crept across the earth. Shadows—no—something tangible like ink bled into the fury-controlled branches. Black devoured the grass, robbing it of color. Life shriveled into something dry and brittle. As the skeins of black flowed over the trapped guards their screams froze my blood.

"What is that?" Stieg repeated.

"Go!" Valen shouted. A true fear in his voice sent a frigid chill down my spine. "Fury will not hold."

Ari didn't hesitate. "Pull back! Run to the ship!"

In a shudder the fury barricade dissolved. Around me, Ari's defenses fled into the darkness. I was almost certain someone called my name. My head spun in a painful flurry, attacking my body, stilling my muscles. What happened here tonight? How had my sister become so cruel, so power mad?

The shock of it all filled my skull, slowing each thought until I could hardly keep up.

"Elise."

Valen. His hands were on my shoulders. He shouted in my face.

"Go. You must run."

Why did he have a blade drawn? Why wasn't he running?

I blinked. "Come with me."

"I will hold them back."

A cold blow to my chest shook me from the fog. I snapped to attention, my heart in my throat. "No, you-you're bound."

I screamed when another hand gripped my wrist. Stieg pulled me back.

Valen was ordering him to.

"No! No, you can't fight this."

The Night Prince ignored me. He turned away too quickly, as though he would not be able to leave otherwise.

The Guild of Shade and the Blood Wraith drew their weapons. The last thing I saw was the black ink devouring some of Ari's fury branches and a new unit of ravens racing down the scorched hillside toward the Guild of Shade.

"Stieg, no!"

"They'll hold them back," he grunted. "Buy us some time. Come on, quit kicking. All gods, you're stubborn."

When the game hall disappeared completely, I gave up. Stieg outmatched my strength three to one. Numb, I allowed him to pull me through the gnarled trees until the soil dampened and the air grew wet with stagnate water and mold.

The longship bobbed a good distance off the bank. Men trudged through the water, others pulled them over the edge and into the ship.

Stieg raced with me into the icy river.

I coughed against the pain of cold but forced my feet to keep moving.

Any moment Valen would break the trees.

He didn't need fury. With his curse he hadn't realized he had fury and he'd survived. He was the Blood Wraith the same as he was the Night Prince.

"*Kvinna*, here." I don't know who pulled me over the edge

of the ship. Korman? Frey? The moment I plodded onto the deck, I turned back to the trees.

"Row," Ari's breathless voice commanded.

"No! Ari, they're still out there."

The king gritted his teeth and cursed. He faced the trees, scanning the shadows like the rest of us.

"We cannot wait," Ulf insisted. "We'll be trapped by their ships."

"Ari," I said, a break in my voice. "Do not leave them. I beg you."

His jaw pulsed. He scanned the riverbank again, flicking his fingers at his sides. After a few tense moments, Ari turned to me. "We cannot remain here, Elise." He hesitated. "I'm sorry."

The oarsmen gave a great pull. The ship lurched forward.

"No." I raced to the bow frantically. In passing my mind registered Siv and Mattis were there. Arabella and Ellis. Junie and Casper. But not Valen. Please. *Please.* I clutched my throat, one foot propped on the ledge of the ship, ready to jump in. "Wait! Stop!"

My finger trembled as I pointed to the trees. Three figures burst from the shadows, sprinting into the river.

"Stop," Ari commanded. The current still carried us away, but slow enough they'd catch up.

The Guild of Shade swam with the flow of the river. Korman, Mattis, and Casper leaned over the edge and caught them by their forearms before the current dragged them down-river. I remained frozen at the bow, hand on my throat as Tor, Halvar, and Valen were dragged on board, soaked, but breathing.

Ari chuckled, but it seemed to come from nervousness. He

clapped Valen on the shoulder as the Night Prince leveraged into sitting. "I knew I would not regret you."

Valen scoffed, shirked the king off, but grinned. "They will follow. I suggest you get us out of here, King."

Once the oarsmen picked up their pace again, the longship settled into a tense calm. Everyone remained alert, but there was a sense of peace the farther downriver we sailed. My fingernails dug into the wood of the ship. From this vantage point I had a clear view of Mattis. He took Siv's face in his hands, whispered something only she could hear, then kissed her.

A grin played with my lips.

He kissed her until she gave in and curled her arms around his neck.

Stubborn fools.

I slid down the side of the ship. My body melted into the wood and damp. Each movement ached.

I looked to Valen. His eyes locked on mine from across the ship. I wanted him to come to me. Wanted him to look away. It didn't take long before men from the game hall swallowed him up and the Guild of Shade with questions and pitiful, bawdy jokes.

He would not come to me.

CHAPTER 24
ROGUE PRINCESS

W e returned to Ruskig before the pale dawn broke through the trees. Those we'd left behind greeted the weary and battered with nettle soups and herb rolls. Ari barked orders to find shelter for those we'd rescued from Mellanstrad.

Siv disappeared into the trees with Mattis, and I doubted I'd see much of them before midday.

Valen, surrounded by the Guild of Shade, looked at me across the great hall. His eyes cut through me like broken glass. How could he control every piece of me with a single glance? How did he keep this power over me when the entire journey back he'd said nothing?

Perhaps the greater question—why did I allow it?

I couldn't find the energy to be in his presence now. Not if he would continue to build walls between us. I'd build my own. Tears threatened to wet my eyes, but I rubbed them away and hurried back to my shanty.

Inside, I dimmed all the light but for one candle, slipped

into a thin chemise, and opened Lilianna's journal. The only way I found nearness with the Night Prince lately was through the memories of his mother.

Two pages in, the door slammed open.

I let out a strangled cry, clutching the journal to my chest, and whirled around to face the intruder.

My pulse quickened.

Valen stood in the doorway, eyes like pure midnight. His dark tunic and trousers faded against the darkness, but the candlelight warmed his bronze skin.

He stepped inside and locked the door behind him.

All at once I was aware my chemise was entirely too diaphanous. I folded my arms over my chest and turned away, saying nothing. Not even the words to ask why he'd come.

His heavy footsteps groaned over the floorboards. With a touch of caution, the Night Prince came to stand in front of me.

He cleared his throat. "I'm sorry. For your father. It is not easy to watch those you love be harmed."

I winced. "My father has little love for me, but he is the only father I have. Why are you here? Could we have not discussed this on the ship?"

Valen shifted on his feet. He stared at his fingernails. "Are you . . . are you injured at all?"

I didn't want to talk about what happened in Mellanstrad. I didn't want to pretend like we hardly knew each other. Not when we knew so much.

"I'm fine." More silence. I pretended to read the journal again. "You?"

He smirked. "They didn't touch me."

I swallowed past a dry scratch and fiddled with a wooden

cup of cold tea on my table. "Is there something I can do for you?"

"Do you wish me to leave?"

No. Stay. I wished I knew why he ran from me, only to come back again and again. I could've said it all out loud. Instead, I pretended to read again.

"What are you reading?"

I bit my lip, desperate not to grin. He kept fidgeting. Lacing his fingers, fiddling with his belt, running a hand through his hair. A prince—a king—lost in nerves was entertaining.

"The journal. The queen has just caught her rakish youngest son and one of the courtier's daughters in the stables. It's scandalous, actually."

The smile couldn't be contained when I flicked my eyes to Valen, and a flush added a layer of pink to his face.

"It's quite funny," I went on. "A mother catching her son in various states of—"

"All right." He hurried and took the journal out of my hands. "My mistake for giving this to you."

"Understandable since you did not know it was written about you at the time."

"Yes. But now that I do, you should know my mother was notorious for writing every detail of her days and had a proclivity to . . . *dramatize* the truth."

I lifted my eyebrows and played indifferent. "Night Prince, are you trying to tell me your mother wrote exaggerations?"

"No," he said, inching closer. "I would not call my mother a liar, but you are wrong about one thing."

"And what's that?"

He didn't answer right away. Valen grinned, a sly kind,

placed the journal on the table, then his arms went on either side of my chair, making a cage around me.

My breath burned in my chest.

His eyes had a magic all their own. The hot black tried to break into the wall I'd carefully built between us. A few cracks splintered my resolve to be indifferent to Valen Ferus. But the clean scent of his skin, the smirk on his mouth, the way dark waves gathered over his brow—I was at risk of crumbling at a single touch.

Weak. I was weak, and there was no other way to describe it.

"I was young," he said, "but I am no rake."

My throat tightened. He'd come so close. I could see the gold and dark green in his eyes. If I did not take care, I would be at his mercy.

"What—" I cleared my throat when my voice cracked. "What are you doing here?"

"I'm tired of distance."

"Distance you have created."

"For good reason. At least I thought so." Valen leaned his forehead to mine, voice low. "I feared for you tonight."

I licked my lips. My skin burned for him to come closer. "Makes some sense. It was frightening."

"I did not fear for anyone else."

His fingertips followed the line of my jaw, down my neck. I drew in a sharp breath.

"Valen," I whispered. "What are you doing?"

He hesitated. "Do you believe I am distant because I am indifferent to you?"

"Yes." I did not hesitate. "I think you enjoy me—or like to

enjoy me. Like at the Black Tomb."

"You make it sound as if you mean nothing and are simply a warm body to me."

I shrugged. No mistake, I'd seen the desire in his gaze, but for me, it was more than want. He was so much more, and I hated that I could not let him go. *Doomed from the beginning.* The damn icy voice raided my thoughts again. I shook my head and turned away.

Valen used his knuckle to tilt my chin. He brought his face nearer. "The curse was broken, so there must be no other reason for me to remain near you, right?"

"You feel indebted."

"Ah," was all he said.

I shook my head, afraid if I did not move, I'd suffocate from want and desire.

I rose from my chair and stepped out of his arms. "Valen, maybe at first you felt differently, but I know you do not wish to be here. I know you—"

Words pinched off. Valen had closed the space between us. His arm surrounded my waist, his hand trapped my cheek. Chests to hips collided. My body burned for him.

"You're wrong." His voice was deep and husky. His thumb brushed my bottom lip. "I wish to be anywhere you are, Elise Lysander. I have lost everyone. I watched them be used against me, watched them be tortured. But the thought of losing you is worse than any agony I've felt in the past. And I hate myself for it."

I curled my fingers around his tunic, holding him close. "Why?"

"Your name alone puts a price on your head. Add me, and the web of risk increases tenfold. How can I do it to you?"

"Who says you are the one who makes the choice alone?"

He coiled his fingers in my hair, tipping my head back. "Distance between us is the safest. It is the best choice. For you."

"Then why are you here?"

A half grin tugged at his mouth. "Because as my mother wrote—I never was one to make the best choices."

Valen crushed my lips with his.

At once my arms curled around his neck. My mouth parted. His tongue was warm and soft. I dug my fingernails into his shoulders.

We staggered together until my back hit the wall.

"You command me." He smiled against my mouth. "All of me. Irritating, since I am a prince."

I kicked his shin. "No. You are a king."

I broke the kiss, breaths heavy, heart racing. His eyes were heated with desire. One of his clever hands slid down my waist; he bunched the satin of my chemise into his grip, then glided his calluses over the smooth skin of my thigh.

A smirk teased the corner of his mouth. "*Kvinna*, if a man were to touch you like this, would you like it?"

Moments when he was Legion Grey, a man forbidden to touch me, a man who did it anyway, filtered through my mind. I closed my eyes and allowed my head to fall back against the wall. My grip on his tunic held me steady as his sly fingers burned across the flesh between my legs.

His teeth scraped over my neck; his tongue ran along the slope of my throat.

"Valen..."

"Or this?" He grinned as he drew his second hand up the curve of my waist, across my ribs.

"Yes," I said in a breathless whisper.

His touch climbed higher, grew more daring. He teased the underside of one breast, then pressed a kiss to the swell of it. Each draw of breath came heavy and deep until my head spun in delight, and I thought my legs might give out.

"I am the man who touches you. The *only* man." His lips drew close to my ear; his voice grew dark and violent. "You're mine, Elise Lysander."

Valen moved his hand from between my legs, leaving me weak and trembling, and tugged the thin fabric of my chemise off one shoulder. A hint to what the Night Prince of Etta had planned.

I arched into him and twisted his hair in my fingers. My body shuddered in desire as his hands claimed every inch of me, and his lips met mine again.

Legion Grey had once ignited a blinding passion in my soul, but to have those moments collide here, in my shanty, with a once-dead prince burned through me in an insatiable need.

Into something deeper.

Something like love.

My fingertips slipped beneath his tunic, tracing the lines of his chest. Valen moaned against my mouth, and his body tightened.

I rested my hand to his heart and pushed him back. The edge of my bed hit his knees, so he fumbled into sitting. I stood before him, fingers numb, body alive.

He was not the Night Prince, was not a vow negotiator. In

this moment, he was simply Valen, a man who'd dug into my heart and never left.

He was mine.

The night in the old schoolhouse at Ravenspire, his hands had claimed my body. He'd earned my loyalty then, but tonight was different. No secrets remained between us. No illusions.

My hands shook as I reached for the sleeves of my chemise. As girls, Runa and I would wonder about lovers and what bedding them would be like. We'd giggle and imagine sweeping, grand gestures of handsome warriors, of lust filled nights on petals and plush furs.

This was not how I imagined.

I would not change any of it.

My chemise slipped off and bunched at my feet. Valen's lips parted; his gaze roamed my naked body. He swallowed, then took my hand and guided me to him.

The Night Prince pulled me onto his lap, leveraging my hips until I straddled him. My center settled over his hard length. Valen pressed his hips against me as if he were fighting the urge to take me right there, and to take me furiously.

"Do not turn from me again, Valen Ferus," I whispered, stroking my fingers down his cheek.

"I could not even if I tried."

"They win if we do not live."

One of his hands traveled the curve of my hip. Again, his fingers slipped between my legs, sinking into my core. He flicked and pinched at my center. I rocked against his hand until I could not breathe, until my head spun in a delirious passion, and all I could do was cling to his neck like a ballast in a whirlwind.

When he pulled his fingers back, he touched them to his lips, licking the tips as if desperate to taste me. I could not hold back, not another moment.

I yanked his tunic over his head. The heat of his skin on mine sent a ripple down my arms. He groaned when my lips grazed his ear.

Valen flipped me onto my back and settled over me, legs tangled, bodies aflame. In a frenzy, he shucked off his trousers. I gasped into his mouth as he filled me in one, rough thrust.

He pulled back, as if he expected me to stop, to turn away from him.

I kissed him instead. Kissed him until his harsh breaths matched my own. I bared my throat, wishing I could be closer, but it would still not be enough. Each touch left bright sparks of heat across my skin.

Valen kissed the sweat from my brow, then kissed down my chest until he took one of my hardened peaks into his mouth.

"Gods, Valen." I dug my fingernails into the flesh of his hips, drawing out a hiss from between his teeth.

Soft gasps filled the night. We moved together, fast and greedy, then slow and tender. With each shift and position in the narrow bed, laughter passed through traded kisses.

All the need and want since we first met collided in a swell of passion and desire and something softer.

Something gentle and lasting.

Valen gripped my leg, and held it around his waist as he deepened every thrust. I let my head fall back. His name rolled off my tongue in a reverent whisper as I whimpered and shuddered while my head spun in a delightful haze.

He dropped his forehead to mine, deep, rough breaths

burned my skin. I bucked my hips, wanting him deeper, wanting him to break me. I was delirious and grounded all at once.

"You're mine, Elise," he grunted again and dragged his tongue along the pulse point in my neck.

My center was drenched in desire; blood pounded in my head, my chest, between my thighs as the sounds of our skin slapped together, until Valen gave a violent thrust and I let out a strangled cry. Any attempt to shout his name tangled on my tongue. No doubt other folk were passing by my little shack, no doubt they could hear my garbled scream.

It only made me want to scream louder.

The Night Prince quickened his pace, keeping me close and breathless, until his fingers curled around the furs of my bed, and he growled his release against my neck.

He let his body slump against me for a few breaths, then rolled to one side, pulling me against his chest.

Valen touched his fingers to the line of my lip, kissing me like it was the first and last all in one. I held his head to my chest. He drew soft lines up and down my arms.

Before sleep took me, Valen whispered in the dark, "Elise. I choose to live."

CHAPTER 25
NIGHT PRINCE

"They w-want you, brother," Sol whispered. His lips had gone blue, and his thick black lashes were crusted in frost. "You h-h-heal the land."

"Stop," I said. My voice was hardly more than a whisper. It hurt to speak, as if each word peeled layers off the back of my throat. "Don't t-talk like this."

Sol cupped a hand around the back of my head. His muscles convulsed in the cold, but he managed to draw my forehead to his. "P-P-Promise me V-V-Valen. Promise me when they f-f-free you, promise me you w-w-will take back the throne."

"Shut up." I slung my arm around his thin shoulders and held him. "Shut up, Sol."

"I am a threat to them, b-b-brother. I frighten them. I knew when they t-t-took Daj they'd kill me too. We cannot s-s-save Etta. Not like your f-f-fury. They will want to use it."

"I won't s-save it. Not for them."

"For us, Valen. For our p-people."

"Fate chose you."

Sol closed his eyes, exhausted. I understood. Staying coherent for too long was taxing. Most days we took turns in our winter cage trying to stay awake and make sure the other didn't stop breathing.

"Fate chose you," I repeated, my palm on the side of his face. Sol would be king. He would take back what was stolen. Still, something in my bones told me fate was only just beginning with her wretched plans.

The sun had chased away the dawn mist. Outside, the chatter of the people of Ruskig gave away that morning was well approaching midday.

I had yet to step outside.

From the chair at the small table, I had a perfect view of her sleeping face. Elise smiled as she slept. Her hair was messy, and I could not remember seeing anything so beautiful.

All night the honor of sleeping beside her, her body in my

arms, belonged to me. I'd hardly moved. Until a thought kept nagging in the back of my mind. Perhaps it was what triggered one of the final memories of my brother.

I needed to speak with the others, but I didn't want to leave.

My fingers traced the rim of the wooden cup in my grip; the herbs were potent. As if she sensed my stare—or perhaps it was the herbs—Elise's eyes fluttered against the morning light. She stretched her arms above her head, looking around until she oriented.

A soft grin spread over her pink lips when she saw me. "Waking to a half-naked prince—I am a lucky woman. Fully naked would be better, but I'll take what I can get."

I narrowed my eyes and went to the bed, kneeling beside it. My fingers tangled in her hair. I drew her mouth close to mine, so my lips caressed hers as I spoke. "Do not tempt me, or I will never leave."

"Then I plan to tempt you all morning." She kissed me, slow, sweet, and sincere.

I held out the cup of herbs. "I, uh, I made this for you. Not to be presumptuous, but if you want it."

She wrinkled her nose. "What is it?"

"My sister used it." I scratched my face. "So a child isn't . . ."

Elise lifted her brow and took a drink. "Wise. I don't want to imagine what Runa would do if I had a child."

My thoughts exactly. "It's not that I wouldn't . . . with you, it's—"

"Valen, please," she said, resting a hand on my arm. "You should be so lucky to father my young ones."

I sneered, snatched the cup from her hand, and pinched her

sides until she went red in the face from laughing. When I pulled back, we settled into a comfortable silence. After a moment, Elise stroked the side of my face. A delightful habit I didn't know I wanted. Her smile faded. "What troubles you?"

My shoulders sagged. I sat on the floor and leaned back against the edge of the bed. Elise's fingertips scraped over my scalp, sending a thrill dancing down the back of my neck. Her touch soothed, and I cursed myself for trying to go without it all this time.

"Valen," she whispered. "I see it in your eyes. Something is bothering you. I cannot forget last night if you are—"

"No." I turned quickly and silenced that terrible line of talk with a kiss. "There is no going back, no regrets, Elise."

"What is it?"

"I need to speak with the guild, you, and I suppose Siv since she knows who I am. No one else."

Elise propped onto one elbow. She didn't question, simply said, "When?"

"As soon as possible."

"I'll go find them. No doubt if you show your face half of Ruskig will want to strategize with you, or Ari will send you on some other dangerous adventure."

I smirked but didn't disagree. The king would not free me from the constant burn of the bindings, yet he wanted me to behave like his first knight, or royal assassin.

She tore the furs off her body and hopped out of the bed. Her pale skin stole my breath. I must've made some feral noise because she glanced over her shoulder, a flush to her cheeks. "What is it, Night Prince? Does the sight of me unsettle you?"

"Captivates is more like it, and I doubt I will be thinking of anything else but the sight of you from here on out."

She laughed and hurried to dress in a simple gown. Before she left the shanty, Elise came to me and pressed a kiss to my mouth, then went to find the Guild of Shade.

I paced the small room, fidgeting, wondering if I'd lost my mind. I made up the bed, tried to hide the evidence of what happened here. I was unashamed, but I didn't know how Elise would feel if everyone suddenly knew we were lovers.

Though, I was sure most suspected.

I even tried to brew tea, but something scorched on the bottom of the pot, and I gave up.

Not long after, the door opened, and Junie led the way inside. Siv followed, then the rest of the guild. Elise locked us in and invited everyone to find a place to sit. Casper and Stieg looked half asleep. Halvar searched for ale which he insisted Elise was hiding. Siv and Junie sat on the bed, and Tor stared out the window.

He'd know if I was losing my head or not.

"Ari is looking for you," Elise said, pressing a hand to my heart as she retrieved the ewer she kept in a chest. Halvar sang her praises when she poured him a horn.

"He can wait," I said.

"Well, you better get to it, then," Junie said. "I think he's rather jumpy since last night and will likely come breaking down doors."

I crossed my arms over my chest, staring at the floor. The thoughts were hard to gather because I didn't know where to begin.

"Something has troubled me since Elise's sister took her father's eye." Tor closed his eyes. His jaw pulsed. I wasn't insane. He thought things, too. "You all saw the darkness that spread, right?"

"No, but it's all Frey and Ari can talk about," Casper said. He shuddered. "Gives me the bleeding chills. What sort of fury does that?"

I pinched my lips, daring to look at Tor. He was pale, and dark circles puffed under his eyes. No doubt, he had little sleep last night.

"Valen?" Elise said when I remained silent too long.

"I've only seen that kind of dark fury—blight is what we called it—in one person." I paused. How would I explain this? It was a secret, only those closest to the Ferus line knew. I hated keeping it, like it was a shameful thing. It wasn't. Simply different. I lifted my eyes, finding Elise. She was the calm in a storm. "My brother."

Elise's mouth opened. "He did have fury then."

I nodded. "He did, but no one spoke of it."

"Ridiculous," Tor grumbled. "As if Sol would ever bring harm to anyone."

I gave Tor a look to keep calm. "Sol was to be king. Through counsel from their seers, our parents thought it best to keep Sol's fury secret. Probably why my mother never truly mentions it in her journals. He was the Sun Prince, the hope of Etta. And his fury brought death, disease, and darkness."

"Only Prince Valen could counter it," Halvar said grimly.

"Wait," Elise said. "The diseased Agitators—on my land. Do you think—"

"Hells," Halvar said. "I'd nearly forgotten, but . . . yes. Valen, I think you took it from them. You were changed through the curse then, but I think somehow you stopped it."

"I don't heal bodies," I said.

"You don't remember, but you drew the blight back and it . . . it didn't heal them, it killed them. It must've been manipulated somehow, but your fury still drew it back."

Elise rested a hand on my arm. "How do you counter such a thing with earth fury?"

"Sol and I were opposites." I shook my head, a burn in my chest. Gods, I missed my brother. "I could bring the world to bloom; he could destroy it. What concerns me, now more than ever after hearing of the Agitators, is that Ravenspire has somehow manipulated blight and has the power to use it against us."

"Sol," Tor said, his voice soft and raw. "They manipulated Sol, and this is his legacy. What is left of his magic is used for evil."

"'We don't know that, brother," Halvar said, clapping Tor on the shoulder.

"We don't," I agreed.

"Do you think—" Stieg hesitated. "Do you think they have a dark fae with the same talent?"

"It's possible, I suppose. But last night was still different. I've never seen it bottled in such a way. I have no power over the body, at least not with Sol's magic. Sol brought disease to the earth, so I could counteract it. But if Ravenspire knows how to kill by fury poisons—we are at greater risk than I thought."

"We need to find the fae they are using," Stieg said.

"And slit his throat," added Casper.

"Or the poisoner," Elise suggested. "Who knows if they have found a way to manufacture this *blight* through their experiments."

"I tell you this to be on guard," I said. "We need to prepare healing potions. Moonvane is powerful and may be our only chance against blight in the body. Everyone should have a supply."

Elise came to my side. "We need to tell Ari."

"Do so, but don't mention Sol," Tor said. "His name will not be muddied by stupid folk who fear fury they don't understand."

Elise left me and went to Tor. He was not one to accept pity, but he gave her a small smile when she clasped his hand and squeezed.

"I think we need to get our fearless king to stop fearing your fury," Halvar said. "We need to get these bindings off."

"You could tell him the truth," Casper said.

I shook my head. "Nothing has changed. I do not want the crown. Ari can lead."

"But Etta did not choose him," Halvar said.

"In time she will," I insisted. "Besides, right now we need the people focused on surviving. Ravenspire will come again, and we need to be ready. Not lost in a battle of who wears the weak crown of an uprising."

The looks on their faces made it clear not one person in the room agreed, but for once no one argued. I had seen what became of people who didn't want to give up power. Ari was not cruel and ambitious, but he was creating a thorn in the side of Castle Ravenspire. I would overturn all the efforts made by stepping forward.

But the fool could take off the bleeding bindings.

If this blight was a remnant of my brother's magic, I might be the only one who could destroy it.

If it was something else, then I prayed to the gods we'd find a way to survive it.

CHAPTER 26
ROGUE PRINCESS

I flipped through the early pages of Lilianna's journal. Most of my reading was in the middle and final pages—after Valen had been born. But I scanned the early passages looking for anything. The queen was clever, though. Carefully wording each passage, but after learning the truth about the Sun Prince, I found a few clues.

> . . . *my heart breaks for the Sun Prince. Such a lonely child. Still, this is for the best. His instruction should be within the walls of the castle until he has matured enough to attend classes at the gentry school . . .*

> . . . *Herja's fever subsided. Sol is once more*

*consolable, no matter how many times we have
explained the troublesome frosts were the cause . . .*

I TUCKED the journal in my satchel with a sigh.

How I wished Lilianna were here. I had so many questions, and not only about her children. Valen's mother was Timoran. She learned how to balance being of both worlds. Her children and husband belonged to magic and Etta, but her people were of the wastelands, of war. My heart lived here, among Night Folk, fury, and Valen. Yet, I still embraced the thrill of war like my ancestors. I loved my people too.

Today the sun was warm, but tensions were high. The time for the royal vows was days away.

From morning until twilight folk in Ruskig worked to prepare. Boisterous costumes were created for those who would be playing the part as traveling bards and court entertainers. Pointed caps with gold threads, curled slippers with bells on the ends, doublets with brass buttons, stockings in black and white stripes.

It took some doing gathering supplies. By gathering I meant stealing. Ari seemed content to move Valen from his role as Blood Wraith, known killer, to his own personal thief.

I didn't hold much guilt, and I'm not sure the Guild of Shade could be called thieves exactly. It was a strange sort of thieving. In most cases, some, or all of Valen's guild would wait by the fjord for traveling longships, or caravans on trade routes, corner them, take what was needed, then leave them with a purse of silver shim, and a vicious threat to speak of them to no one.

I didn't like the way Ari used the Night Prince like a common scoundrel.

But when he crawled into my bed, night after night, the heir of Etta was sure to remind me this was a temporary moment. If we wanted to live—truly live—we would need to overthrow Castle Ravenspire.

My fingers tingled in anticipation. Already, Ulf and his scouting party had brought back information about sightings of the fate witch. Relief was sharp and potent knowing Calista was free of her cage and alive. The girl had risked herself for strangers. She'd known of Valen's curse, she knew he was important, and she wrote his story to freedom.

When we met again, I would not leave her behind. She would be free of that place. As much as the others wanted to slaughter whatever dark fae Calder was using to cause the blight, I believed we needed to save them as much as Calista.

Who could say what torture they endured?

Tor insisted as much as Valen, that even with dark fury, Prince Sol had been kind and loving. Odds were good this dark fae would be much the same but forced to act on behalf of enemies.

"Elise." Junius waved at me. She sat in front of a large tub next to Siv and half a dozen healers. "We're ready for more."

"On my way," I said and held up my satchel.

Junius nodded, then returned to the tub, smashing a soupy mix of petals, soils, and juices from herbs with a thick rod.

At least Ari listened to Valen about using moonvane as an antidote against any poisons. All it took was a few healers to agree to the healing properties of the blossoms, and for days folk had been filling skins and vials with the elixir.

I enjoyed gathering the blossoms. It took me out of the bustle and into the quiet trees.

Hedges of moonvane grew thick and lush near the creek. I kneeled beside one selecting the silkiest of the silver flowers.

A grunt at my back lifted the hair on my neck. I snatched the dagger from my pack, and crept through the shallow creek, careful not to step on branches or dead leaves, then peered over a row of hedges.

Nerves faded at once, and a rush of warmth swelled in my chest.

A row of children sat in a line, giggling, fidgeting, and clapping for their playmates who sparred in a circle of twigs.

They did not spar with just anyone.

"Block, here," Valen said, adjusting the wooden practice sword in front of Ellis's narrow chest. "Now, tell me, what areas do you guard at all times?"

"Head, heart, and manhood!" Ellis shouted.

Valen shot a glare at Halvar who barked a laugh. With a sigh, Valen placed the practice sword over the boy's middle. "Close, but you protect your innards. Don't listen to fools, boy."

"Fools!" Halvar said, wiping his eyes. "Would you want to take a stab there?"

At Halvar's side was a nervous looking Kari, but her eyes brightened with a shy smile. The raven had gained her strength in the last few days, and with Brant busy with the cartographers mapping out routes of the castle, she remained close to Halvar. I'd only spoken to her briefly, and she was shy and respectful. Her time in the guard had built her stronger than most women, but she had gentle features and kind eyes.

"Who's next?" Valen said, ruffling Ellis's hair as the boy returned to the line.

A girl with dirty cheeks, pointed ears, and silver eyes hopped up. "Dagger!"

Valen tipped his head and reached for a shorter practice blade. He handed it to the girl who swung the blade at once, she giggled when Valen pretended to take a hit.

"Seems the Blood Wraith is no match for Inge." Mattis—I had to look twice—yes, Mattis shouted. He smiled and laughed when the children chanted for Inge to best the Wraith. A few swings and instruction later, Valen went to his knees as Inge cut across his chest.

He fell back, dead on the ground.

At Halvar's encouragement the swarm of littles pounced on the Night Prince. Laughter rang in my head. These children had no idea who took the time to teach them to defend themselves. They didn't know he was their king, that he had fought this war longer than any of us.

My chest squeezed. Valen was finding his place among his people again. The very thought of it burned through me until I could cry.

I had never cared for anyone this way. In a way that led me to think strangely, to imagine a life beyond battle and curses. Where each night and each morning his face was mine to see. Where we could be lovers, friends, and laugh this way always.

I wanted it all—with him. I'd never loved anyone before, but the feelings I'd developed for Legion Grey awakened again for Valen Ferus.

I loved him.

I loved the Night Prince of Etta.

He is a king and what are you? I winced at the chilly voice that always carried doubt. But today, I steeled myself. True, he was the heir of this land, making him king. But that king chose *me*. The fallen *Kvinna* with no name, no land, no place. He chose me.

I took a step to join the fun but stopped at the sound of a horn.

Blood drained from my face. I whipped around toward the townships. An attack warning. How . . . how was it possible? The fury guarding Ruskig it . . . it couldn't be broken unless someone let them in.

I broke through the hedges for the children. Valen was already on his feet, true blade in hand. Kari opened her arms for the littles to follow her, face pale as she watched Halvar tug on his mask and withdraw his sword.

Valen took hold of my arm. "What is it?"

"I don't know," I said. "I was gathering and—I don't know."

His palm covered my cheek; the pleading in his eyes broke me. "Go with Kari. Hide the children."

"No." I shook my head. "I'm not leaving you—"

"Elise, I beg of you. Protect them, Kari is not strong enough on her own."

I wanted to protest, wanted to accuse him of sending me away because he feared for me. But he was collected. As he did as Legion Grey once, he removed the dagger from my satchel, and handed me the blade.

"Remember, you promised."

The moment when we stood close in my father's study,

after surviving an Agitator attack replayed in my head. *I have made a vow to defend you,* he told me, *but I must know you will also protect yourself. At all costs. Promise me.*

Nothing about that vow had changed.

I took the dagger, the pain of leaving him overwhelming.

He didn't care about anyone watching when he pulled me close and kissed me. Not long enough, and the kiss came from a place of fear. A tremble darkened his voice when he whispered against the curve of my ear, "Never doubt for whom my heart beats."

Valen released me and took another seax from Mattis before he pulled the red half mask over his chin and became the Blood Wraith.

It would be selfish to follow him. Reckless to disregard his plea out of fear of losing him. We had roles to fulfill, we knew the risks. We chose to live despite them. A chill raced up my spine when screams rang in the distance. Desperation demanded I run to the township, to my friends. Duty demanded otherwise.

Tears in my eyes, I spun on my heel. The crunch of twigs and leaves shattered the stillness of the wood as I sprinted after Kari. The raven was swift and had already disappeared into the trees.

I found them a moment later at a slope where mudslides had toppled logs all down one side. My mistake was coming up behind Kari. Before I could move, the raven deftly notched the edge of a knife high beneath my chin.

A flame simmered in her gaze. She breathed heavily and ripped the knife back. "Sorry, *Kvinna*."

"You are terrifying," I said and lifted a tiny girl over a log and tucked her next to Ellis.

"I promised myself I would never be overpowered again." Her jaw pulsed as she covered the children's heads.

"Kari, you must hide here," I told her. "You are still recovering."

"I will fight if needed, *Kvinna* Elise," she said with vigor. "I may not be trusted here, but children are children. I will not hesitate to defend them. You have my vow."

I believed her. I tried to ignore the faint cries carried on the wind. Through the haze of tears, I looked at the frightened faces under the logs. "No one is to make a sound. You shall think tiny as little, quiet mice. No matter what you see or hear, you do not move. You do not speak." I held a finger to my lips. "Understand?"

"Yes, *Kvinna*," Ellis's voice came from the left.

I touched Kari's arm. "I will go behind the trees and keep watch. If I see anything, I will signal in a whistle like a jay. Get in, I'll cover you."

Kari crouched in a spot within the log pile. If needed she could guide the children out to one side and flee. When her head was hidden well enough, I hunched behind trees a fair distance away and waited.

Smoke burned my nose. Blood pounded in my skull. The forest was still, but my soul was a frenzy of emotion. All I could think of was if those in the township had a fighting chance against whatever had come. Siv, Junius—did they have time to fight back? Would Ari's guard be enough?

Valen and the Guild of Shade knew how to fight. I forced

myself to remember the folk of Ruskig were also the Agitators of Timoran. They knew how to hold a blade.

A shadow drifted in the corner of my eyes. My senses jolted alive. I saw nothing, but something, someone was there.

Movement. The barest snap of a branch.

In a group of trees to the left, a figure hunched low, creeping with great care toward the slope where Kari was hidden.

If I moved just so, I could take them from behind.

For a silent kill, cover the mouth first. Slit the throat second. Soft points of Ravenspire armor: the joints where guarders overlapped, the underarms, the neck. With a shield, aim for the legs, the back. Lessons over the months of living outside of noble life reeled in a cycle as I stalked the figure— now, clearly an armed raven.

There had to be more. I kept my sights open for anyone else in the trees. No point in sending a single guard out here. But no one came into view. That unnerved me more than anything. The raven gained ground to where Kari was hidden. I doubted he knew children and a former raven were there, but he was clearly searching for runaways.

Twelve paces. Ten.

My legs ached from crouching. Ways to kill him darkened my mind. The first kill nearly ruined me. Now, I would kill for anyone in Ruskig. I would not think twice. Terrible as it was, I craved death for those who threatened anyone I loved. A tiny glimpse into what I imagine the curse of bloodlust would be like.

Five paces. Three.

At his back, I raised my dagger.

The raven turned on me so fast I stumbled backward. My body didn't strike the ground, no, I fell into arms. Leather guarders, gloved hands, rank herbs on the breath. A raven crushed me in his grip, and soon the trees were alive with more guards, shouting commands and laughing.

I screamed, kicked, twisted in his grip. My voice broke, but I whistled. A talent I'd had since childhood; I could make the call of jaybirds. A mix between a raven's caw and a songbird's melody.

The guard tossed me on the ground when my elbow smashed into a soft space below his arms. He kicked my ribs, then straddled me, pinning my hands over my head. Another guard roughly pushed my hair off my face.

They shared a look, then together bared smoke-yellowed teeth. The raven pinning me to the ground shouted over his shoulder, "We've got the *Kvinna*! We've got her." He glared at me. "Come on, you."

I didn't cry out a protest. What was the point of screaming *no, please*? Did anyone ever listen when a captive said those things?

No words came, but I kept my promise to Valen. I fought. I fought with every drop of warrior blood in my veins. When the ravens tried to pick me off the ground, my fingernails sliced over one's cheek. He slapped me. I kicked the other's knee from my place on the ground.

They cursed me, kicked me, struggled with me.

I found a rock and threw it at one guard's head. I fought until, at last, a guard grabbed my braid, and yanked me back. Together, the ravens rolled me onto my stomach, and kneeled on my back, holding me still.

After a struggle, they managed to tether my arms behind my back, then lift me. I still kicked, still took their strikes. A raven covered my mouth, his companion grabbed my ankles. They carried me between them like one of the fallen logs. I knew I was bested.

They would take me, but no mistake, I would die fighting.

CHAPTER 27

NIGHT PRINCE

The township was in shambles. Shanties burned, a full unit of ravens ravaged the shops, toppled carts, spilled blood.

The grass was no longer vibrant and green, but rusted in puddles of blood and flesh and bodies. Darkness roared inside me. Fury in my blood scorched under my skin, desperate to break free. I could do nothing about the bindings on my wrists, but I could have a weapon.

Before we crossed over the border of town, I grabbed Mattis by the collar, and drew his face next to mine. "My axes. Now."

Mattis didn't fall into petulance. He nodded and sprinted to the stables where he kept my weapons locked away.

"Night Prince," Halvar said at my side. "We fight for our people today."

I rolled the sword in my hand. A newly lit fire erupted in my chest. These people were mine! These were the folk my father, my family, died defending in the raids. For the first time since my memories returned, the crushing sense of duty shifted, and the honor of the burden pierced through my heart.

This land chose my line, my blood. It chose me.

Fight Valen! You fight like you've never fought before! Fight like the gods! Sol's voice empowered me.

"Legion." Mattis returned and handed me both black axes. They gleamed, polished and unused.

I gave the carpenter the sword and wasted no time. We raced into the chaos.

Fury boiled in the ground. Roots, vines, and earth tangled around the ravens. Night Folk fought as they knew, but it wasn't enough. The guards were too many. Soon the fae realized the more they paused to use fury, the more they died by the swift cut of a sword.

I came behind a guard and buried one axe in his spine. The woman he'd been after scrambled back to her feet. She sneered a little wickedly, took up the raven's sword and thrust it into a nearby guard.

It didn't take long before calls of notice were drawn to the Guild of Shade. Across the town square, Junius fought beside Stieg and Casper. Near the royal longhouse, Tor, masked and ruthless, fought with Ari and Frey.

My axes were a calm to me. Each blade tempered, while also taunting the dark lust for death I kept inside. With them I had control. I could kill and pull back with a clearer head. Maybe I created their power all in my mind, but did it matter? I was nimble and deadly with my axes restored.

Three guards rushed me. I cut deep into one thigh. As he fell, I opened another guard's chest. I spun around and drew an axe blade on the back of the first raven's throat. Two dead before the third skidded to a stop.

I gave him time to let out a breath, then I threw both axes, burying them deep in his middle.

By the time he hit the ground, I'd ripped out the blades and moved on to the next.

Two ravens rushed me. All my training with the knights of the courts served me well as the Blood Wraith, even if I hadn't known who had taught me. Quick steps kept me out of reach. A guard swung his broadsword. I stepped backward, a whip of wind from the swing on my face. He reeled back, expecting me to parry, no doubt. I didn't move. My intent was to gauge his skill. He didn't impress, and his companion guard impressed me even less.

"Fane!" the raven who'd tried to take me down shouted, out of breath and bleeding from his lip. "Are you going to just stand there?"

The words snapped his companion into action. He lunged with a short blade, aiming at my heart.

Make them stumble, My Prince.

I grinned at the memory of Dagar. Halvar's father taught me many steps. Precise, strategic, maneuvers with my body to upend an opponent's footwork. The blade came from the front. I bowed my middle backward to avoid the strike.

He tried a downward blow. I ducked. When he staggered forward, I swung one axe up, slicing through his cheek. With a kick to his back, I shoved him aside. Let him bleed. Beneath my mask, a grin twisted over my mouth when the first raven picked up where the other left off.

This raven had surer marks. It took more thought. Bend, jab, parry, cut. Steel rang on steel as his sword met my axes.

Make them stumble. Even after centuries, Ravenspire had not taught their warriors to guard their feet. The guard made a strong strike. At the last moment, I dodged, then kicked out the back of his knees.

The raven stumbled. His shoulders heaved as he straightened off the ground. "Kill me with a warrior's honor, Wraith. It is all I ask."

I kicked his sword away. "Thieves of this land do not deserve the great hall of the gods."

He did not have his blade, but I granted him a swift death. My mask was soaked with blood. The fight raged. I raced toward the royal longhouse, striking and dodging blows as I ran to aid Ari and Tor.

Then, the low rumble of a horn carried over the battle. Almost at once, the Ravenspire guards pulled back. They rushed for the boundary, leaving a stun over Ruskig. It took a few breaths before the folk cheered. They bellowed our victory.

My grip tightened on my axes. Something was off. Ravenspire didn't pull back for no reason.

A scream, all too familiar, rang over the horn. Followed by a shrill cry that shot a hole through my chest.

All gods, no.

At the gates, a huddle of ravens carried a thrashing Elise between them. She screamed and kicked. She snapped her teeth when one tried to cover her mouth.

"Elise!" I roared and darted for her.

"Legion!" By the hells, she fought, but when her eyes found me, they were bright with fear she tried to hide.

A few remaining guards stood in my way. I swung my axes, not killing most, more shoving them aside. The more I tried to reach her, the more bleeding bodies seemed to stand in my path.

"Elise!" Desperation pulsed through me, heavy as iron. They were taking her. They'd come for her, and I'd left her out there *alone*.

A raven pounced in front of me. He was dead at my next step, his blood on my face.

The guards had her halfway through the gates. I was at least a hundred paces from her. I wouldn't make it. My body weakened, as if the whole world pressed down on my back. "Elise! You fight! I will come for you! I'll come!"

She was gone. The moment the invaders fled through the gates, the fury wall of stone, thorns, and briars repaired itself.

I fell to my knees. Breath wouldn't come. Soil broke between my fingers as I dug into the earth.

"Fight," I said, haggard and broken. "Please fight."

Time didn't matter, so I had no idea how long I remained there before Tor's grip pulled me upright. My body trembled in unmanaged rage when I looked at my friend. "I won't let them take anyone else."

"You will not feel the pain of losing your *hjärta*."

I didn't dispute it. I could not. Elise Lysander stole my heart when it was still cursed. I never took it back. I slammed both axes into the earth. Rage ripped through me like a second being lived inside of me.

"Ari!" I bellowed. Elise was gone, and not another moment would pass that did not involve me getting her back. The king was near his longhouse. Blood speckled his face, his body weary as he helped the wounded. "Ari!"

He faced me. The smugness he'd always had was gone. Now he was a beaten and broken man.

I didn't care and held up my wrists in his face. "Release me! Do it now or I slit your throat."

He scoffed, but there was no humor in it. "Legion, *I* cannot release you. I do not hold the key. Perhaps that is a good thing for now. You cannot run after her without a plan. Be logical."

He turned away, but I gripped his tunic and forced him to face me. "You said you had the key. Find a way to release me, you bastard."

A shadow passed over his features. "We are not straying from the plan, Legion Grey! We will go to Ravenspire, we will fight back, we will take their fury. We will do all we can to retrieve Elise. I assure you."

"I don't want your bleeding assurances. Give me my fury, and I will handle the rest."

"Brother." Halvar shoved his way through a few bystanders. He pressed a firm hand over my racing heart. He rarely addressed me like the knights once did, but I needed it now. I looked at him, fists clenched. He didn't blink. "You know we have one chance. If we rush, she'll die for certain."

"You think they won't kill her if we move slowly?"

"They want her, remember? You saw it in her sister's face in Mellanstrad. I could sense it. They want Elise alive. For now."

I turned away, dragging my fingers through my hair.

"Legion," Ari said. "Help us tend to our dead, then we will make our retaliation."

He didn't command me, truth be told, Ari hardly sounded

like the king he was playing. I looked at him, shoved my finger in his face. "You will follow my order. I will lead us there. I will be the one to stand against the false king."

I would knock him off *my* throne.

Part of me wondered if Ari sensed something had shifted in me. He didn't argue. He dipped his chin. "I could not protect my people. If you can lead us there, if you can fight more than I can, then you lead. I want no more death."

"You will rid me of these bindings."

"If I do, if I retrieve the key," he said, "will you tell me who you are, really? Someone betrayed us today. I need to know who I can trust."

I leaned in close, so our heads nearly touched. "Release me, and I will be known soon enough."

Ari nodded. "Legion, do not make the mistake that you are the only one who cares. Elise matters, but there are bigger things than any of us in this battle."

He was right. This fight was greater than any one life. I knew it. Even Elise knew it. But only one life mattered more than the rest to me.

"We all care," Frey added.

Doubtless an attempt to be soothing, instead it fueled my anger. I shouted my rage at the sky. For a moment the bindings on my wrist squeezed. They glowed. Hells, my fury nearly burst through them. Ari and Frey wore matching expressions of stun and intrigue.

"You might care with the best intentions, but I *love* her," I shouted at them, finishing the rest over my shoulder as I walked away. "Go to Ravenspire for your reasons. I go for Elise Lysander."

No one followed me. No one tried to soothe me again.

I stormed back to her shanty, locked the door. My back scraped over the wood as I slid to the ground.

To the eaves I made a silent vow. By the end of tomorrow, I would find Elise. I could not stand any longer than that.

By the end of tomorrow, I would be king.

THE PYRE ROSE high over shattered rooftops. We stood in a somber line as the dead burned to ash.

Children cried for lost mothers and fathers. Mothers and fathers cried for their littles. Ellis stood next to Halvar. His chin trembled as he watched the flames. Arabella had been found behind their shanty, likely one of the first to fall. Kari had her hands on the boy's shoulders.

I went to him and lowered to my haunches.

He stared at me with glassy eyes. "*Herr* Grey," he said, bravely. His voice shuddered.

From my boot I took out a narrow switchblade. The hilt was made of bone and had an arrow carved into the steel. "This knife has served me well. You fought well today. You protected the other children. Kari told me how, at Elise's call, you helped with the small ones. Your mother would be proud."

He blinked and a tear dropped on his cheek. I handed him the knife and began to stand.

"*Herr* Grey," he said softly. I returned to my crouch. "*Kvinna* Elise, she believed you were stronger than the false king. I heard her talking to Maj about trusting you, about believing in you. I trust you too."

I choked on my words. All I could manage was, "You take care of that knife. It brings new responsibility."

Later, the Guild of Shade packed the inside of Elise's shanty. Being there allowed me to feel close to her. It took half the night to tend to the dead and ensure the borders were completely secure. Ulf was due to return with his scouting party so we could make alternate plans on how to return to Ravenspire during the vows. Tomorrow was the highest moon, and it would be the last the false king would sit upon the throne.

A knock cut into my mad steps.

Junius hurried to the door, then stepped aside as Ari entered with Mattis and Siv.

Ari looked around the room. "I want a vow that you will not kill me when you have your fury restored. Try to understand why we blocked it to begin with."

Tor glowered, but Casper let out a loud chuckle. "Ah, we like you, Kingling. We won't kill you. But remember—we could."

Siv came around and handed each of us wooden bowls. She had tear tracks on her cheeks when she met my eye. With a slight bow of her head, she handed me the bowl then shuttered the windows.

"Remind me again why we must be so secretive," Ari said. "Don't mistake me, I'm wholly intrigued, but also unsettled."

"You have a traitor among you," Halvar said. "It will be to our benefit if you are the only one who knows our fury is restored. Trust me, you'll understand soon enough."

"But what about Mattis, here?"

I looked at the carpenter. "We trust him."

He ruffled at the praise and took Siv's hand.

"Good," Ari said. "Because he has the key to the bindings."

"What?" Now I glared at Mattis.

He stepped forward sheepishly. "I was the angriest, so King Ari thought I would be the one who surely would never give in and unbind you."

Mattis went to Casper first, a silver rune piece in his hand.

"Grab your bowls," Ari said. "It is rather unpleasant having bindings removed and most people turn their guts inside out."

"We've all endured bindings before," I muttered, but did ready the bowl.

Casper and Stieg drew in sharp breaths and doubled over when Mattis removed their fetters. Stieg was the one to vomit first, but Casper was the loudest. Junie backed to the door with a look of disgust.

Tor and Halvar resisted the longest, but even they succumbed, clinging to their bowls. Mattis hesitated when he came to me.

"I trust you too," he told me. "I will stand with you. Whatever fury you have."

The way he spoke, I got the feeling he believed me to be a dark fae. Easy to suspect, I supposed, since I knew about the blight.

He ran the rune over the bindings. They clattered on the floor. Hot, white pain throbbed in my blood. Bile burned my throat. I groaned and leaned over my knees, breathing through my nose. I didn't vomit as much as the others, but even kings struggled with bindings.

After a moment the rush eased, and I straightened. Tor

grinned as he opened his palm, and a bright blue flame snaked around his fingers.

Ari let out a long breath. "Powerful fae. All of you. I've either made a wise choice or a deadly mistake."

My body felt whole. My head clearer. I went to Siv first thing, wishing I could've done this with Elise. "I release you from your fury lock."

She closed her eyes, her shoulders relaxed.

"Ah, that answers a few questions," Ari said. "I assume, dear Elise was also tongue tied, then. Now I am even more curious, Legion Grey. Her little warnings about my games and threats. What kind of dangerous man are you? What is it you do? You assured me you would be known once fury was restored."

I held Ari's stare for a long moment. He had proven he could be trusted, but how would he react when he learned his rule as king was at an end? He'd given me leadership even without knowing. I had to trust he was loyal to Etta, no matter who ruled.

I went to the center of the room. "Stand back."

The others pressed against the walls when I kneeled. Fury strengthened as my mind imagined what I wanted. I pressed my palm to the floor, careful to control the bend so the rest of the township wouldn't take notice.

The shanty rattled. Ari and Mattis were the only ones who looked uneasy. Mattis even cursed when wood splintered and cracked.

Elise would need to forgive me for destroying her hovel. It was hardly an effort, but soon enough the wood split, and a deep fissure opened the soil and stone of the ground beneath the house.

I opened my eyes and stood, brushing the dust from my palms.

Ari and Mattis gawked at the crack in the ground. Then gaped at me.

"You're . . . you're a Bender," Ari whispered.

"I am."

"This is fun," Halvar murmured to Tor.

"But the only one in a thousand turns was . . ." Mattis tried, but he faded. He stared at Siv. She simply took his hand.

Ari lifted his gaze to me again. "What is your name? Your true name."

No secrets. It was time. For Elise, for Etta, it was time.

"I have several," I said evenly. "But most know me as Valen Ferus, the Night Prince."

CHAPTER 28
ROGUE PRINCESS

Dungeons at the fury quarries were how I imagined most would be. But at Castle Ravenspire the cells were mostly devoid of prisoners. Lonely, damp, and filthy. In one corner of my cell a constant stream of water left a trail of black moss on the stone and perfumed the air in a moldy stink. The locks on the doors were large with visible levers. I'd spent the better half of the hour trying to snap it out of place. All I'd gained was a crick in my neck and a sliced fingertip.

When the pin from my braid slipped again, the cold iron opened a second finger. "All hells," I cursed loudly.

Another exasperated sigh came from somewhere down the line of cells. "You're not smart. If you could pick these locks, don't you think I'd be outta here forever ago? They're impossible."

I knew that voice. "Calista?" She giggled. My heart back-flipped. "All gods, Calista. I've imagined you locked at the Black Tomb still."

"Nope. Not that it's much better being locked away in the smelly innards of the castle."

"I went there," I said softly. "I returned to the Black Tomb, and . . . I thought I might've left you behind again."

She hesitated. The girl was young, but I had few doubts had lived a dark life. Still, I noticed when she tried to hide emotion in her voice, and she was trying desperately to remain casual and detached.

"Don't see how it's your problem to come after me anyway," she said.

"You helped us. The Night Prince."

"I wrote a story to help me. If he got free—which is another reason it's annoying to see you here—then so be it. Why'd you go and get snatched and ruin all my masterful work?"

I fought the urge to laugh. Calista was a strange girl, but even knowing she'd cursed my own father, she'd twisted fate so I would be tossed into this fight, I liked her a great deal. "When did they bring you here?"

"Right after the last time."

"Do they know what happened at the tomb?"

"They're too stupid. But they made me finally fess up about what I can do." Pain was in her voice. I closed my eyes. Doubtless what she meant was they hurt her until she broke. Calista sighed loudly. "They think I did something and messed with the magic at the Tomb, so they had me curse it again, then tossed me in here. Not before I scared them so they were pissing themselves, though."

She snickered and reminded me of Ellis. Sly, mischievous, a child trying to survive a harsh world.

"So, you did curse it for me."

"Yes, and you're bleeding welcome." She shifted; the scrape of feet echoed down the cell block. "Your folk wanted to maim you, but I made those shadow guardians thick and slow. I couldn't exactly write, *don't touch her*. No, I had to be careful with my wording, but I've been learning new words. I tossed in a few things like 'apathetic to their strength' and 'clutched their leaden' –it means heavy – 'blades'. Made them slow, but also made them sound fierce to these sods."

I grinned. All gods, this girl would be a force to be reckoned with someday. "But why did they want to curse me?"

"To trap you, I guess."

"Not kill me?"

"Well, not after I convinced them otherwise."

"What did you do?"

She hesitated, then let out a frustrated sigh. "I might've copied an idea from an old storyteller's work. I know, I know. Unoriginal and lazy, you don't need to tell me. But, I mean, it was a *good* idea."

"Calista, what did you do?" A laugh was in my voice. If I had to be locked in a smelly pit, torn from friends and Valen, I held a bit of gladness it was with her. She seemed hardly aware of her dire situation and held her chin high. Perhaps it was her way of surviving, but there was almost a childlike innocence about her still in there.

"I told that new queen sister of yours that if the lost royal of her blood were killed, the land would weep. It would deaden its heart and return to the wastes that once were. I changed the wording a bit because I'm not *that* lazy, but it was the same idea as the storyteller who cursed the prince. You know she did that to stop the killing, right? All those old royals, I've learned, they kept killing them, so she saved them by lying about what would happen if they died. I did the same. Your mean hearted sister needs you alive. At least she thinks she does."

"I'll live?" It was more a question of disbelief than a statement.

Calista snorted. "I guess. From what it sounds like, she doesn't want you to live *comfortably*."

Chills raced down my arms. I pressed my forehead to the bars of my cell, hoping to get a look at the girl. All I could make out were her arms poking from her bars, and I discovered we were not alone down here. In a cell across the block, and to the left of Calista's a broad bundle crouched in the corner, wrapped head to foot in a dirty, woolen blanket.

I didn't bother with the third prisoner. They had not moved, had not said a word. "We need to get out of here. Can you write another story?"

"No," Calista pouted. "They took my scrolls and runes."

I closed my eyes. Think. "There is water coming in. We might be able to find holes and send a signal, or perhaps when they come to take waste buckets we could—"

"Overpower them? Come on, Kind Heart, they aren't fools. They come prepared."

"We can't do nothing. There is an uprising not far from here. *He* is there." Curse the fury lock. I could not say Valen's name, but it might be a good thing if Runa planned to torture me.

Calista snickered again. "Sheesh, I wish I could've seen his face when he figured it all out. Is he a snob now? Or is he bossy? Maybe he's a quiet prince."

"He's . . ." My throat tightened with thoughts of Valen. As

they'd taken me away, his desperate cries were all I heard. "He does not want to take the throne. But he is none of those things. He is strong, yet unsure. He is brutal, yet gentle."

"Huh," she said. "Sounds like he's got no idea who he is and needs to just pick one way or the other."

I laughed now. It scraped at my parched throat. "Yes, maybe he should."

"It comes," a throaty, raspy voice came from the third cell.

The prisoner didn't move, didn't pull back the blanket. For a moment I wasn't sure they'd even spoken until Calista giggled.

"Oh, that's Lumpy, at least I call him Lumpy because he looks like a lump just sitting there all the time." She giggled again. "He's always saying things like that."

"Who, who is he?" I asked, certain the covered prisoner wouldn't tell me.

"Don't know. They come for him a lot, but he never tells me what they do. He doesn't fight, though. He listens to them good, but he's really, really old, so I guess it happens when you're stuck here too long."

"They never use a name when they come?"

"Oh, yeah. Mean ones. Like they call me witch, but they call him all kinds of names. I usually tell them to shut up, but I think it makes them laugh more."

"You're kind to him," I said. "It is you who is the kind heart, Calista."

"Am not," she insisted. "I'm ominous and I survive. But Lumpy doesn't hurt anyone, and he teaches me words sometimes, so I don't like when they call him names."

My brows lifted. I looked to the unmoving prisoner again. "He's been helping you with your stories?"

Was this prisoner an ally?

"Nah, only when I get stuck on a word. He knows words better than me, isn't that right, Lump?"

The prisoner simply tightened the blanket around their shoulders.

A door clanged down the cell block. We fell silent at heavy footsteps. I steeled myself for what was to come. If this is when I faced whatever torture Runa had in mind, I would do it without a curve in my spine. I would look her in the eyes and never bend. Not to her.

Even still, when three ravens stopped in front of my cell, my stomach twisted in fear. They grinned viciously as they unlocked my cell.

"Come on, now," said a guard. He snatched my arm, pinching my skin. "The queen has asked for her sister."

"Last we met she told me she had no sister," I said dryly, wincing as the guard tightened his grip.

"I'd learn to shut up if you have any brains, girl."

"I don't, so I plan to talk until you spin into madness."

Calista snickered until the guard slapped a rod against her cell bars.

They didn't speak to me again. I was dragged out of the chilled dungeons and led through the halls of the castle. Memories of running through these with innocence played out in my head. When I still enjoyed Calder as a cousin, when Runa and I snuggled in each other's beds at night and giggled to sleep.

I lifted my chin as the guards led me into the throne room.

Do not bow. Do not cower. This is not the king. The true king lies by your side at night.

On a raised dais, seated in high-backed chairs, Runa and Calder watched my pitiful procession. Calder had dark gold scruff on his chin. Rings on his fingers. The fur mantles were soft and white. His face was trim and sharp and cold.

Runa favored gold, down to her dress. Around her eyes gold powder brightened the blue, and her hair was adorned in dainty gold chains.

I tried not to look, but was utterly aware, at her side, my mother and father stood stalwart. My father's right eye was covered in a frightful patch. My mother was joints and bones wrapped in thin skin. She looked pale and worried, not the proud Mara Lysander she had always been.

The ravens forced me to my knees, then stepped away.

"Cousin," Calder said after a long pause. "Good to see you. It has been so long."

"I wish I could say it had been long enough."

A raven made a move to strike me, but Calder held up a hand. He grinned viciously. "Elise, your sharp tongue is always entertaining."

"I'd like to return to my cell," I said. "It is more pleasant than here."

Calder rose, jaw tight, but a cruel gleam in his eyes. He descended the stairs and stood before me. "My cousin, my soon-to-be sister, will not whither in a cell. Not when there is so much to celebrate. Vows are always enjoyable."

The vows. My insides twisted. Ari and the others in Ruskig were expecting the vows at the high moon. That was still two days off. I avoided Calder's gaze. I kept quiet.

"Runa would be heartbroken if her sister were not there with her," Calder went on. "And I live to please my queen."

Doubtless by sneaking away with a dozen different consorts.

"So, I devised a way to make the vows even more . . . perfect." Calder sneered at me as a raven opened a side door. Jarl stepped into the throne room. My stomach heated in sick. I turned away, refusing to look at his horrid face. Calder rested a hand on Jarl's shoulder. "Elise, I promised to care for your family, and I plan to keep that promise. A strong match for you will ease my bride's troubled heart over her wayward sister. It will bring you back to us." Calder chuckled darkly, then lowered so his eyes were level with mine. "Isn't it a brilliant idea, cousin?"

I clenched my fists, rising to his bait. "What idea?"

"Two vows at once."

No. The sick abandoned my stomach and burned my throat. No, he couldn't mean—

"I have given you to Jarl. A wife to tame is a welcome challenge for an esteemed warrior. And if I remember right, you once were fond of each other. Perhaps in time, he will make you fond of him again."

Runa wore a cruel smile. Calista was right—she would let me live, but in a life of pain and suffering.

"I will never take vows with Jarl," I said. "I thought the last time he attempted this he had learned his lesson. I do not keep weak company."

The mood shifted. Jarl narrowed his eyes, and his hand went to his side. I hoped because he remembered the bolt of Halvar's bow piercing his body.

"Yes," Calder said airily. "What a fascinating tale my queen retold after Mellanstrad. The Blood Wraith is your ally. But then, he is not just the Blood Wraith, is he?"

"He will come," I warned. "He'll slaughter you."

Calder returned to his throne. "Oh, I plan on him coming. I plan on his entire guild to show. We'll be ready. You see, Elise, I did not become king in the way I did—"

"Through murder."

Calder's eyes darkened. "I did not earn the throne because I am weak. You underestimate me, cousin. I have eyes all around, even in your pitiful refuge."

Movement at my side, drew me to look. A scorch of betrayal warped into murderous anger. I trembled with hate. "Ulf."

Ari's guard met my eye. He was hardened and looked more Timoran than Ettan. "Elise," he said with a nod.

I chuckled, a little mad, a little muddled by rage. "I hope he finds you first, traitor."

"Oh, your little fae king and the Blood Wraith have no idea," Calder says. "After seeing our forces at Mellanstrad this Ettan grew some brains and knew which side would win in the end. Your friends will be sure to know what we plan to do with you. If Jarl and your sister are correct, Legion Grey will come for you. No doubt they all will come to attack our vows. And when their trusted scout leads them in, we will be waiting."

"You're a fool. Do you really think you will best the Blood Wraith? He has evaded you and your father for turns."

"Yes, but that was before he had something to lose."

I bit down on my tongue. Calder would dangle me in front of Valen, and I had no idea how it would unfold. What the Night Prince feared was losing more people close to his heart.

He'd avoided me, ignored me, all to prevent this moment. Would he be clear-headed? Would he be a frenzy of rage and get himself killed?

Calder flicked his fingers and Ulf left the throne room. He left to lie, and lie, and lie to those in Ruskig. I imagined his death a hundred different ways.

"I see you are worried, sister," Runa says. "Perhaps you can hide it from others, but you are unsettled. There is a way you can ensure Legion Grey is not harmed. Take vows with Jarl without protest, and the Blood Wraith will not be killed."

I closed my eyes. He would live, but in a cell. They would never let him go free. He'd be bound for the rest of his days. But if Calder had more cunning than I thought, could I watch him die?

"We've given Elise much to think about," Calder said and held out a hand for Runa. She rose in a rustle of fabric. "Go. There isn't much time to prepare. Your mother will assist you and the queen for the vow ceremonies."

I was lifted to my feet, a raven holding my arm. My sister led us from the throne room; my mother walked at my back.

Each step brought the weight of the risk and pushed me lower until I forced myself to slip into numbness.

"How can you stand by this, Maj?" I asked bitterly. I didn't look at her.

She sighed. "Elise, you have no idea what you speak of."

"You are a coward."

Silence deafened the space between us until she whispered, "If doing what I can to save my child is cowardly, then so be it."

I lifted my chin. My mother had faults, but she was compliant now on my behalf. I disagreed and would prefer we fought for our lives or died trying. Her silence would sentence me to a fate worse than death. Even a night as Jarl Magnus's wife would be worse than the hells. Either I would not survive, or by morning I would wish I were dead.

I never told Valen I loved him. I should've told him, should've held him a little longer. All I could do was pray that if I died, he did not lose himself. I prayed to silent gods that he would find his place, he would heal Etta. He'd find love again.

A tear fell for the Night Prince. For what might've been.

CHAPTER 29
NIGHT PRINCE

"Ari wants to see you," Tor said, tapping the tip of his blade back and forth on the table. "Finally."

I scoffed and finished buckling the weapon belt around my waist.

After I gave my name, Ari laughed, like I'd told a joke. When no one else even smiled, slowly, the color drained from his face. He studied me for a long pause, then left faster than he'd come.

I hadn't seen him in hours. Mattis took the news differently. He'd been mostly quiet but had asked to know everything. From my time as Legion Grey, why I needed Elise Lysander, the curse, to why I had not claimed the throne. He'd not left us since he heard the tale.

I added my axes to my belt, then looked at the room. The Guild of Shade was there, along with Mattis and Siv. "Prepare to leave when I return."

The air outside was still heavy with death and blood. Most folk remained in their shanties, afraid to face a dawn after the attack. I did not blame them, but they would need to find a way to stand in this fight. Doubtless more death would come before it was over.

The royal longhouse was empty in the hall, but in the back chamber boots scuffed over the wood floorboards.

I tossed aside the hanging fur over the doorway. Ari stopped pacing, his hand on his chin. He met my gaze with a bit of awe and a heap of trepidation. "You came."

"You asked for me."

"I—" He shook out his hands. "I did not command it, I merely asked if you would be willing and—"

"Ari," I interrupted. "What did you need? Have you heard anything?"

"Uh, well, I expect Ulf to return with his report soon. But there is . . . there is more I wanted to speak about if, if you would allow—"

"All gods," I said, "say what you must say. I am as accustomed to ruling as you are to humility. Do not snivel, I beg of you, and be the leader you have been."

"Forgive me," he said with touch of annoyance, "but I am still grappling with the fact that the dead prince I have served, and believed in until months ago, is actually alive and has been all this time. I am still accepting that I have been dreadfully wrong, that I did not bring life to this land. Mere coincidence led me here. Not to mention, I am replaying every demand, every harsh word I've spoken, and hoping you will not take my head."

If Elise were not in mortal danger and my desperation to leave was not so potent, I might take the time to laugh. He was nothing more than a body of nerves and it was amusing.

"I have no plans to take your head."

"Well, that is one good thing, I suppose." Ari crossed the room and unfurled a hand drawn map on a piece of vellum. "Before the attack, Ulf delivered these from a contact of his in Lower Mellanstrad. He told me there are passages at the back of Ravenspire. They would be the simplest way inside, but I figured, well, since you once *lived* there—what do you think?"

I took the vellum. "They have changed parts of the castle, you know."

Ari shrugged. "Still, you might know better than a sketch."

I studied the drawing in silence, trying to read it through my own memories of Ravenspire. Not long ago I'd fled through those halls, but we hadn't gone deep in the back, or in the lower levels at the coup. What did I remember about it as my home, though? I'd never stopped long to try to recall days when Ravenspire was Ferus land.

It didn't help my process to have the burn of Ari's stare breaking into my skull.

"What is it, Ari?" I asked without looking up.

He shifted on his feet and came to my side. "Elise knew."

Muscles in my jaw ticked. "She knew. I did not lie when I said Elise saved me. She sacrificed everything to keep me breathing, and she . . . kept me from choosing hatred."

"I was born the turn the Timorans raided Etta." Ari stared at the table. "But my sisters were old enough to remember days of peace, when your folk ruled our land. My folk never lost faith in yours."

I furrowed my brow, embarrassed by the strike of emotion gathering in my throat.

"When—" Ari took a long breath. "When I lost my family, I

kept that devotion." He leaned his back against the edge of the table. "I think—forgive me—but I think the people should know too. Like me, they will serve you willingly. Truth be told, it will light a fire beneath them. I don't want to question, but I don't understand why you do not take the throne. I will abdicate this very moment."

"You still do not know who betrayed you, and Ravenspire does not know of me. It will be to our benefit to keep it that way until the right moment." I gripped his shoulder, feeling him tense under my hand. "You must still lead here, Ari. You have been a good king, and these people deserve that king to lead them through this. You see a broader picture than I can right now, and I—" I struggled to find the words. "I am glad to call you an ally."

A faint smile curled his lips. "Always. *My* King."

I rolled my eyes. "Just keep your mouth shut a little longer. Hard, no doubt, for you, but do it."

"Yes, My King." He laughed softly, then pointed to the vellum. "So, what do you think?"

"It's unfamiliar," I admitted. "It doesn't seem right in some ways."

I couldn't explain more before the fur was thrown back. Frey, Ulf, and a few of Ari's guards filled his chamber. It took him a moment, but after I shot him a pointed look, Ari stood straight and regal. "What is the report?

Ulf stepped forward, dirty and sweaty from his journey. "There is talk in Lyx. The vows have been moved to tonight's moon, My King."

"What?" Ari moved around the table. "You're certain?"

Ulf nodded; his eyes turned to me. "That isn't all." The man shifted nervously. "The false king plans to . . . give his queen's sister to his High Captain in vows at the same time."

At first, relief that Elise was alive caught me by the chest and tightened. But in another heartbeat, fury numbed every inch of me. Numbed my tongue, blinded me to nothing but rage. "He plans to force Elise's vows?"

Ulf nodded and stared at the floor. "She will have no choice. They hold Ruskig over the *Kvinna's* head, and the lives of her parents."

"Dammit!" I kicked the table leg and raked my fingers through my hair. What did I tell Elise not long ago? Even she would do what was necessary to protect Etta and these people. I'd meant she might agree to take vows with Ari, but now, I had few doubts to save all of us, Elise would trap herself to the cruel hands of Jarl.

I made grand plans to cut off each of his fingers.

"They destroyed our textiles," Ari said. "We do not have the supplies to go under the guise as performers."

"I care little," I snarled. "I will attack the bleeding front gates."

"But that will not help Elise, nor will it give us the opportunity to take their fury. A plan we ought to keep," Ari said, his voice stern and direct. "None of it will matter if you are dead."

I heard the underlying meaning. The others would only hear their king clipping the Blood Wraith.

"I agree we have a new challenge," Ulf said. "But there is a way we can take." He pointed at the open vellum scroll. "Here in this partition, there are few guards because of the risk of flooding from the river. It is low, and in constant repair against the nearness of the banks. But we can get in there."

"Yes. Isn't one of your Shade a water fae?" Ari asked, even though he knew the answer. My wrists were covered by my tunic. Ulf and Frey didn't know we'd been released.

"Yes," I said through gritted teeth.

"Then, I will release you, Blood Wraith. You and your guild will help us through these tunnels." He placed a hand on my shoulder. Ari knew the truth, but he played his part well. I almost believed him to be more friend than anything in the moment. "We take the river. Our ship is fast, and with the help of fury and fate, we will break through their strongholds. We can make it. We can succeed."

"Ulf," I said, still looking at Ari.

"What?"

Ari flinched; no doubt unsettled at the venom in the guard's voice. I'd grown accustomed to venom; it was the respect I still had to make peace with.

"Where do the back tunnels lead?"

"I believe they come out in the dungeons."

That brought me to pause. I had not been in the dungeons of the castle since boyhood when my father insisted I learn of them. I might easily be remembering wrong, or perhaps something had been added, but I couldn't recall any sort of passage that led to the river, or the back of the castle from the dungeons.

"With the vows," Ulf went on. "I doubt many ravens will be in the lower levels."

"We can't assume that," Ari said. "We take all we can in the longship. We take the rafts. We make a fleet, and we prepare for the most resistance."

He looked to me, and I guessed he wanted my nod of

approval. After our journey upriver to Mellanstrad we had made plans to build more ships and had a few roughly constructed rafts that survived the attack. We had little time, but we needed as many hands as we could.

"I'll see that they're finished," I told Ari.

"Right. We all will help. Ulf, Frey, tell the people and see to it every able body has a tool or rope. We have no time to waste."

WE HAD fifty to our number. Three rafts were able to be hastily made enough to float with the weight of a dozen men. The rest squeezed onto the longship, leading the way upriver. I wrapped my arm around the tack at the stempost and peered into the murky fog. Together, Halvar and Casper worked their fury around the wet air to shield us in gray mist and force the current to push us forward swiftly.

The way their muscles flexed and trembled, it wouldn't be long before they were both spent.

"I don't know why Ari keeps the two ravens tied," Junius said. She watched as Kari, bound at her ankles, brought Casper and Halvar water. Brant sharpened swords and axes near the sternpost. "You could tell him to release them, and he would comply."

"He is playing his role," I said. "A distrusting king. In truth, I don't blame him. They are ravens, who is to say they don't run the second we get to Ravenspire?"

"Because I say they won't," Junie insisted. "I've asked them if they wish to return. They said no. I asked if they were loyal to King Calder. They said they hated him. The brother has magic, the sister was brutalized. They are loyal here. I tasted nothing but the truth. I know they are here to guide us, but it would help to have two more skilled fighters."

"Your word is enough for me. I'll tell Ari." Junie picked at a seed roll, appeased, but distant. "Something else troubling you?"

"I have come to realize the world is small. The troubles here are much the same back home, except there are no true rulers there. Merely overlords and prophecies that have long become myths. But magic is bought and used, my people are changed into monsters, or they hide. But being here I feel as if this fight is bigger than your land. Perhaps this will somehow bring about change for my folk too." Junie shrugged and faced the river. "I only wish Niklas were here to see it. He delights in agitating wealthy folk."

I smiled and leaned over the edge of the ship on my elbows. "If somehow fate brings us through this alive, if I am ever on a throne again, I promise you, Junius, you and your folk will always have friends here."

She didn't say anything, simply smiled.

"Blood Wraith." Ulf stepped up to my side. "King Ari tells me you will be the one to lead us to the castle."

"I am."

"Then you ought to know ravens have been camping on the east side of the riverbanks. Although the west will take a slightly longer route, we should dock there."

Junius flinched and turned away. Ulf waited patiently for some response. He glared at me, likely irritated he once more needed to answer to my word.

"Fine," was all I said. Once we were alone, I nudged Junie. "What is it?"

She flicked her eyes to the back of the longship, eyeing Ulf. "He was lying, Valen."

"You're certain."

"I want only to wash out my mouth after hearing him. Every word dripped in smoke and rot."

Ulf lied about ravens. If he was the traitor . . .

"Junie, speak to Frey, anyone close to Ulf. Ask general questions, see if he is lying about the attack on Ruskig, and try to find anyone else who might be in on it with him."

She wasted no time. At my back, Junie's laughter carried as she spoke with the men, passed around bits of seed bread and ale. I could not look. If I did, my face would give too much away. Doubtless Ulf would earn an axe to the neck.

One length from the bank we were to dock at, Junie returned. Her face revealed nothing, she leaned casually against the side. "Frey spoke true. He holds genuine anger for the invasion. Ulf speculated with him. Valen, he lied. At the very least he knows who arranged the attack. But if I were to place a bet—and I am a marvelous gambler—it was him."

I licked my lips. This needed to be carried out right. We couldn't let him know we knew anything in the event he sent a warning to anyone involved, or any ravens positioned and waiting.

"Get Ari. Tell him to behave as if he is giving me directions."

Again, Junie left only to return a moment later with Ari at her back.

"I admit it is unsettling to be told to pretend anything," Ari said. He stared into the night, smiling. "Tell me, should I be forceful? Am I reprimanding you? I can, you know. I'm rather good at reprimands. I think it is the kingliest thing about me."

I shake my head. "We found your traitor."

"All gods." Ari didn't drop his smile, even spoke with his hands as if giving orders. "They are on the ship, aren't they?"

"Ulf."

Ari glared at me, but I took it as part of his show. "I'll kill him."

"No, that is for me. We will be ambushed on the west bank, but we must dock there."

"But—"

"Trust me. We fall into his plans, but in truth, his allies will fall into ours. I need word spread to my guild. Junie will help. Tell them we fight with fury at my signal."

Ari pinched his mouth into a tight line. "As you say, My King."

"Oh, and Ari," I whispered. "Release the ravens and give them a blade."

The mists settled the nearer we came to the bank. The west was littered in trees. Countless places for ravens to lie in wait. My axes were sheathed. This was a risk, but if all went well, no one would be returning to Ravenspire to tell their story.

"Ready, Wraith?" Ulf asked.

I held his stare, longer than I should. "More than ready."

Ari stood with Frey. Tor and Halvar came to me. Kari and Brant handed out weapons to the others before taking their own. I disembarked first. My guild spread out, ready to act. Ulf kept a quick pace, shouting for everyone on the rafts to hurry ashore. Ari moved along the line, muttering to the others, giving them his own directive while I kept Ulf leading.

"Won't be long until we find the path, Wraith," Ulf said.

No. It wouldn't be long.

Ulf led us around a bend and the trees erupted in shadows. Ravens dressed all in black burst from the brush, roaring their cries. They raised swords. Fiery arrows pointed at our ship. The archers let them loose. Stieg and Casper were ready.

With one foot still in the river, the water fae raised a curling wall and devoured half the arrows. Stieg gathered wind and blew the rest of them off course. A roar of ravens charged, swords in hand.

"Let them come!" I shouted. "All of them! Hold!"

Ari repeated my command. We needed to draw out every raven.

"You can't win this, Wraith. Even I could see that," Ulf shouted at me. He slowly reached for his sword, a wash of torment on his face. He would die with his guilt soon enough.

"Tell me, how did it feel at the funeral pyre knowing you killed your folk?" Ravens still charged. A final line broke through the trees. I held up my hand. Ari shouted to hold steady and for the first time, Ulf seemed to realize we knew more than we let on.

"I tried to save lives, Wraith! Ravenspire wants you and your blades for themselves. Turn yourself in and your woman will be saved. Lives will be saved."

"Such a fool. Pity." I opened my palms, calling the heat of fury. The first line of ravens were only twenty paces away. A few more steps. A few more breaths. "You should've had more faith in your own people. You know, traitors made me a prisoner once. I hate traitors."

I clenched my fists and a rush of wind burst from my body.

Magic called to the trees. Roots tangled. Heavy oaks and aspens tore from the soil. They toppled over ravens and screams shattered the night.

"Tor, now!"

Tor sprinted into the chaos of shattering forest. Palms alight with blue flames, he blasted a line of pyre. A coiling serpent of fire wrapped around the back line of ravens, trapping them in my net.

Ulf staggered back. Junius and Brant were there to catch him.

Hands on the cold earth, I commanded a final surge of fury to bend the soil, the bedrock. To open the pits to the gods of the hells. Stone cracked. Rocks rumbled down the hillsides. Heavy trees snapped and fell. The people of Ruskig screamed with the ravens. Over the rush of my fury and the shredding forest, Ari cried for his people to hold.

The ground split. Ravens trapped in the pyre ring screamed and wailed as the earth swallowed them whole. Some tried to leap over the crack but were dragged down by the hooks of my magic.

My body trembled. Muscles ached. Fury would exhaust me if I didn't pace myself, and I would need it to face Ravenspire.

With a grimace I curled my fists and ripped my palms off the ground. After a moment the shudders ceased. Dust and smoke floated over the hole. What ravens remained were broken, stunned, and slow. Ari shouted the advance.

It took only a few bloody moments before every guard was dead or buried in the ground. Frey wiped his brow with the back of his hand, gaping at me as I stalked toward the riverbank. Stares burned into me. A few people startled and jumped out of my way. They could fear me, it didn't matter. I didn't have time to explain again.

Brant and Junie held Ulf near the ship. He met my eye with a look of horror when I butted my chest to his. "Who, who are you?"

I grinned, a cruel sort. "I am the man who is going to kill you. But not just yet." I signaled to Brant. "Ready to lead us?"

"I am," he said, a cautious grin spreading over his face.

I gripped the back of Ulf's neck until he winced. "Come on, then. We have a party to attend at the castle."

CHAPTER 30
ROGUE PRINCESS

My mother pinned the iridescent headdress over my hair. She smiled at my reflection in the mirror. I remained stone faced and unmoved. After a moment she turned away and pointed her attention at the hem of the blue gown. Fine beading glimmered on the bodice. The satin like cream.

It sickened me.

As my mother stood from the floor, she grabbed my hand and placed something cold in it. "For your marriage night."

I dropped my gaze to a small knife. One slight enough to hide on my thigh without being noticeable. I pointed my confusion at her.

She pressed a kiss to my forehead, the gentlest she'd ever been. "Use it well."

Bleeding hells, was she telling me to kill Jarl? I hardly knew what to think.

Runa chirped a shrill laugh across the room as she returned

her rings to her fingers. "Ah, mother, I doubt Elise needs advice on bedding anyone. Tell me sister, what is it like being the whore of such a violent man?"

My mother closed her eyes and paled.

"I wouldn't know," I said. Even if Runa taunted me, talk of Valen helped calm my racing heart. "I have only known him to be loyal. Gentle. The most *attentive* man I've met. You wish to shame me for being his lover, but I could never bear shame for such a thing. Anything I ask, he would give it unconditionally."

I chose my words carefully. True as they were, I enjoyed how Runa's smile faded. "In fact, he is only brutal when those he loves are threatened. I do hope you realize *that*, sister."

Runa frowned and turned away, adding a silver tiara to her head.

"Have I upset you?" I asked with a bite. "Is Calder not satisfying? Or has he not yet come to his queen, and instead spends his nights elsewhere?"

"Shut up, Elise!" Runa burst to her feet. "You think you're so clever, so strong. Well, let me tell you something little sister, by morning your precious Blood Wraith will belong to Castle Ravenspire. Either he serves us, or you will watch him carved to pieces on the rack. I do hope you realize *that*."

She insisted we leave, then stormed away. My mother scurried around the room, gathering blossoms to place in my hair, or on the hem of my gown during vows. It only irritated me.

"Stop Maj," I said. "You do not walk me to a blessed vow ceremony. You walk me toward death."

My mother stopped. A look I'd never seen in her eyes flashed like a spark of embers. "Do I? I must've been mistaken, then. If I had a love as you described, I imagine I would find the strength to keep living until I took it back. Forgive me if I misjudged your conviction."

She left me with nothing but the sting of her last words. All my life my mother, though she outranked my father, was a silent partner. A prize won by a wealthy man's son. But for a moment, just now, she bore the fire of a warrior. A fighter.

I gathered my gown, a new burn in my heart. Today, even if vows were forced, it changed nothing. There would be one man who held my heart, and I would fight until the day I could tell him the depths of mine.

Even if it killed me. Even if those were my final words. Valen Ferus would know I was his. I always had been.

THE CELEBRATION WAS rife with colors and music and tart sweetness. Minstrels hummed to lutes, lyres, and a cheery panpipe beneath a black canopy. Linens woven in sun red, sea blue, and honeysuckle orange draped the tall posts around the guest seating. Lanterns with pale flames brightened the fading sunlight in an Otherwordly glow. As if sunlight had been trapped and bottled for our use.

As guests waited, bards danced between rows singing tales of wonderment of our land and people. They spun on toes, clambered atop chairs, and entertained. At the end of songs, the bards tipped hats for shim or glittering things, and the entertained obliged.

Across the sides of the courtyard were tables toppled in too much food. Candied pears smothered in sugar sauce. Rolls and cakes drizzled in icings of all kinds: berry, sweet butter, bitter chocolate, tart jellies. Roasted hens with herb sauce lined silver platters. And endless fountains of sour wines and honey ales would keep guests drenched through the night.

I stood behind the bladed staffs of two ravens. My ankles were fettered beneath my gown, my wrists bound under the flowing sleeves. At my side my mother waited, unmoved. She made no sound as we watched Runa and Calder stand beneath an archway of moonvane.

I grinned at the blossoms. Even on this day of pain, Valen would be here.

The clergy of the All Father stood before them, draped in red robes, repeating the vows to my sister and the king. Another holy man placed gold crowns of raven wings atop their heads when they kneeled.

"*Stig upp vär herre och dam,*" the holy man said. Calder and Runa stood, hand in hand, king and queen.

Applause and praises to the king rose over the peaceful music. After a turn around the courtyard, Calder and Runa were directed to the black oak thrones seated at the top of a royal dais. At their feet were stacks of gifts. From gold, silver, purses of shim, to glittering exotic fabric and shoes.

My sister grinned at her newly acquired power, then turned her wretchedness to me. A single nod and my fate was sealed.

The ravens moved their staffs and took me under each arm. My mother insisted she be at my side but was refused. I shared a look with her. We had never been close, never been affection-ate, but in that single glance I saw her fear, her heartbreak for me. Not as a second, insignificant princess, but as *her* daughter.

Jarl waited in front of the king and queen and the same clergyman. He forced me to take his hand. I was sure those observing the vows could see how my wrists were bound, and it was disgusting how no one even made the slightest gasp. Doubtless everyone here believed me to be undeserving to vow with such a man as Jarl Magnus. I would be better suited with my head on a pike, traitor as I was.

"Wait, holy man," Calder said when the clergyman opened his mouth. "I want to be sure my dear sister does not have any doubt."

With a signal to the left wing of the dais, a raven dragged out a skinny girl dressed in a white robe, her face veiled. My heart dropped.

"Now, my little witch, make sure this goes forward."

Calista smoothed her robe and cleared her throat, her voice rife with irony. "Oh, gods who listen, gods who command the fates. Make sure these stupid folk get exactly what they deserve."

She squeaked when the nearest guard punched his fist into the back of her head.

"Stop!" I shouted. "Leave her alone."

Runa chuckled. "One might think you had sympathy for strange Night Folk, sister."

Calista rubbed the back of her head and straightened her shoulders again. I'm sure she cursed Runa for calling her Night Folk but kept quiet to avoid being hit again.

"She's a child," I said. "Leave her be."

Calder grinned. He'd won. "As you say, *Kvinna* Elise. Behave yourself, do as your king demands, and the little witch will not be forced to cast her spells of fate. She'll be untouched."

"Don't listen to them, Kind Heart. I can take it."

"It would seem, husband, my pathetic sister has been making friends during her time in the dungeons."

Calder laughed and the crowd followed his lead. Runa wished to humiliate me. These people meant nothing to me, not anymore. Let them laugh. They did not know what that child could do, nor whose rage awaited them outside these walls.

"Continue," Calder demanded.

The red robed holy man turned to Jarl and me and began his old language ritual. Jarl's eyes devoured me; he did not even hide it.

"I've wanted this for a long time. To know what it felt like to have *Kvinna* Elise. You should've chosen me long ago and we might've avoided all this unpleasantness."

"I never would've chosen you," I said.

"Because you believed you could love your vow negotiator?"

"Because your soul is black, and I would have seen you for what you are eventually."

Jarl grinned. "I look forward to meeting the Blood Wraith again. The king has given me the first blow. We have ways of twisting him, you know. Ways of making him compliant."

"Your fury poisons? He is stronger than whatever you have."

Jarl leaned forward, perhaps a romantic gesture from the outside, but his words were nothing but ice. "You have no idea what fury lives in this castle."

"And you have no idea what fury lives beyond it."

A sneer tightened Jarl's face. He lowered his voice. "I will break you, Elise. I will make you forget how to use your voice until you live to obey my word. It begins tonight, *wife*."

I said nothing but held his contempt with my own. Fight. I would fight. There was more to say, more I needed to do before this man wiped me from the earth. I grew lost in my own thoughts and hardly noticed when the clergyman finished speaking. He named us vowed. My pulse quickened and Jarl narrowed his eyes into something ferocious and cruel. He gripped the back of my head and forced my mouth to his. I bit his lip until I tasted the tang of his blood.

He pulled back in a hiss, dabbed his lip, and raised his fist. Before he landed the strike a shudder caused the posts around the guests to groan.

Jarl stared at the ground, confused, but the moment passed. He took me by the hair, grinning, blood on his teeth. "My King. I ask permission to leave with my wife. To show her how a true woman of Timoran is to behave."

Calder chuckled darkly. "Take your leave. And may the gods grant you luck."

I tried to keep quiet, but Jarl tugged on my hair with such force, I let out a cry of pain as he dragged me off the vow podium.

The knife my mother had given me was hot against my skin. Jarl would have it in his back soon enough. I'd murder, I'd run, I'd do it all to be free of this place and back with Valen Ferus.

A collective gasp ran up through the crowd when the ground seized once again. Sharper this time, enough to topple the fattest hen from its platter.

Jarl kept his hand in my hair but drew us to a pause. I

smiled, unguarded. Tears of relief gathered in the corners of my eyes when I tilted my face at Jarl and laughed. "You did not find him, Jarl Magnus. He found *you*."

It was then the ravens at the front portcullis shouted alarms. Calder rose from his seat and commanded the nearby ravens to surround the courtyard. I laughed harder when a violent tremble drew the guests to their feet, screaming.

Jarl glared at me. He adjusted, so his arm was tight around my neck, his blade pointed at my ribs.

From the low place in the courtyard, it was difficult to make out the front gates. Screams vibrated down the slope. Shouts came. Smoke rose. Steel crashed. I didn't know how much time passed, a few breaths, a full clock turn, but when a figure broke through the rising smoke, my knees gave under my weight. I let a tear fall.

Valen, dressed in black, one axe on his waist, the other notched under Ulf's chin, dragged the whimpering traitor through the clouds. The guards around the courtyard raised their swords in a warning.

Our distance made it difficult to see his face, but his voice carried. Deep, harsh, demanding. "Were you expecting us to come from the back, false king? We found your spy and decided to bring him through the front door."

Jarl turned back to the royal dais, forcing me to go with him. Runa was stiff, her grip white on the arms of her throne. Calder's face tightened. He glowered at me, then back at Valen. "Legion Grey, you are outnumbered. Stop whatever foolish attack you think you have started. Come, let us talk as dignified men."

"I am neither dignified nor here to talk to you, false king."

"If you've come for *Kvinna* Elise," Calder shouted, "I'm afraid she has taken vows with another. You are too late."

I could not see it, but a grin coated Valen's voice. "A few forced words change nothing for me. I wish to return your spy." The crowd gasped and screamed when Valen ripped his axe across Ulf's throat. For a moment the bulky man choked on his own blood until Valen shoved his lifeless body down the hillside. "Next, I will tell you Elise *will* be coming with me."

Calder muttered to his guards to make the capture or kill if necessary. "Anything else, Blood Wraith? Any other demands you have when you have no leg to stand on in my court?"

"Yes," he said. The ground shuddered, and even Calder staggered back when a crack drove down the center of the courtyard. "I would have you cease calling me Blood Wraith and Legion Grey. Those names grow old and irritating."

Calder scoffed, but there was a twinge of nervousness in it. "Oh, please, then. Tell us what we should know you by, so we might mark your grave correctly."

The crack widened. Jarl was forced to dodge. We landed in a heap beside one of the wooden posts. I elbowed him, but he held my head in the dirt. It didn't matter, I stopped struggling, desperate to hear every coming word.

"My name is Valen Ferus, the Night Prince of Etta! And you, false king, you are in my seat."

CHAPTER 31
ROGUE PRINCESS

A calm came, the briefest silence. Moments where the words soaked into the skulls of every soul in the court of Ravenspire until they settled like jagged points and brought the screams. Women and men cried out in terror—either believing Valen to be mad or true—they fought to be free of their seats and run.

All around colors blurred. The earth shattered as Valen used his fury. I'd never seen the full wonder he was, and watching the stone of the courtyard crack and mold into new shapes, new walls, new deadly pits, it was no wonder why he was called a Bender.

At my side, the cobbles of a pathway shattered and opened in a wide gash. I used the chaos to crack my elbow against Jarl's ribs. He grunted and loosened his grip. I rolled away and kicked, trying to knock him into the open ground. Jarl was swift and caught my foot. "He'll watch you die."

Teeth clenched, he battled to clamber over the top of me.

"I warned you," I panted. "I warned that you did not know the fury beyond Ravenspire. He will hate you most."

I dragged the skirt of my gown up, reached for the knife, and jabbed. The point nicked the side of his face, startling him enough he rolled aside. I ran, unfinished with Jarl Magnus, and if fate brought me to him again, I prayed I had a deadlier weapon in hand.

I wheeled to the royal dais. My heart stilled. Calder had his hands on the person I'd been after. He held Calista by the throat and shouted in her face.

"You lied, little witch!"

"About . . . about what?" Calista argued.

"You said Ravenspire had the oldest fury! I'll take your eyes!"

"I didn't lie," Calista whimpered, then in the next breath she giggled. "I just didn't tell you they had the next oldest."

All gods! Calder lifted his blade. He was going to kill the girl. My head spun, I had little time to work out what I would do before I threw the knife. The point didn't even touch the false king, merely distracted him.

With a curse on my lips for my poor aim, I darted for the dais as Calista slipped out of his grasp.

"Calista!" I shouted.

She spun on her heel, tore back the veil, and flashed a crooked smile. The girl ran for me. I breathed easier when my hand curled around hers.

Another shudder knocked those of us near the dais off our feet.

Roars filled the night. At the portcullis a dark line of invaders overtook the line of ravens. My heart leapt in my chest. Ruskig, Night Folk, Ettans—they'd all come. Blue flames sprouted from the cracks in the ground. Tor.

A hot surge of angry wind spread the flames, catching hems, the linens, the shrubs of the garden in the fury pyre. Walls of dancing blue flames trapped folk or tormented them. As if Tor's magic had a twisted love of torture, dancing flames chased fleeing Timorans and ravens until it devoured them, or they curled on the ground praying to silent gods.

"Hurry," I told Calista. "We must get to the gates."

I scanned the chaos, searching for Valen. Smoke and flame buried most faces. But next, a thundering boom stilled the courtyard. Smoke thinned enough for me to get a view of the gates. In one side of the front, a gaping hole broke the wall. A flood of invaders burst into the courtyard, led by the Night Prince.

I knew Prince Valen was trained to be the defender of Etta. He was his family's blade. To witness it now, no pretenses, no masks, it was a terribly mesmerizing sight. As the Blood Wraith he had little control when he was cursed. Now, the black axes carved through flesh and bone in a bloody dance. He'd open a gullet, then bend the ground.

With fury unleashed, he'd become an unbreakable force.

"Valen!" I cried his name. "Three hells, I can say it."

"Sort of no point of a secret when he blurted it out for everyone," Calista muttered.

I grinned and kept pulling us away from the dais. I shouted his name again. This time he snapped his eyes across the court-yard, finding me in the smoke.

"Elise!" A new determination dug into his features. He

struck at ravens to clear a path, leaving some wounded and breathing, as he carved his path to me.

Calista screamed. Behind us a raven lifted a short blade. I shoved the girl, then jumped away from the strike. The raven fumbled against the momentum of his swing. He was thick and broad, but off balance. I took the risk and dug my shoulder into his side, knocking the raven to the ground. At once, I pounced on his back, grappling for his sword. My knee pressed into the back of his neck. I dug his face into the soil. He cursed me and rolled, tossing me aside. When we both oriented and faced each other, neither of us had the sword.

The raven sneered, taking out a dagger from its sheath. I was weaponless. Valen still stabbed and cut his way through guards.

The raven handled his dagger, ready to strike, but he gasped at his next step.

A glint of a sword tip pierced through his chest. He fell forward, dragging Calista down over his back. She held the hilt of his blade wrong, and the way she clung to it, she must've used every ounce of strength to drive the blade through. She screamed and swatted, desperate to get off his body.

I scooped her up under her arms, holding her tightly. For a child who had seen too much already, she buried her face into me and sobbed.

"It's all right," I said, smoothing her hair. Keeping her close, I tore the sword free from the raven's back. "We must go, shh, we must keep going."

She sniffed and nodded, burying the pain beneath her steely countenance again. I pointed us at the gates and smashed into an armored body. On instinct, I tried to raise the sword in defense, but his dark eyes drew me to a stunned pause.

"Valen." His name came out in a breathless whisper. I rested one hand over his heart. Up close his features were wrapped in kohl and runes. His eyes like black fire with his fury raging. He was real.

The forces of Ruskig were taking the upper hand. More ravens were dead and bloody than were standing. Valen didn't check over his shoulder, he seemed to care little about the fight around us when he kissed me, hard and fierce. Teeth and lips crashed for a moment of heat and need. It ended too soon.

"Get free of the wall," he shouted. "I will face the king."

"I am standing with you!"

"*Elise*," he warned.

"Do not take the throne today dark prince!" Calista shouted, her eyes glassy. She rubbed her head.

Valen stared at her strangely. I rested my hands on her shoulders. "What did you say?'

She shook her head and stammered, "Don't, don't take the throne today. I-I-I don't know, it just came to me. Something . . . is coming."

I clung to Valen's arm. "She's the enchantress. She feels things, Valen. Heed her."

His jaw clenched. He swept his gaze to the dais with a hint of greed and lust in his eyes. "I do not let Calder live. I cannot, fate owes me that, at least. Get her free of here."

Bloodlust lived in his eyes. In a deep place, but there all the same. The call to avenge his folk, his family, dug deep inside the Night Prince. But if he took the throne, what would happen? Calista had never lied, not to me. She had no reason to start now.

But I would not let him face it alone.

I wheeled on her. "Calista, you run to the gates, find a place to hide. If I do not come back, look for a woman—Siv—tell her you are the storyteller. She will help you. Or a man, Mattis. They will look after you if I cannot."

Her eyes brimmed in tears again, then widened. A haze covered the bright blue, like white smoke. "It's coming, Kind Heart."

"Night Prince!" Calder's voice roared over the fading sounds of death and battle.

Steel silenced. Shouts of battle were echoes in the night. A path cleared around the cracks in the soil, leading to an opening from where I stood beside Valen and the dais.

The Timoran king stood in the center, a hand gripping the cloak of a hunched figure.

"All gods—Lumpy," Calista said, the haze breaking.

"Give up your crown, false king," Valen shouted, gripping both his axes. "This land is no longer yours."

"Are you so sure? You think I do not have power to end you? Do you think kings before did not have the power to keep *our* land, *our* kingdom? You underestimate the strength of Timoran. It will be your downfall, yet again."

"I warn you again, false king. Step down. This land is not yours."

A roar of agreement rose from the people of Ruskig.

"You think you are clever hiding in plain sight. True, I did not know of you," Calder admitted. "But I knew of *him*. I wonder—did you?"

Calder removed the hood of the third prisoner in the dungeons. Where I expected an old, withered man, instead a young, pallid, sunken face shone in the firelight. Dark hair to his shoulders, ears tapered to a point, and a black tint to his lips. If fed properly, doubtless he'd be broad, tall, and fierce. His gaze was empty, but for a bit of red rimming the pitch of his irises.

I didn't know him, but Valen—he stumbled. As if the strength were knocked from him and he had to force his legs to hold him.

I reached for him, a hand on his back. He trembled. Eyes wide, almost horrified. The Night Prince shook his head in disbelief.

Some great trick had gone on, though, for Calder laughed. A cold, unfeeling sound I felt to my bones. Valen took a step back, hand to his heart. I opened my mouth to ask him what had happened, but my blood turned to ice when he uttered a name, soft and dangerously low.

"Sol?"

CHAPTER 32

NIGHT PRINCE

"Fate had different plans, little brother." Sol's blue eyes grew dark, like the black parts of the sea. "Fight Valen! You fight like you've never fought before! Fight like the gods! I'll save a space for you in the great hall!"

My final glimpse at my older brother raced through my head, trying to make sense of what I was seeing now.

"Sol?" His name slipped from my lips.

How? Was it an illusion? This haggard, empty creature was a shadow of what Sol Ferus once was. Bold, cunning, always filled with laughter. No. I would've known if my brother still lived. I would've felt something. The land would not have bloomed for me.

Elise's hands braced me. I hardly noticed, but somehow knew she was keeping me steady.

The initial stun began to shatter. What had they done to him? Why did he look at me like he didn't know me? My heart shot to my head when a painful cry shattered the rest of my daze. Tor raced for the front.

"Sol!" Tor cried. "Dammit, Sol what have they done?"

Tor's pain seared into me. Halvar reached for him, but Tor flashed his pyre at anyone who tried to stop him. The hollow eyes of Sol found Tor in the bloody crowd. Did he know him? Care at all? Was he nothing but emptiness? I'd rather he be dead if they'd slaughtered the goodness of his soul.

My brother—what was now my brother—lifted his hand. Black mist wrapped around his fingers. He aimed them at Tor.

"No!" I shouted and rushed for Tor, but he was too far ahead. "Sol, no!"

The black mist crept from Sol's palms and like skeins of dark ribbon the inky blight seeped into the soil at Tor's feet. His consort stiffened and fumbled to his knees. Black veins slithered up the back of Tor's neck, around his eyes. His lips turned a ghastly shade of blue.

I gripped my axes. No. No, this wasn't Sol. Poisoned land could sicken folk, true enough. It was a battle strategy we'd planned on using during the raids before our own courtiers betrayed us to the first false king. Sol never had the chance to test it. But watching Tor weaken as the blight soiled the earth, it was sickening.

"Sol, no! This . . . this is not—"

"You are not the only one with secrets, Night Prince," Calder interrupted, grinning. "What is a Night Prince when we have the death magic of the Sun Prince?" The Timoran king looked at my brother. "The woman."

It happened so quickly. A second dart of black shot from the dais, destroying a narrow piece of shattered soil until it struck beneath Elise's feet. She coughed, clutched her throat, then crumbled the same as Tor.

"No!" A frenzy of panic wrapped around my throat. I reached for Elise, but Halvar pulled me back.

"Don't touch her," he hissed at me.

Elise's smooth skin was overtaken by black, poisonous veins. The whites of her eyes turned gray and yellow.

I rushed for the dais, the black eyes of my brother following me the entire way. "Sol, release them. Release them, damn you. He is yours—" I pointed at Tor. "Remember him, brother? He is yours. And she, she is mine. Sol, look at me! She is my *hjärta*. Stop, I beg of you."

"I do love when royals beg," Calder said. "You cannot beat this, Night Prince. We hold the oldest fury."

I ignored him. "Sol, release them. Release them, please. You are *killing* Torsten!"

For the slightest moment, his gaze twitched to the place Tor struggled to breathe. A hint of light colored his eyes. The barest flicker of light blue. Our mother's eyes. One heartbeat is all he had before blackness struck again.

The Sun Prince glared at me. He spoke as if each word ripped from the back of his throat. "I *can't*. Bend it. Go!"

An instant to make a choice. I understood what he meant, what needed to be done, what Calder did not understand about two brothers' fury. But it would mean choosing—a choice I did not know how to make now that the truth was here.

I prayed I'd be able to live with it.

My fingernails dug into the soil. From the battle, my arms ached, fury had exhausted most of my energy, but I had a bit more. I had enough.

I did not crack the earth, but it shuddered all the same. A gust of wind shot at the dais when Calder ordered his guards to take me. The ravens toppled with their king. Halvar, Stieg, and Ari stalked toward the dais. Cries of vicious sights came from the ravens as Ari twisted their minds in illusion. Stieg and Halvar tossed a whirlwind about. I held my grip on the ground until the blackness drew back. Bits of poison and blight faded against my healing fury.

Torsten drew in a sharp breath. The painful poison pulled away from his blood. Ten paces away, Elise coughed and rolled onto her side.

I turned to the dais, heart breaking. Sol's unnaturally dark eyes drank me in. It might've been my imagination, but I thought he nodded. As if he knew what I needed to do and agreed. But on second glance only his flat, unfeeling gaze met mine as he lifted his hands to strike again.

"Back to the boats!" I shouted at Ari.

He nodded and called a retreat as Halvar slung Tor's arm over his shoulder. My hands trembled. I needed to do this. It wasn't over, but the false king was right about one thing: I could not beat this, not today. Not wholly unprepared.

One final time, I pressed my hands to the ground until stone split. Instead of carving ravines and valleys, I bent the earth until a jagged, stone wall sprung from the ground like rows of teeth. It would not be enough to stop Calder's units forever, but it would give us time.

With Ari, I demanded our folk run for the shore. My body ached from using too much fury, but I gripped my axes and took what few ravens remained. Most didn't engage; they ran. Those who fought didn't live long.

I reached Elise as she found her feet. She trembled and was pale. I drew her against me, kissing the sweat on her brow.

"Valen," she said, voice hoarse.

I shook my head. We'd speak of what happened here later, but I couldn't now. Not when I was abandoning my own brother to the cruel hands of enemies.

"Elise Lysander!"

We turned together. My stomach plummeted when that bastard, Jarl, raised a crossbow. Bloodied, and covered in ash, hate burned in his eyes. He pointed his bolt at Elise's heart, but before he fired, a woman used a fallen scrap of a wooden post against Jarl's head.

"No, Maj!" Elise shouted.

I hadn't recognized Elise's mother, but at my next step, I ran for her.

Jarl rebounded quickly. His anger pointed at Lady Lysander when he stuffed her heart with a curved knife. I tore him off her and swung a frenzied strike with an axe. He dodged, and like the coward he was, fled with the ravens to the safety I'd created with my own bleeding walls.

Elise's mother shuddered, knife in her chest. She reached for me. We had no time, but I clasped her hand and held the back of her head as blood dripped over her lips. "You'll c-c-care for her?"

I nodded, blinking rapidly. The knife went deep. Too deep.

"Swear to me."

"I swear," I said. "I swear she will never fear me. She will have all of me."

She smiled. It was a frightening sight with all the blood.

Her grip tightened on mine; her voice soft. At peace. "I hope fate returns your crown, Prince."

Mara Lysander died with a soft smile. I rested her on the ground gently, then gathered my axe, and faced Elise. Her cheeks were lined in tears, her fists clenched. She lifted her eyes to mine when I tilted her chin.

"We must leave," I whispered. "Her last hopes were for you."

Elise closed her eyes, more tears fell, but she allowed me to guide her away. Away from the stolen throne. From Castle Ravenspire.

Away from the Sun Prince. The true king of Etta.

CHAPTER 33
ROGUE PRINCESS

Heady, endless black faced us on the journey downriver. We kept lanterns doused, voices soft. The only light came from the flicker of starlight and the nearly full moon above. My skin reeked of smoke and blood. The horrors of the night clung to me like a new layer.

From the sternpost, a bucket of fresh water hung for the taking. My hands shook as I ladled a horn. The cool drip scorched against my rough throat. I ladled more. Valen's fury had robbed him of strength, then to add the revelation that Sol —I could hardly think it—his brother lived. It was a wonder he was standing at the bow at all.

"Elise." My gaze dropped to the back notch. Ari grinned, his face dripping in smeared kohl and smoke. I blinked through tears and reached for his hand. He kissed the top of mine. "I am glad you live, dear *Kvinna*."

"I am glad you were wise and freed them," I said, voice rough. "No doubt it was a surprise."

Ari grinned. "That I had imprisoned the Night Prince? Yes, you could say it was a bit of a shock. Yet, the more I think on it, somewhere inside I always knew he was a leader. It's why I always included him or wanted him to be involved in all my schemes."

"You helped him find himself again by trusting him."

"No," Ari said. "You did all that. Only you drew him back to Ravenspire. I'm afraid I had no choice but to release the bindings. I was certain he would slaughter us all if I didn't. Alas, who knew I would secure my own abdication by releasing them. I have grown accustomed to ordering folk around."

I scoffed, though nothing was funny, not really. "You are a fine leader, Ari. You will always have my respect."

"Then I shall die a happy man." He squeezed my hand again. "And I have mighty plans to continue irritating our dear prince by insisting you take vows with me and not him."

I grinned and pressed a kiss to his forehead. "So long as you say it when he isn't holding his axes."

I left him and made my way through the oarsmen, back to the front. The wreckage of the battle was grave.

Calista slept beneath a heavy fur. Kari busied with a bandage over a deep wound in Halvar's side. He grinned through it all, demanding she take note of his naked chest, and admire his handsomeness until she was laughing.

Brant held a bloody cloth to his face. I doubted he'd keep his eye. Frey, Stieg, Casper. They all bore wounds and scars. Junie hugged her knees to her chest, tears on her cheeks. Siv and Mattis held each other, eyes closed against what had happened.

Tor. My chest squeezed. He had not spoken; he'd not

looked at anyone. His eyes were locked at the destruction we'd left in the dark. No one asked him to speak. No one bothered him. What was there to say? Still, I could not pass by without mourning with him. If the tables had turned, if once again, I'd been torn from Valen, I could not imagine the sorrow.

I took his hand and curled it around a horn of water. His eyes were wet and broken. But he squeezed my hand once before he turned away again.

The Night Prince stared at the expanse of river before us. Distant. Alone. I rested a hand between his shoulders. He startled slightly, then curled me against his side. We were silent for a long while. Any words I thought to say fell short.

At long last, Valen leaned his head to mine and whispered, "Elise, I don't know what to do. What to think."

I wrapped an arm around his waist. "I think there is only one way forward."

Vulnerability and fear burdened his gaze. In this moment, with me, he could be a normal man. I'd read about his mother's love for his father, but especially in those moments when King Arvad confessed his fears to her, when he was her lover and companion more than a king.

"You go forward, Valen Ferus. You take the crown; you fight to free your brother. You are his only chance."

He closed his eyes. "You do not wish him dead?"

"Why would I?"

"I hear whispers," he said. "People seething betrayal from a son of Etta."

"Valen," I said, resting one hand to his cheek. "They have manipulated Sol. I was with him in the dungeon without knowing, and he was docile. It was only after Calder called him that he . . ." I shook my head. "We will free him."

He covered my hand with his and pressed a kiss to my palm. "You should know, *Kvinna*, my heart and soul are yours for the taking."

"Then, I have all I could want." I kissed him, unashamed. A raw need built in my chest to restore all he had lost, to heal the scars this land had left behind.

When we returned to Ruskig, reparations were made to the fury barriers. With Valen and his guild unbound, the walls were higher and stronger than before. I escaped after discovering the children left behind were well and seeing that Calista was welcomed with Ellis. He mourned his mother; she was an outcast who was more afraid than she let on. Until we figured out what to do with the storyteller, perhaps the children could be a comfort to each other.

My shanty had been split in two, but I took Siv's since she would be with Mattis. Alone, I bathed and cried. My mother was dead. She'd died for me. I cried for Sol. Calista had, in a way, befriended the Sun Prince. He had goodness inside him, he must have goodness. To help a child with words for her fate spells, maybe he understood she was helping his brother.

His fury was horrifying. I shuddered, remembering the pain of his poison. As if each muscle, each vein in my body were bursting with fire.

Ravenspire used him as a weapon. No mistake, the poison that had taken my father's eye came from some torture and manipulation of the Sun Prince. For centuries he'd been Ravenspire's greatest secret—more than the cursed prince. They held tight to the death fury. Truth be told, it made a great deal of sense now how Ravenspire had always frightened Night Folk or found ways to control them.

With fury like Sol's—there was no telling what they could do.

I'd just wrapped a linen towel around my body when my door opened, and Valen stepped inside.

His eyes flashed in a heat of desire when he took me in, then his lips curled. "I've come to beg you for mercy that you might allow me to stay in here. Ari will not stop insisting I take the royal longhouse, and I am simply not ready to face it yet."

"I'm not sure that's wise, Prince Valen."

He closed the space between us, one brow lifted. "Oh? Why is that?"

My fingers traced the planes of his chest as he pulled me against him. "I have a very protective lover, you see. He has these axes that are terrifying. The type of man who wears a mask and causes havoc."

Valen brushed his lips along the curve of my ear, smiling. "He sounds awful, and you should consider loving a prince instead."

I closed my eyes when he left a trail of kisses down my neck. "You make a compelling point."

He claimed my mouth as his own. Then, held me closer, loved deeper. We'd faced what it would mean to lose each other, and it came out in every touch, every kiss, every movement. His hands, his mouth, wiped away the marks left by Runa's cruelty. They healed the fear of being Jarl's body to ruin.

I did not release him until the sun rose the next morning.

By the time we made our way to the longhouse, already a crowd had gathered as a council in the hall. Halvar had spent the early hours of the morning explaining what had become of the Night Prince. He explained the curse and lack of memory. I think Valen breathed a little easier knowing he didn't need to relive the curse yet again.

Still, the walls were crowded. Everyone wished to hear from the Night Prince. I'd since learned he'd made his declaration during a bloody battle and had not explained anything to the people of Ruskig. To know they'd followed him into battle without knowing his full tale meant something.

It gave me hope.

"I abdicate," Ari said when everyone had settled. "I willingly give the crown to Va—"

"Wait," Valen said, raising a hand. "Before you do, it should be known I am no longer the heir."

"Valen," Halvar said with a touch of sadness.

"I know what you're going to say. I also know that . . . Sol is not in a place to take his birthright, but our laws of Etta stated if a king or queen could not rule in their mind, but still lived, the power would fall to their consort."

My mouth dropped.

Tor shrunk a bit into the wall. Other eyes followed as Valen went to Tor's side and placed a hand on his shoulder. "Perhaps some do not realize, but Torsten is my brother's consort. The crown falls to him."

Ari let out a long breath and scrubbed his face. "There are too many bleeding people with claim to this bleeding crown."

Tor lifted his gaze, only looking at Valen. "I am no king. I do not want his crown, or yours. But I will fight for and serve the Ferus line until my last breath."

327

"All right, then. Wonderful. Settled," Ari said. "May I abdicate, now?"

"What of Herja?" Valen folded his arms over his chest. "Sol is alive, who is to say they have not hidden my sister somewhere?"

"Valen," Halvar said gently. "Herja was not Night Folk."

"She had other talents; you know this. She would be valuable, so shouldn't we make sure she is dead before we assume?"

Halvar nodded. "But until we know for certain, these folk—all of us—we need a king, a leader. You are that leader."

Valen studied the room, he stood at the front. "If it is your wish, I will serve you, but we do all we can to retrieve the Sun Prince—"

"He serves Ravenspire," a voice shouted at the back of the room.

"By force," I shouted back. "Don't be fools. You think the Sun Prince would willingly fight for the people who killed his family?" Valen wore a bemused grin and stepped back as I stomped forward. "You do not know what my people are capable of. How desperate they are to keep the throne. Calista, come here." I turned to the corner where the girl sat beside Ellis and Kari. She jumped but obeyed. "Tell them what you know of the Sun Prince. You spent the most time with him."

She licked her chapped lips, gave Valen a shy look, then met the eager faces in the hall. "I . . . I didn't know he was a prince. Thought there was only one, even though I guessed he had old fury. Still, I didn't know his name, but he sometimes talked to me. He helped me cast, uh, spells that helped us break out. If he was so bad, he wouldn't have helped me. Don't be stupid folk. He's one of you, just a little twisted because those sods at the castle feed him his own poison. They torture him."

Tor seemed ready to faint. He pulled out a chair, sat, and dragged his fingers through his hair, avoiding any glances.

Valen cleared his throat. "Can you write anything? A story that will ensure we get to him?"

Calista paled and shook her head. "It doesn't work like that. I think I've crossed too many lines. My magic is sort of a push and pull with fate. She doesn't like to be manipulated, by me or anyone. I tried to write something the second we got here, but it burned me in my head, and in my heart. It's like at this point, in this story, your fate is in your hands. I have done all she will allow."

"Then, we do what we can to rescue him," Valen said. "But . . . if he is gone, then my brother would rather not live."

I rested a gentle hand on his arm. All gods, I prayed he would not be faced with killing Sol. But, it seemed, the burden of a kingdom, of an entire people, had fallen atop his shoulders at last. He would do what was needed to protect them above all else.

The people grew quiet and somber. Ari cleared his throat and stood. "At the high moon, then. We'll make it official."

AT DUSK, Valen, his guild, and I stood at the edge of the sea. A trader's ship bobbed in the tide, a skiff being loaded with textiles and herbs for distant kingdoms waited to embark into the waves. Junie shouldered a satchel and tightened a fur mantle around Calista's shoulders.

"I'll see her to her homeland. In the west, right girl?"

"I live in Raven Row," she said, dryly. "Some say it was the first kingdom, you know."

Junie snorted. "Well, your highness, I shall see you to this Raven Row then."

I wrapped my arms around Junius, holding her tightly. "You did not need to fight, but you did. I will always be grateful to you. And I hope you keep your husband from burning the world."

She grinned, longing in her eyes as she handed me a parchment with a post for a foreign land.

"Should you need me, you need only ask." Junie looked to Valen. "My guild at home, we call ourselves the Falkyns, but it has been an honor to be a Shade. Do not forget us. I know you will come to mean a great deal to my people. I don't know how, but I do not think this will be the last time we meet."

"A king is a good friend to have, after all," Valen said. "Even a temporary one."

"It is. I mean it," she said, pointing to the parchment in my hands, "should you need anything, ask. You have foreign allies now."

"Goodbye, Kind Heart," Calista said. When she lifted her gaze, her eyes grew stormy, like pale clouds covered the irises. "Your battle ends when his begins."

My stomach twisted. "Calista? When whose battle begins?"

Valen came to my side, watching the girl curiously. When she spoke again, her voice was hushed, her words changed.

"The breaker of night and fear begins his fight when yours ends." Calista blinked rapidly, then smiled as if nothing were amiss in the slightest. "Goodbye, cursed prince. Don't forget what I did for you. The good things, I mean."

Valen and I shared a look.

"What was that?" he whispered as Calista darted down to the boat.

"She sees things. I don't know what it means. I'm not sure she even realizes she said it."

He let out a long sigh, jaw tight. "Knowing the tricks of fate, we'll find out soon enough."

"And as uncomfortably as she can manage, no doubt," I grumbled.

Valen grinned, kissed the side of my head, and paid the dock men an extra purse of silver shim to ensure Junie and Calista made it to their lands safely, with an added threat if they did not, the Guild of Shade would destroy their trade, then their lives.

A glimpse at the pyre on Tor's palms was enough to get the dock man to nod and make a hundred assurances before they rowed into the waves.

I slipped my fingers into Valen's and watched the horizon. "Are you ready?"

He pressed a kiss to my knuckles. "As much as I ever will be."

THE CORONATION PYRE raged into the black velvet sky.

Women were crowned in moonvane, men wore crowns made of smoothed twigs. Everyone was dressed in their best gowns, best tunics. They wore bones in their ears and runes on their hands and faces.

I stood near the empty chair beneath a white canopy and moonvane archway. Tor and Halvar remained beside me, the royal advisor, and first knight. Siv clung to Mattis's arm, beaming at me. She'd lived with the clans her entire life. This was a night she'd trusted would come, and it struck me that this meant more than an ascension to these people. It meant freedom.

The crowd silenced when Valen, Ari, and Elder Klok stepped into the light.

Valen wore a fur cloak, and Klok carried in his hands the silver circlet Ari had worn as king. My stomach clenched. How long ago it seemed from the night Legion Grey became my vow negotiator. I'd resisted him, then fell for him. Together we survived a coup, we survived lies, a curse. Now, in this moment, when his eyes met mine, I had no doubt whatever fate had in store, we could face it together.

Ari turned to the people. "For centuries we have believed our true royals, the family of Etta, the Ferus line would rise again. Their magic never died. We knew it. We felt it. We held onto it. It is my honor to abdicate this crown to our true king, Valen Ferus."

Valen lowered to one knee. The very wind stilled as Klok placed the circlet on his head. A sheen of light gathered across the moonvane blossoms. As if the earth were celebrating our victory.

When Valen rose, the people cheered. Siv jumped on her toes, then kissed Mattis like it was the last. Stieg and Casper roared their pleasure. Frey pounded a fist over his chest, as did Ari. Halvar smiled and winked at me. Tor—even Tor smiled.

Valen went to the throne. His face was calm, but the way he shook out his hands, he was no doubt filled with hot anxiety.

"What is the first order, King Valen?" Ari asked.

Valen studied his people. He looked to me. I didn't blink. When he turned back to the crowd, he lifted his chin. "I declare war on Castle Ravenspire, on the new king and queen of Timoran."

A battle cry that rocked me to my core rose with the embers into the night.

A confident grin spread over Valen's mouth. His voice deepened. "Prepare to fight for your families! For your people and your land. This war never ended, but I swear to the gods, it will end with us. It begins now."

READY FOR MORE?

Keep reading with Valen and Elise in Crown of Blood and Ruin by scanning the QR code below.

WANT SOME EXTRA?

Scan the QR code below for a sexy bonus scene with Valen and Elise.

THANK YOU

I am so grateful to so many people. This series has been a long time in the making, and it wouldn't have been possible without the help of others.

First, to my husband for bouncing a thousand ideas back and forth. I don't know how many times you've heard about this world and these characters, but I'm so grateful you never stopped chatting with me. It's blown this up into something I never saw coming.

To my kiddos for your patience and your support. I love how you get excited every time one of my books comes in the mail. You are my reasons.

To Jennifer Murgia for helping me smooth out the edges, saving my comma mistakes, and catching all those times I put 'form' instead of 'from'. Thank you to Clara Stone at Author Tree for your beautiful formatting skills. You are amazing. And to Bianca at Moonpress Co. for your beautiful covers. Thank you to Eric for your spectacular map and header art.

As always, thank you to my readers. Without you these worlds wouldn't be possible. I'm so grateful for you, and my opportunity to share these words and characters with you!

May we all be the good,

LJ

Printed in Great Britain
by Amazon